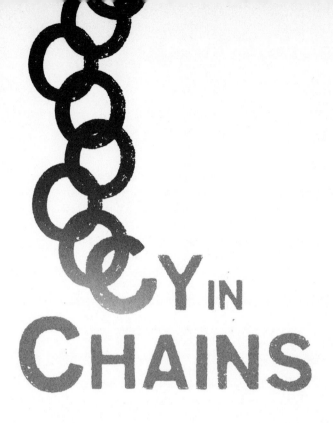

Y IN

CHAINS

A NOVEL BY

DAVID L. DUDLEY

Clarion Books ▪ Houghton Mifflin Harcourt ▪ Boston   New York

CLARION BOOKS
215 Park Avenue South
New York, New York 10003

Clarion Books is an imprint of
Houghton Mifflin Harcourt Publishing Company.

www.hmhbooks.com

The text was set in Letterpress.

Library of Congress Cataloging-in-Publication Data
Dudley, David L.
Cy in chains / by David L. Dudley.
p. cm
Summary: In the post–Civil War South, a seventeen-year-old
African American boy, accused of a crime, is living
in a labor camp where brutality, near starvation,
humiliation, and rape are commonplace.
ISBN 978-0-547-91068-0 (hardcover)
[1. Chain gangs—Fiction.
2. Prisoners—Fiction.
3. Race relations—Fiction.
4. African Americans—Fiction.] I. Title.
PZ7.D86826Cy 2013
[Fic]—dc23
2012046026

Manufactured in the United States of America
DOC 10 9 8 7 6 5 4 3 2 1
4500443031

For my children:

Chris, Joy, Michael, and Will

warriors all

ONE

THERE WAS NO WAY TO ESCAPE THE SHOUTING and the noises of animal terror bursting from Teufel's stall. The crack of the whip against the stallion's side, the horse's maddened whinnying of rage and fear, the curses from John Strong's mouth.

Cy put an arm around Travis, who pushed closer to him. Travis had his hands over his ears, like that would do any good. *I tried to tell you we shouldn't of sneaked down here,* Cy thought, feeling the younger boy trembling. *But you had to have your way, and see the mess we in?*

Cy was afraid too—his pounding heart told him so—but his fear was mixed with hatred for John Strong and pity for the man's son. As much as he wished to, Cy couldn't stop Strong from tormenting the horse. Trying to leave the barn was too risky now, so he and Travis would have to stay and listen until Strong's craziness had eased or his arm was too tired to strike another blow.

Both boys were huddled in the corner of the stall that

had been Rex's before the roan had been sold to help pay John Strong's bills. The familiar barn smells—dung, urine, and hay—came up faintly from the red clay floor. Dust particles hung in the yellow shaft of warm April light filtering through an open window.

"Why won't Daddy *stop?*" Travis asked. "Teufel didn't mean to lose the race."

"Keep yo' voice down," Cy warned. "If Mist' John find us here, we be in big trouble."

"He'd whip us too."

"I hope not, but they's no tellin' what yo' daddy do when he been drinkin' so hard. Don't worry. I ain't gon' let nothin' bad happen to you."

"I'm scared, Cy. Ain't you?"

He couldn't let on that he was. Travis counted on him to be the brave one, and most of the time, that was fine.

"He ain't gon' do nothin' to you, Travis. I promise."

From the far end of the barn, the shouts of the man and shrieks of his horse continued.

"I'm gonna run away from here," Travis whispered fiercely. "Tonight! You come with me."

"Ain't no way you can do that. You only eleven."

"Twelve, next month! And you're thirteen. We can do it! Wait until late tonight, and take Teufel with us."

"That's crazy talk, and you knows it. Yo' daddy come after us, and then we both get it." *'Specially me*, Cy thought.

"We'll get across the river! Daddy couldn't follow us then."

"Shhh!" Cy put his hand over Travis's mouth. "Sound like he done."

The door to Teufel's stall creaked on its hinges, then slammed shut. John Strong's curses had turned to the broken ramblings of a drunken man. The sounds grew fainter as he left the barn.

"You all right?" Cy asked.

Travis didn't move, didn't answer, but sat with his knees drawn up to his chest. He wiped his runny nose on his shirtsleeve.

"It over now," Cy assured him.

"Until next time Daddy gets drunk."

Cy listened. The barn was quiet. When he was sure Strong had gone, he led Travis to Teufel's stall. Cy lifted the latch and eased the door open. Right away, the stallion kicked at the wooden walls and snorted a warning.

"There now, boy," Cy told the horse. "You know me. I ain't gon' hurt you. Quiet, now."

Teufel lowered his head and stood, quivering.

"Come on in," Cy told Travis. "He calm down."

Travis entered the stall, but pressed close to the door.

"Sweet Jesus," Cy said. "Look at the way Mist' John done cut you up." What he saw made him want to cry. The horse's right flank and quarters were crisscrossed with bleeding wounds.

He had to take charge. "Travis, get the salve from the tack room. We got to tend to these cuts." Cy dug into the pocket of his overalls and brought out two shriveled apples. He offered one to the injured animal, who took it and began chewing it slowly. Even now, his side torn up by John Strong's cat-o'-nine-tails, Teufel was the handsomest horse Cy had ever seen. And when he ran, it seemed like his hooves never touched the red clay under him. *Mist' John ain't got no right to hurt you so bad*, Cy thought. *I sho' would like to steal that damn cat and—*

Use it on that son of a bitch, he wanted to say, but even thinking such thoughts was dangerous. *Steal that damn whip and bury it somewhere*, Cy corrected himself. Before Strong ever got another chance with it.

Travis came back with the jar of salve. He held Teufel's head while Cy applied the medicine to the cuts. Every time he touched a hurt place, the horse flinched, but he let Cy go on. The whole time, Cy whispered gentle words, and slowly the trembling stopped. Helping Teufel made him feel better. Uncle Daniel said he had a real knack with horses and that was something you couldn't buy or learn. Either it was yours, or it wasn't.

Cy handed Travis the second apple. "You give him this one. Let him know you his friend too." Travis held the apple on the flat of his palm, fingers pointing downward, out of the way of Teufel's enormous ivory teeth.

"You think we should put him in the pasture?" Travis asked. "Let him get some grass?"

"Better not. Yo' daddy probably be mad enough when he find out we played horse doctor. We could get him some water, though, and maybe a few oats, if they is any."

They filled Teufel's water bucket, but the feed bin was empty.

"I best get home," Cy told Travis when they were done.

"I'll come with you. We could get the poles and go fishing."

"Too late for that. I got to think about gettin' supper goin'. Daddy been plowin' all day and sure to be starvin'."

"I could help you," Travis offered. He had the pitiful look in his eyes that Cy knew well.

Cy was ready not to have Travis hanging around, but he wouldn't hurt the boy's feelings. "They ain't anything much to do," he replied. "Besides, soon as I get a couple yams in to bake, I's gonna try and rest some. You go on home. Ain't nothin' gon' happen. Your daddy for sure gone up to bed. You ain't gon' see him till tomorrow."

"*Please* come to the house, Cy."

"Oh, all right. But you wait and see. Things gonna look better in the mornin'."

"No, they won't," Travis mumbled.

"You ain't still thinkin' 'bout runnin' away, is you?"

Travis fixed his eyes on the hard-packed earth of the barn floor. "Naw. It was just talk. I reckon I'll see if Aunt Dorcas has somethin' cooked."

As they left the barn, Travis took Cy's hand, something he hadn't done in a long time.

For a second, Cy wanted to pull away. *Mist' John sho' wouldn't like to see us like this*, he thought. He glanced at their clasped hands, his a deep brown, so different from Travis's, which was pale, almost pink, and he knew it was all right. They were unlikely friends, for sure: Travis, son of a plantation master, and himself, poor and black, the son of a man who farmed a few acres of that plantation just to put food on the table. But they had grown up with no friends except each other, and that was more important than the different colors of their skin.

Cy knew that most folks didn't agree with him about that, especially John Strong, but at the moment, he didn't care. Travis's hand felt good in his. He remembered once overhearing Strong warn Travis that it wasn't fitting for him to be so friendly with a nigger, that niggers needed to remember their place, that they got wrong ideas in their kinky-haired heads if white folks were too *familiar* with them. That gave Cy yet another reason to despise the man.

Cy waited by the back door of the house. Travis went in, then came back after a minute and said everything was all right, his daddy must be asleep like Cy had predicted.

"Thanks," Travis said. "See you tomorrow." He went inside and pushed the door shut. In all the years they'd been friends, Cy had never been invited farther inside Travis's place than the kitchen.

Cy started down the hill toward what everyone still called "the quarter," where the slaves used to live, back in the day when John Strong's granddaddy was owner of the biggest plantation in those parts. He walked through the grove of oak trees, kicking a sweet-gum ball as he went. He wished he could take that cat-o'-nine-tails to John Strong, let him know what it felt like to have your skin torn to pieces by its twisted cords. He came into the clearing where the colored folks' cabins circled an open space around the old well. The red clay ground was packed iron hard by the feet of the black people who had lived there since slavery times. Slavery was gone now, and so were most of the people. Some were dead and buried in the weed-choked graveyard nearby. Others had headed off long ago for better chances in Savannah or Augusta, or had been forced to seek land to sharecrop for a landlord better off than Mr. John Strong, master of what little was left of Warren Hall Plantation.

Most of the cabins were empty and sagging; others nothing more than collapsed piles of rotting boards brooded over by crumbling chimneys. Aunt Dorcas and Uncle Daniel's was one of the few that looked neat and tidy. They both worked up at the big house, as the old colored folks still called the shabby white-columned mansion where the Strongs, father and son, lived. Mrs. Strong had been dead two years—summer fever and too little love, Aunt Dorcas declared.

A few other families lived in the quarter, but Cy didn't know them well, and he didn't much want to. They were strangers, empty-eyed black folks who showed up in early spring looking for a few acres to sharecrop, tried their best to raise some cotton or tobacco, and left after harvest, when it was clear they couldn't get through a winter on what little they made working for a man as mean as John Strong.

Cy stepped into the empty one-room cabin. He didn't look for his father to be home, not with so much plowing to be done. A rainy spring had made it too muddy earlier to get into the bottom land, the only acres on Strong's place where a man had a chance to raise a crop and come out at least even. Strong let Cy's father, Pete Williams, farm that land even though it was prime. There was no one else to do it, not anymore. Strong could have, but he'd lost interest in growing things since his wife died. That was when he discovered his love of betting on the races and had the bad luck to get his hands on the horse of his dreams, the stallion he'd named Teufel. Travis said it meant "devil" in some foreign language.

Cy sat down on the crude bench by the table where he and his father ate. His eyes landed where they always did sooner or later: on the pink calico sunbonnet that had belonged to his mama, hanging there by the door. A familiar ache settled over his heart, then a surge of anger, the anger that had made him take his mama's glass bead necklace, the only other thing she'd left behind, and hurl it down the hole in the outhouse. Many a time he'd wished he hadn't done that, but nothing was going to make him try and get it back. Gone was gone.

He wondered, as he always did, why his mama left her bonnet the morning she walked out of the cabin and out of his life. Where had she gone, and why? His father said she was homesick for her people downstate near Valdosta, where she was from, yet he never bothered to go down there and see. At first, Cy thought he himself must have done something to make her unhappy enough to leave, something real bad. But no matter how many nights he lay awake searching for a reason, he couldn't think of anything. He loved his mama—she had to know that. So why would she abandon him? He didn't understand, and he was afraid to ask his father.

Cy did know that after his mother left, something changed in Pete Williams. He used to work on the land all day and in the evenings still have energy to play checkers and then sit on the front stoop and entertain folks by playing his mouth organ and singing. Now he was silent most evenings, sitting by the fireplace repairing tack or carving spoons out of the dry, hard oak he stored in the corner. Days, he was always on the move, mending fences, chopping weeds, hauling firewood—staying busy.

A change in the light meant evening was coming on, and it was past time to start supper. Preparing their meals was one thing Cy had been forced to learn in the last two years. The day after his wife left, Pete Williams informed his son he wasn't no cook, and if Cy wanted to eat decent from then on, he'd have to learn to do for himself.

Do for himself. That had meant a lot more than figuring out how to get a fire going in the cookstove and how to keep it just hot enough so it would cook a cornpone all the way through without charring the bottom or top. It meant washing his own clothes, what few there were— just a couple pairs of drawers, denim overalls, a blue cotton work shirt, and a jacket.

It meant getting along without the jokes his daddy used to tell, without the games of catch they used to play with the tattered baseball Pete had found somewhere and brought home. It meant not feeling his daddy's arms, strong as iron, around him at bedtime the way they always used to be when he was young. The last time Cy had wanted his father to hug him, he'd been told he was too old for that foolishness now.

So Cy had started spending even more time with the puny white boy he'd known as long as he could remember. They hunted everything from mourning doves and squirrels to white-tailed deer, but not the sharp-tusked wild hogs—they were too dangerous. They fished in the Ogeechee for redbreast. Shared stories about what they'd do one day when they were grown men. They made their own world of secret hideouts with hidden treasure-troves of iron railroad spikes, turtle shells, the skulls of small animals, spear points left behind by the Indians Uncle Daniel claimed once roamed this land until the white folks drove them away or gave them bad diseases so they all died.

I hope to God Mist' John don't wake up till he sober, Cy thought as he put a match to the fatwood in the stove. When he was sure the fire was well started, he rummaged in the food bin. Now, what we got for supper? he asked the plank walls of the cabin. Same stuff as always, they seemed to reply.

The food was ready when Pete Williams came into the cabin. His work shirt was dark under the arms and even the bib of his overalls was wet with sweat, and he hadn't bothered to wash up. When his wife was around, he'd never come into the house dirty and smelling bad, but these days there was no reason for that nice stuff, he said.

Cy eyed his father, wondering what kind of night it would be. A moonshine night, with the man slowly drinking himself into a rage and then into tears of self-pity, falling asleep in his chair, his mouth slack and spit dribbling from its corners? Or the kind when he would eat without a word, then get up and leave, not to return until dawn? Cy guessed he had a woman somewhere, but who she was and what she saw in Pete Williams, he didn't know.

"What's with you?" the man asked.

"Nothin', Daddy. Why?" Cy could feel his muscles tense. These days, he never knew what to expect from his father.

"Don't tell me nothin', boy. You got some misery written all over yo' face. What is it?"

There was no point in lying. "Teufel lost the race, and when they come home, Mist' John put him in his stall and whipped the hide off 'im."

"Shit! I ain't never knowed no man have worse luck with horses than John Strong. You know what this mean, don't you?"

"No, sir."

"Mean Strong done lost this place at last. I heard tell he bet every cent he got left on that damn horse, and see how he end up. God in heaven! I don't give a damn what that man do to hisself, but what about the rest of us? What about Dorcas an' Daniel? We all gon' have to leave now, 'less we wants to beg the new owners to let us stay. And after all that damn plowin' these last five days!"

Pete Williams went for the crockery jug he kept on the high shelf by the bed where he slept alone. He pulled out the stopper, raised the jug to his lips, and drank deeply. So it would be that kind of night. "Supper ready?" he asked.

"Yes, sir."

"Dish it up, then."

Cy served his father a plateful of beans, a piece of pone, a slice of fried fatback, and some dandelion greens.

"Lord, I's so tired o' beans," his father complained. He used his spoon to push the sticky mass to one side of his plate. "We got any syrup?"

Cy went for the pitcher. "Bring the salt, too," his father told him. He covered his pone with the thick brown syrup and poured salt on the beans. "That's better," he declared. "Next time, be sure to cook them beans with plenty o' water."

"Yes, sir." Cy had given up a long time ago trying to cook food the way Pete Williams liked it. Whatever he cooked was usually too this or too that, but he noticed that his father always cleaned his plate. There was too little of anything to waste it.

The man took to pushing his beans into small mounds. "Guess we be leavin' here real soon," he said bitterly.

"Why, Daddy? Even if Mist' John lost the place, we can stay."

"For what? So I can break my back slavin' for some new master? Hell, no! I's done. Somebody else can kill hisself to make money for the white man. I been thinkin' of headin' over to Savannah anyway, get me a job on the docks. You, too. You almost old enough."

Cy put down his spoon. *Maybe I don't want to go to Savannah*, he thought. *Maybe I wants to stay here. If Mama ever come back lookin' for us, and we was gone . . .*

But Cy didn't dare say this to his father.

"What's a matter?" Williams asked. "Don't you want to get outta here?"

"Sure, Daddy. But—"

"But nothin'! The sooner we go, the better I like it. Savannah can't be no worse than this hole."

"How we get there? Mule belong to Strong."

"You got two feet that work, ain't you?"

"Yes, sir."

"Well, then." Pete took a bite of fatback, then spit it out. "Ain't I told you 'bout cuttin' off the rind 'fore you fry this up?"

"Sorry, Daddy."

"Fetch me the jug."

Cy brought the moonshine, and the man took another long swig. They finished their meal in silence. Williams kept drinking, and soon after he'd eaten, his head dropped onto his chest. He began to snore.

"Come on, Daddy," Cy urged. "Lemme help you."

He half carried the big man to the bed and let him drop onto it. Cy lifted his father's legs from the floor and got him to roll onto his side. The snoring wasn't as bad that way. Then he cleaned up the dishes and put some wood in the fireplace. After a warm day, the evening was surprisingly chilly. Cy sat staring into the fire, brooding.

Had John Strong really lost everything this time? Would a new owner take over the place? Would Travis have to leave?

Hatred stirred in Cy's belly. John Strong had so much, and Cy and his daddy had so little. Black folks tried to hold tight to what little they *did* have, while a sorry man like Strong went and threw away everything. Travis said everyone had told his daddy not to buy that horse. Yeah, he was fast, fastest ever seen in those parts. But there was something devilish about him, something no man could trust. And now see how it had turned out.

The fire burnt low in the hearth, and Cy went to bed.

TWO

A LIGHT BUT URGENT TOUCH ON HIS SHOULDER
woke him out of sad dreams. He flinched, but then he recognized Uncle Daniel's voice, whispering close to his ear.

Cy sat up, wondering what the old man wanted. It had
to be something important for him to come into the cabin
in the dark of night. "Uncle Daniel?"

"I tapped on the door, but I didn't see no light, so I figured y'all was asleep. When they warn't no answer, I stuck
my head inside the door and heard him snorin' the way he
do when he been drinkin'."

"I put him to bed."

"It's a shame. But you the one I got to talk to. Can you
come with me fo' a moment? We needs yo' help."

Cy followed Uncle Daniel outside. The air was colder
than inside the cabin.

"What is it?"

"Travis gone! Took Teufel with him."

"Naw! He promised me he warn't gon' do nothin' like that."

"Y'all talked about it?"

"After Mist' John whipped Teufel so bad, Travis said he was gon' run away. I made him promise he wouldn't."

"Well, he ain't kept his word. He took off, him and that damned horse. I was done with my work up at the big house and was headed home when I heard noises in the barn."

"Ain't it real late?"

"Naw. I stayed 'round tonight to finish puttin' fresh mortar between them bricks in the kitchen fireplace. Had to wait for the hearth to cool down enough fo' me to work. Like I said, I heard these noises, and when I went to check up on things, Travis come bustin' outta the barn, ridin' bareback on that black devil! I shouted at him, but he didn't pay me no mind, just kept goin', headin' for the road."

"Travis was *ridin' on* Teufel? He ain't never been on that horse's back! He ain't big enough to get up there."

"I'd of said the same thing if I hadn't seen it with my own two eyes. But that ain't the point. We got to go after him, bring him back 'fore Mist' John wake up and find him gone. If he catch him, they's gon' be hell to pay."

"What can I do?"

"Son, I hates to ask you this, but I wants you to go look for him. I's too old to come with you. I just slow you down. Them young legs o' yours can carry you fast."

Uncle Daniel's request was crazy, impossible. "I can't! He on a horse—fastest one around. Travis bound to be long gone by now."

"Gone where? Don't you see? He ain't really runnin' away. Boy that age got nowhere *to* run. I reckon he just gone off somewhere close, somewhere to calm down. In the mornin', I bet he come home by hisself, but we can't take the chance of his daddy findin' out he left and took that horse."

"I can't, Uncle Daniel! Where I even begin to look for him?"

The old man put his hand on Cy's shoulder. "I know you boys got you a secret hideout somewhere not too far off. Ain't I right?"

How did Uncle Daniel know? Cy and Travis did have a place of their own, down on the river, but they'd sworn a blood oath not to tell anyone about it.

"I's right, ain't I?" Uncle Daniel asked again.

"Yes, sir."

"I bet if you go there, you find him wishin' he hadn't

done such a thing. That boy probably scared o' the dark, and cold, too. You go get him, and he follow you home like a little lost puppy. With any luck, we can get Teufel put up and Travis in his own bed without Mist' John ever findin' out. Please, Cy! Go an' fetch him home. You know he look up to you."

Yes, Travis would listen to him, but Cy felt uneasy. This was between Travis and his father. How many times had his own father said that the black man must *never* get in the middle of white folks' business? If he did, when everything was settled, somehow the black man was the one who ended up in trouble. No, best keep out of it. Let Travis come home on his own.

But Cy couldn't leave Travis out there somewhere in the dark with a horse he couldn't really handle. Not with Uncle Daniel begging him to find the boy and bring him home. And what if Travis really *was* gone for good, if he hadn't gone to their secret place near where the Ogeechee was extra wide, the spot folks called the Bull Hole? At the least, he'd have to try and find Travis, see if Uncle Daniel was correct.

"All right," Cy told the old man.

"Oh, thank you, son! You can use my lantern. This place o' yours, it ain't too far, I hope?"

"No, sir. It gon' take time to get there in the dark, though."

"All right. You best hurry along. Sooner we have that boy home safe, the easier I can rest. Dorcas an' me be sittin' up, waitin' on you."

Cy eased back inside the cabin. His father was snoring hard. He'd be out cold for hours. Cy grabbed his coat and closed the door behind him. Outside, Uncle Daniel gave him the lantern and put a piece of pound cake in his hand. "From Aunt Dorcas," he said. "She always say a nice sweet make things seem better."

Cy left the clearing and headed for the Bull Hole, cutting through the woods on a narrow path only he and Travis knew about. Even in the dark, he could go pretty quickly because he knew the way so well. Still, it took what seemed a long time to get to the river, which he heard before he came up to it. Spring rains had been heavy, and the water was running high and fast.

Cy slowed to a cautious walk as he came to the place. There was no light except from his lantern, but when he stood still, he could hear another sound besides the movement of the water surging to his right. The soft nickering of a horse. It had to be Teufel.

"Travis, that you? It me, Cy."

For a moment, there was no answer. Then, "Cy? You alone?"

"Yeah."

"You swear? Daddy ain't with you?"

"I swear. Uncle Daniel saw you hightail it outta the barn, and he come get me, asked me to find you. I got to bring you home 'fore your daddy wake up."

"I ain't coming home!"

Cy moved forward into the small clearing. Travis stood facing him, Teufel beside him, his reins tied to a tree. In the lantern light, Cy could see the boy had been crying. His face was smeared with dirt, and the hair hanging on his forehead was wet with sweat, even in the cool night air.

"Hey," Cy said. "You all right? And Teufel?"

Travis nodded. "He's okay."

"Uncle Daniel claimed he saw you *ridin'* him. That the truth?"

"Uh-huh. I didn't think I could do it. But I did like I've seen you do—talked to him quiet, told him we were going to run away, that Daddy wouldn't touch him ever again. He understood me, Cy! I know he did."

Cy went to the horse. He held out the piece of pound cake, which Teufel took and swallowed in one bite.

"We got to go home now," Cy said.

"I told you, I ain't goin' back there."

Cy stepped toward Travis, who turned his face away.

"Let me see you," Cy said, and Travis turned back. In the lantern light, a red slash mark stood out clearly on the side of Travis's face. "Yo' daddy do that?"

"He was asleep on the sofa in his study when I went in the house the first time, but after you left, I started upstairs, and he come charging out into the hall like some kind of crazy man! I tried to get away without a fight, but he got hold of me and cut me with that whip."

"What for?"

"He ain't needed a reason since Mama died. Just because he was so bad drunk. He gets the devil in him when he's drunk. That's when . . . he beats me."

"Aw, Travis! You never told me about that."

"Come morning, I'm heading out. You *got* to come with me, Cy. I'd go now, but I'm so tired, and it's so dark. Cy, please! I got to go, but I need you."

Cy reached for Travis's hand, and the boy crumpled onto the soft sand. Cy sat down beside him. "Go on an' cry some. You feel better after you do. Mama always say so. Then, when you calmed down, we go home."

"I'm not going back there. You got to believe me."

"All right. Let's just sit here quiet awhile." Cy kept his

hand on Travis's shoulder. After a few minutes, Travis's muscles began to relax and his breathing got slower. He lay down on his side and was quickly asleep.

Cy stood up and went to Teufel. The horse nuzzled his hand, looking for more pound cake. "Well, boy, what we gon' do now? I got to get him home 'fore morning, but he so wore out, I hates to rouse him." He stroked the horse's nose. "You had a bad day, too, ain't you? I reckon you don't want to go back any more'n Travis do."

Cy stood in the glow of the lantern, not sure what to do. Part of him wanted to run away with Travis. There was nothing left at Warren Hall, not with the place lost to strangers. But how could he and Travis get away? All they had was a horse, a horse famous in those parts. Somebody would recognize them the very next day and send word to John Strong.

The night air was growing colder. Cy sat down again beside the sleeping boy. He'd let Travis rest for a while, then rouse him and make him return home. He wouldn't want to, but Cy could persuade him. Travis sighed in his sleep and pulled his arms closer to his chest. Cy was cold now too, but at least he had a coat. Travis was wearing only a shirt. He'd done a bad job of running away.

Cy took off his coat and put it over Travis. The

glowing lantern gave off a bit of heat, but the kerosene was more than half gone. They'd need its light to find their way home. He had to wake Travis soon, but he'd let him sleep while he, Cy, kept watch. Right away, his own eyes grew heavy, then closed. That was all he knew until dawn.

THREE

A SHARP PROD TO HIS BACK JOLTED CY FROM
sleep. For an instant, he didn't know where he was. The
world was predawn gray, his face wet with dew. Travis lay
facing him, his arm draped across Cy's neck. That was the
one place on Cy's body that felt warm.

"Wake up, you!" John Strong commanded. His tone
was menacing. "Get away from my boy! Jesus God, I never
thought . . ."

Cy moved and got to his knees. A second man stood
nearby, holding a brown and white hound straining against
its rope. Jeff Sconyers, a cracker farmer who messed with
a few acres down the road from Warren Hall.

"Get up, Travis!" Strong cried.

Travis stirred, and Cy tried to stand, but Sconyers
pushed him back to the ground. Nearby, Teufel, still tied
to the tree, snorted in fear.

"You want me to signal Burwell, Mr. Strong?" Sconyers
asked.

"Yeah. He'll know to meet us back at the house."

Sconyers pulled a pistol from his belt and fired into the air.

Travis jumped like he'd been hit. His pants and drawers were lying piled next to him. Except for his shirt and Cy's jacket over his shoulders, he was naked.

"Travis! Cover yourself," Strong ordered. "My God . . ."

Travis started to pull Cy's coat down over himself.

The cat-o'-nine-tails appeared from nowhere and came down on Cy's shoulders. He cried out as the knotted leather thongs tore his skin.

"Don't, Daddy!" Travis shouted. Then the whip caught him across his back and he crumpled to the earth, face-down.

Teufel pulled against the tree, frantic to get away. Sconyers stood back and watched, his face a blank.

Strong came at Cy again, whip raised. Cy put his arm over his face to shield himself from the next blow. It bit through his shirt, cutting the flesh on his forearm.

"Please, Mist' John, stop! I knows Travis done wrong, runnin' away and all—"

"Shut your goddamn mouth! You ain't got a thing to say that I want to hear."

From the corner of his eye, Cy noticed Travis moving. *Stay where you is. Don't call attention to yourself*, he thought.

To distract Strong, he kept talking. "We was gon' come home last night. Uncle Daniel saw Travis run off with Teufel and ask me to find him—"

Strong flailed at Cy and missed.

"I was gon' bring Travis back last night, but he was so tuckered out he fell 'sleep, and then I reckon I did, too. I meant to bring him home last night."

Strong turned on his son. "What kind of white man are you?" he snarled. "Lyin' like that with a *nigger?*"

Suddenly Cy understood. Travis without pants . . . Strong thought he and Travis were—he searched for the word and couldn't come up with it. But such a notion was all wrong, crazy. He and Travis weren't like that. They were friends, sure—brothers, even. But not that other thing.

"What is it, Daddy?"

"What *is* it? I got eyes! Why ain't you wearin' your britches?"

"I took 'em off. I—wet myself in the night and didn't want to sleep in my pants. Cy's tellin' you the truth. I run off. He found me, that's all. I didn't want to come home, but Cy made me promise I would. We didn't mean to fall asleep."

Strong's answer was to raise the whip yet again. Travis

cowered like a cur dog, trying to protect himself, but the whip fell on his back and he cried out.

Cy jumped up. He had to save Travis. But his father's warning leaped into his mind: *The black man don't never dare mess in white folks' business*. He couldn't move. "Leave him alone!" he shouted. "He only run away 'cause he tired o' you beatin' him!"

Strong's arm stopped in midstroke. He fixed his eyes on Cy, then started toward him.

I can take him, Cy thought. But the look of poisonous hatred in the white man's eyes drained his courage. And there was Jeff Sconyers, pistol in hand. Two white men, one crazy, the other itching to use his gun.

Cy broke and bolted for the river. When he came to the bank, he hesitated, for the water was surging by with terrifying speed. But Strong was right behind him. He jumped. Murky water closed over his head, and for a second, panic threatened, but he pushed back to the surface. The water was bitingly cold, so cold he could hardly catch his breath, and the current was more powerful than any force he'd ever felt. It was pushing him downstream, and he had to swim against it with all his strength just to stay where he was. Even so, with every stroke, he was losing ground.

Behind him, Cy heard Strong cry, "No, Travis!" and

then a splash as someone plunged into the water. Cy looked back and saw Travis bob to the surface, terror on his face.

"Go back!" Cy shouted. "Go back!"

Travis clawed against the current.

"Travis!" shouted John Strong from the top of the embankment. "Swim for it, boy! Swim hard!"

"You can make it!" Cy cried, treading water.

"Get him!" Strong shouted at Sconyers.

"I cain't," the man said. "I ain't never learned how to swim."

Travis looked frantically at Cy, then at the men on the shore. Every second, the river was pushing him farther and farther away.

Cy went after Travis, but even though he was swimming with the current, its power was draining his strength. Travis's head appeared above the surface, then went under, only to resurface farther downstream. He didn't even seem to be trying to help himself now.

Strong and Sconyers scrambled alongside, crashing through the web of small trees and wild grapevines, Strong shouting to his son to make an effort, try and swim back to the riverbank.

Cy kept swimming. Straight ahead he could see a wall of floating debris that wasn't moving. Travis was swept past it and disappeared. Cy was slammed directly against it, and the force of the current held him there. Slowly, he began making his way back toward the open channel, grabbing on to branches and pulling himself forward. Just beyond where he was about to take his next handhold, a snake dropped into the river. *Let it not be a water moccasin,* Cy thought. *Last thing I needs is for a poison snake to bite me.*

Finally, Cy reached the end of the snarled debris. Only open water lay between him and the riverbank. The current was pulling ferociously toward his left, but maybe he could swim across it and get back to safety.

He took a huge breath and made himself let go of the log he'd been clinging to. Right away, the current seized him, but he swam with all he had. Slowly, he made progress toward the land. He struggled on, forcing himself to take the next breath, the next stroke. When he finally made it to the water's edge, he dragged himself through a mat of slimy leaves and grass and up the muddy bank, then collapsed on top, his chest heaving. He retched and vomited up water as brown and thick as the river itself. His body heaved with sobs. "I tried to save you," he moaned. "I tried."

A kick made him cry out. "Get up, nigger," Strong commanded, his voice hoarse.

"I—I don't know if I can," he gasped.

Strong stood over him, silent, while Cy labored to catch his breath.

In a moment, Cy pushed himself to his knees and tried to speak. "I do anything you want—Mist' John—but—but please, sir, don't make me—"

"Make you what?"

Cy looked at the mess of mud and vomit where he'd been lying. "Don't make me get back in that water. Please!"

"Who said anything about that? Travis got ashore somewhere downstream. All we got to do is find him. Durned if I ain't gonna tan that boy's hide for playin' me such a mean trick. Now let's go. I'm too old for this kind of nonsense."

The man done lost his mind for sure, Cy thought. Did he really think Travis would be playing a game with him? Cy, too, wanted to believe that somewhere they'd come across Travis, wet and all tuckered out, scared half to death, yet safe. But he knew that couldn't be. Travis had drowned. Cy was the better swimmer, and the river had almost beaten him.

Strong brought a coil of rope out from his rucksack and shoved it into Sconyers's hands. "Tie him first," he said.

The man looked down at Cy with disgust. "On your

feet," he growled. Cy managed to stand, but his legs felt wobbly. "Hands behind your back."

"Mist' John, why I got to be tied? I ain't gon' try nothin'."

"You sure as hell ain't. You caused me enough trouble already, and I ain't taking no chances with you."

Sconyers bound Cy's hands so tightly that his wrists throbbed.

"Let's go," Strong ordered.

Cy took a few steps downstream. He was afraid now. With his hands tied, there was nothing he could do. If Strong decided to push him back into the water, he was done for. Something hard poked him in the back. The barrel of Sconyers's pistol.

Cy kept moving, watching every step so he wouldn't slip and tumble down the embankment. If he was going to die in the river, he didn't want it to be from his own mistake.

The maze of vines and low-hanging branches made the going slow. Branches snapped Cy in the face because he had no way of pushing them aside. Strong kept shouting for Travis. Nothing. They stopped often and scanned the river. Still nothing. A long time passed, and the fear in Cy's belly grew.

"There!" Sconyers shouted. Travis, his shirt torn away by the force of the water, was caught on a dead cypress tree sticking up like a bony finger from the middle of the river. The boy's face was pressed against the trunk, his left arm pinned, and his right floating free and seeming to point downstream.

Strong cried out, then bit his own knuckles.

Cy felt his legs buckle, and he collapsed onto his knees.

"No time for prayin'," Strong cried. "Get up!"

Cy obeyed. "I's sorry, Mist' John. Oh, God, I's so sorry."

"You ain't got time to be sorry just now. There's a job to do."

"Sir?"

"Go get my boy! You think I'm gonna leave him out there for the fish to eat?"

"How can I—"

"Let him go!"

Sconyers undid the rope.

"Now tie one end around his waist."

Sconyers did that, too.

Cy shrank from the white man's touch, but at least his hands were free.

"You're gonna swim out there," Strong told him, "get the bod—get my boy, and bring him back. We'll hold the rope."

Cy wanted to run away, hide, be anywhere except here by the river that had killed his friend, being forced to go back into it by a man mad with grief.

"I got to piss first," Cy whispered. "Please, sir."

"Go on, then. I ain't stopping you."

They turned away while Cy relieved himself. His bowels wanted to move too, but that would have to wait. So would the vomit that rose in his mouth again. So would his tears.

"All right, Mist' John. I's ready."

"Remember: You swim out there, get him, and hold him tight. We'll pull you back. Got that?"

He nodded. "Yes, sir."

Cy stumbled down the bank and tried to hold his footing just above the water. There was nowhere to wade in; he'd have to jump. His body begged him not to do it. The first time he told himself to go, his legs refused. *Come on,* he commanded them. When he hit the water, the cold shock jolted him just as hard as it had before. The men put tension on the rope to keep him from being pulled downstream. That helped.

When he reached Travis, a sob rose in his throat. It took all the strength he had to free the boy's arm, catch him around the waist, and pull him close. He hated how Travis's eyes, the color of a robin's egg, gazed unseeing into his own. The dead boy's head fell forward against Cy's left shoulder. Having him so close was almost more than Cy could stand, and for a second, he considered simply letting the body go. But Travis deserved better.

Cy couldn't swim now, not with both arms wrapped around Travis's body. He hoped Strong and Sconyers would be able to haul him back to shore.

"Ready?" Strong shouted.

"Yes, sir."

It took a while, but finally Cy and his burden reached the bank. The father, oddly calm, seized his son's body and cradled it against his heaving chest. With careful steps, he made his way up the embankment.

"C'mon, you," Sconyers told Cy. He waved the pistol toward the top of the embankment. "Up there."

Above them, Strong was sobbing. When they reached the top, he was standing over the naked body of his son, which he had laid on the ground. Cy approached and looked down at his friend. The eyes were open yet, and the mouth, too. In death, Travis looked small and defenseless, his ribs showing under the pale, thin skin of his chest, his arms and legs like sticks. Cy grasped for the right words to let Strong know how much he ached for Travis, how sad and sick he was over what had happened. But there were no words.

"Give me your shirt," Strong ordered him.

Cy undid his overalls and peeled the filthy, tattered rag from his chest, which was heaving with sorrow. Strong wrapped it tenderly around his son's nakedness, then lifted the body and held it to himself. "Let's go," he said. "Tie the nigger, Jeff."

They struggled back the way they had come. From time to time, the barrel of Sconyers's pistol nudged Cy's back, as if reminding him how much the man would enjoy pulling the trigger.

When they came to where the boys had slept, Strong draped Travis over Teufel's back. "Let's go home," he said gently. "Your mama's waiting on us."

Strong's words made a chill run up Cy's back. How could Travis's mother be waiting back at Warren Hall? She'd been lying in the family graveyard for two years. *Strong outta his head*, Cy thought. *And a crazy man be likely to do anything* . . .

As they went, Cy's thoughts tormented him. Why had he let Uncle Daniel talk him into going to find Travis? He'd messed in the white man's business, and just as his father had warned, he was in bad trouble now—the worst trouble of his life. Most of all, Cy wished he hadn't run when Strong came at him—hadn't turned yellow. If he hadn't jumped into the river, Travis wouldn't have followed him. He'd be alive now, instead of lying limp and pitiful across Teufel's back.

Teufel. This was all really *his* fault. If he hadn't lost the race, none of this would have happened. No, it was Travis's fault! If he hadn't run away, he'd be alive this minute. *No.* It was all his own fault. If he, Cy, had stood and faced Strong like a man, maybe he *could* have held his own. Maybe Travis would have come and helped him fight. Maybe together they could have gotten Strong to listen to the truth . . .

Maybe. What a cruel word. It was all too late; all the maybes in the world couldn't help Travis now . . .

Cy felt as if he were trapped in one of those dreams that are so terrifying you wake up pouring sweat, scared to death but grateful it was only a dream. Only this was real, and it wasn't over yet. Something terrible was going to happen. He felt it in his bones.

When they approached Warren Hall, Aunt Dorcas appeared at the kitchen door. She screamed and covered her face with her hands. Uncle Daniel hurried from the stable and eased the body off of Teufel's back.

"Take him upstairs," Strong ordered. He turned to Aunt Dorcas. "I need your help," he said. "You know what to do. I'll be up shortly."

Sobbing, she followed Uncle Daniel into the house.

Strong turned his attention to Burwell Sconyers, Jeff's brother, who had been waiting for them. The two men walked toward the barn and stood close together. Strong talked, and Burwell listened and nodded. Cy felt jittery and wished he knew what was going on. His bowels demanded relief. Next to him, Jeff Sconyers kept fiddling with his pistol. At last Strong dismissed Burwell and trudged into the house.

Burwell sauntered up to his brother. "Strong says to untie him, let him go back to the quarter."

Again, Jeff did as he was told.

"Mr. Strong says for you to git home," Burwell said. "Wait at your place till he sends word."

Cy was suspicious. This was all? Strong wasn't going to whip him, tell him to clear out? "He ain't mad at me?"

"How the hell should I know? That's all he said. Just do like the man says. If I was you, I'd sure want me a bath. You stink, boy!"

The two men walked away. The hound sniffed at Cy's leg and then, losing interest, followed his masters to the barn.

Free, Cy raced to the outhouse, where he sat in the half-light. His chest was heaving, and he stayed there long after he'd finished his business, trying to calm down and figure out what to do next. Something wasn't right. He didn't know whether or not to believe what the Sconyers boys had told him. But he couldn't think of anything else to do but go to the cabin.

He was headed down the hill when he heard Uncle Daniel calling. The old man caught up with him. Cy could tell he'd been crying. Together, they walked toward the quarter.

"They told me to go home and stay there," Cy told him.

"That's right. Mist' John say for me to tell you the same thing. He tol' Dorcas an' me what happen. I's suppos' to take that horse and rub him down good. They gon' wash and dress that po' child, and Mist' John say we got to dig his grave next to Miz Annie's."

"What happened, Uncle Daniel? How Mist' John find Travis an' me?" Cy had been wondering this on and off ever since the point of Strong's boot had wakened him at dawn. Had Uncle Daniel betrayed the two boys? He didn't want to believe it, but how else could Strong have known how to find them?

"He come 'round to our place 'bout four in the mornin', knockin' on the door fit to bust it down and shoutin', 'Where Travis?' I didn't like to let him know the truth, but I was afeared to lie, so I told him."

"Aw, *why* you do that? You shouldn't o' said nothin'!"

"Please don't be angry with me, son. I cain't stand it if you is. I never thought things could turn out thisaway." Tears coursed down his cheeks.

Cy felt sorry for him. "It's all right, Uncle Daniel. You didn't mean no harm. What happen then?"

The old man wiped his nose on his sleeve. "Mist' John an' me went over to yo' place and looked in, and we didn't see you, so I knowed you wasn't back yet. Yo' daddy was still sound asleep, so Mist' John say to leave him be."

"Where Daddy now?"

"I's comin' to that. Strong say he was gon' to get some help to look for you boys and for me to stay 'round the place. At dawn I was suppos' to find Pete and tell him to get to work first thing and see to the plowin', considerin' how the wet weather done kept him outta the field till now and it so important to get that seed into the ground. I did like he told me. Mist' John was actin' calmed down by then, like you boys bein' gone warn't really no big thing—he just wanted to find y'all, and them Sconyers boys got theyselves a good trackin' dog."

Uncle Daniel's explanation still didn't make sense. "He for sure ain't mad at me?" Cy asked.

"Not now, son. He allowed that maybe back at the river he was mad, but he don't blame you none. He say he had time to think it over while y'all was walkin' back, and he realize it all jus' a accident. 'A terrible accident,' is how he put it. And he say he 'preciate how you tried to save his boy."

"Is that really what he say?" None of it sounded like the John Strong Cy knew.

"God's truth. And also he know you must be all tuckered out after tryin' to save Travis and for you to rest. You can tell yo' daddy what happen when he get back from the fields. Strong say he send word later when he finish makin' plans 'bout when we gon' bury Travis."

The thought of burying Travis was too much. Now it was Cy's turn to cry.

"It *was* a accident, Uncle Daniel! The whole thing. I found Travis just where you say he be, and I try to make him come home, and he didn't want to, and he cry and then he fell asleep and I did too . . ."

"Hush now. I knows you done what you could. And remember, I's the one who sent you to find him."

Cy could feel his stomach knotting. He retched and threw up another mouthful of river water. "I's scared. What he told you—it don't feel right. He wanted to hurt me. Look!" Cy pointed to the slash marks the cat-o'-nine-tails had left on his back and arms. "He kept hittin' us. Then he started for me. He wanted to kill me! That's why I jumped into the river. And then Travis did too—"

"Easy there, son. Mist' John ain't hisself. First losin' that race, now this—"

"Somethin' bad gon' happen. I know it, Uncle Daniel. I got to get away from here! Daddy too." His mind was running like a scared rabbit, trying to think of what to grab and throw into a sack, then where to find his father and escape before—

Uncle Daniel placed a gnarled hand on his shoulder. "Easy, son. Strong give his word that things between you and him is okay. Jes' do like he say. You all to pieces 'cause you so tired and grieved. Besides, would yo' daddy let anyone mess with you?"

That was some comfort. Uncle Daniel was right—his father would protect him.

"Go on now. You 'bout to drop in yo' tracks. Anybody can see that. I check on you later."

They'd gotten to Cy's cabin. His head was pounding, and the tears continued sliding down his face. He wished his father would be home, but he knew that wasn't likely. For a moment, he simply wanted to run—run anywhere— the swamp, a hollow tree, a hole in the ground. Or go into the fields and find his father. But he was too tired.

A silent, empty cabin greeted him. The sight of his mother's pink bonnet brought a new wave of tears, and Cy dropped onto his narrow bed. His body craved sleep, but he had to get out of his wet clothes. He stripped them off and let them lie where they fell. A bath would feel good, but he was too tired for that too. Instead, he put on his other drawers and overalls. The only shirt and jacket he owned were lost now. Cy dropped onto the bed. He would sleep just a little, he told himself, and then he would go find his father.

FOUR

CY WAS SWIMMING TO REACH TRAVIS, WHOSE body kept floating away from him, just beyond his grasp. The force of rough hands pinning his shoulders to the straw tick woke him from his nightmare. He looked up into Jeff Sconyers's eyes, and their gray emptiness frightened him. Cy tried to sit up, but two more hands forced him back. Burwell Sconyers. Cy struggled for all he was worth, but the brothers flipped him face-down and bound his hands.

"You fight us, nigger, I'll kill you here and now, understand?" Jeff warned.

Cy fought to roll onto his back, to free himself, then took a slap to the side of his face.

"Quit, 'less you lookin' to die, which would be a shame after how hard you worked to save that sorry kid this morning."

He let himself go limp. They were too strong for him,

and he believed Jeff Sconyers's threat. The man had been looking for an excuse to shoot him all morning.

"That's better," Jeff said. "Do like you're told, boy, and it'll go easier on you."

"Lemme turn over. I won't fight you."

"Promise?"

"Yes."

"Yes, what?"

"Yessir." The word was bitter in his mouth, but he had to say it.

"Let him up, Burwell."

Cy turned over and sat up. "Please, sir! Don't do this," he begged. "I didn't mean for none o' this to happen. Strong told Uncle Daniel he didn't blame me."

The white men looked at him with cold eyes.

"What you gon' do with me?"

Jeff Sconyers chuckled. "Ain't you the curious one. Don't worry, boy. You'll find out soon enough."

"Kill me?"

"Naw. Nothin' bad as that."

Cy fought down a scream. He was desperate to escape. "Did Mist' John tell you to do this?"

Jeff snorted. "Keep your mouth shut and do like I say unless you want more trouble'n you can handle in a hundred years. Understand me?"

Cy nodded. He yearned for his father. Surely Pete Williams would be wondering if he'd found Travis and brought him home. Surely he'd be back any moment to see.

"We best be gettin' on," Burwell declared. "Strong said we got a lot o' miles to cover."

What was he talking about?

"The sack," Jeff said.

Burwell produced a small gunnysack and yanked it down over Cy's head.

"No!"

Cy could feel a cord being wrapped around his neck, tight at first, and then tighter. Panic seized him. "Please, get it off!" he shouted. "I's chokin'!"

"No you ain't," Jeff assured him. "If you can yell, you can breathe. Just relax, boy. Fightin' back and gettin' all upset only gonna make it worse."

"I ain't goin' nowhere with you! My daddy comin' home any minute—"

"Hey, what y'all doin' in here? You git away from that boy!" It was Uncle Daniel's voice. Relief swept over Cy. He would be rescued now. Uncle Daniel would save him.

"This ain't your concern, uncle," Jeff growled. "Don't try and stop us. We got our orders direct from John Strong."

"I won't let you hurt that boy," Uncle Daniel cried. "What happen at the river warn't his fault."

"Stand aside," Burwell said. "We ain't got time to mess with you."

There were sounds of a scuffle, Uncle Daniel ordering the men to stop, the men trying to force him out of the cabin. Then the crack of a fist on flesh, a groan, and Cy heard a body hit the floor.

"I told the ol' fool to leave us alone," Burwell declared.

"They ain't never gonna learn," Jeff replied. "No wonder they live like they do. Animals, all of 'em."

"Come on," Burwell told Cy. "On yer feet. We got to get goin'."

Cy was pulled up and dragged out of the cabin. Outside, he could tell it was still day; light filtered through the sack over his head. He started to yell for help.

"Shut up, you!" Jeff cried. "I knowed we should of gagged him."

"It ain't too late," Burwell said. "Hold still," he told Cy. The sack was untied and a cloth gag forced into Cy's mouth. It was tied, and then the sack replaced.

Cy tried again to shout, but he'd been silenced. Terror overwhelmed him, and he began to thrash, desperate to get his hands free, the choking gag out of his mouth, the stifling bag off of his head. Nothing helped. He gave up and dropped to the ground.

"Let him be," he heard Jeff say. "He'll behave if he knows what's good for him."

I got to get hold o' myself, Cy thought. *Figure this thing out. There got to be a way.*

But nothing came to him.

"You ready to cooperate?" Burwell's voice came from above him.

Cy sat up and nodded.

"Get up, then." Cy struggled to his feet. Sweat was pouring into his eyes, and he had to keep swallowing so he wouldn't choke on his own spit. Burwell prodded him to move, then after a few steps, ordered him to stop. "We're at the wagon."

Wagon? *Why is there a wagon?*

"You're gonna get in, and you ain't gonna cause no trouble, see?" Jeff told him. "Right here."

Cy was pushed forward until his chest hit what he guessed was the back of the wagon. Then the men hefted him up and onto a flat wagon bed. There they held him on his side while his ankles were tied.

"Don't try and get off," Jeff warned him.

"Like to see him try it," Burwell said.

"Just you lie still now," Jeff advised. "Might as well catch you some sleep. We got a long ways to go."

Cy heard them climb onto the wagon seat. Then the horse was urged forward, the wagon jolted ahead, and the nightmare of that day resumed.

They went without stopping for what seemed like hours. Eventually, Cy gave up the battle with his body and urinated in his pants. The scratchy cloth sack was torture against his face, and his hands throbbed from being tied so tightly. The gag was the worst. His stomach wanted to empty itself, but if he let it, he'd choke to death on his own vomit.

More than anything he'd ever wanted in his life, Cy wanted his father. By now Pete Williams had gotten back from plowing, heard from Uncle Daniel what had happened, run to the big house, and forced Strong to tell him where to find his son. *Hurry*, Cy pleaded silently.

Then Travis's image rose up in Cy's mind, the boy's pale eyes staring into his own, his hands covering himself, embarrassed that Cy should see him naked and helpless. At last sleep came, and forgetfulness.

Cy woke when the wagon stopped. It was full dark. The men pulled him out of the wagon bed, took the sack off his head, and unbound his gag. Right away, Cy began to dry heave. When he was done, they untied his wrists and let him go off a ways and relieve himself. When he returned, he was told to sit on the ground, and Jeff tied his ankles together. Burwell gave him water from a tin cup and a plate of cold beans. He was too upset to eat, but he drank cup after cup of water.

Cy finally found the courage to ask a question. "Where we goin'?"

"Nowhere that'd mean anything to you," Jeff said. "You might call it a post office."

"Sir?"

"Place to make deliveries!" Burwell exclaimed. "*You*."

"Don't say too much," Jeff warned.

"My daddy's comin' after me," Cy said.

Jeff laughed. "Only if he figures a way to get outta that curing barn we locked him in!"

Hope died. Cy knew they were telling him the truth. Strong had planned it all out.

"You gon' kill me, right?"

"I told you not," Jeff replied. "We ain't no murderers."

"What then?"

"Just wait and see," Burwell said. "Wait and see."

Cy spent the night tied in the wagon bed. When Jeff said they wouldn't make him have the gag and the sack on his head if he'd cooperate and keep his mouth shut, he almost cried. Not that it mattered—they were stopped way off in deep forest with nobody around to hear anything. As soon as it was quiet, Cy fell toward sleep, praying he wouldn't dream. He didn't.

The next morning, he was allowed to relieve himself and was given water and bread, which he devoured. Again he was gagged, the hateful sack was pulled over his head, his hands were tied, and he was laid on the wagon bed. A tarpaulin was thrown over him, and another torturous day began. At midday they stopped in dense woods, and Cy was allowed to stand up, to quench his thirst, to gobble the food the brothers gave him.

As the afternoon wore on, as the sack rubbed the skin of his face raw and the sweat poured off of him in the dense heat, the agony in Cy's body crowded out the torment in his mind. More than anything now, he wanted relief from the gag and freedom from the sack over his head, the rope binding his hands, the suffocating cloth that concealed his body from any curious travelers his kidnappers might meet on the road.

The next time they stopped, it was dark. Never had Cy been so thankful for ordinary things like relieving himself, stretching his arms and legs, and putting some food in his belly. Again, sleep brought forgetfulness.

The third day, Cy began to believe that this journey was Strong's revenge. The Sconyers boys would go on and on until he died, then throw him away into a shallow grave. Then they could say they hadn't actually murdered him, he'd just—died. With the passing hours, any lingering hope that his father would save him drained like water into dry sand, and he began to wish that he *would* die.

This was his reward for being Travis's friend. For finding him in the night and trying to get him to come home. For telling Strong to stop whipping him. And for almost drowning while trying to save him. If by some chance he lived, Cy promised himself, never again would he try and fix the messes of other people, especially white folks. From now on, he'd look out for himself, and other folks could do the same.

On the third night, when Cy knew he wouldn't last much longer, the wagon stopped and he could hear the men jump down. One began pounding on something; it sounded like a wooden door. Then strange voices, the sound of a lock clicking open, a heavy door or gate swinging on rusty hinges, and Jeff telling the horse to walk on. Cy was hauled out of the wagon bed. The sack was taken from his head, his gag removed, and he was made to step forward.

He was in a large open space. In the dim light thrown by a single lantern, he could just make out a fence of barbed wire fastened to tall wooden poles. In front of him were a couple of long, low wooden buildings.

Two white men, one holding a lantern, came forward and stood looking him over the way a horse breeder looks at a gelding up for sale. "So who's this?" the man with the lantern said, touching Cy under the chin and making him raise his head. "And who might you fellas be?"

"Our names ain't important," Jeff replied. "Let's just say we work for a rich man up in Davis County. He hired us to deliver this nigger to you, and he don't want no questions asked."

"Davis County? That's a long ways from here. How'd this rich boss of yours find out about my place?"

Jeff shrugged. "I dunno. Maybe you got a big reputation, Mr. Cain. Mr. Str—" He caught himself before he gave away the name. "He told us just where to find you. Said you're famous all over for bein' an old-time nigger catcher, like them patrollers before the war."

Cain threw him an ugly look. "Don't try my patience if you want to do business. If I got a reputation, ain't none of your affair how I come by it. Understand?"

Jeff lowered his eyes. "Yessir."

"This big boss of yours . . . He send you with any . . . *incentive* for me to take this boy off his hands?"

"If you mean money, yessir."

"Let's see it, then."

Jeff dug in a pocket and came up with a pouch. Cain

handed the lantern to his helper, untied the string, and poured some coins into his hand. "This boy ain't sick, is he? Ain't got the consumption or swamp fever?"

"No, sir. He's fit. Can put in a big day's work. No doubt about that."

Cain jingled the coins. "Open your mouth," he ordered Cy. His helper held the lantern close, and Cain peered down Cy's throat. "Turn around." Cy did. "Unhitch them britches so I can get a good look at you."

Cy obeyed. He hated the white men's eyes on his body. Cain looked him over, again like he was inspecting a cow or hog. "He'll do, I reckon . . ."

"So you'll take him?" Jeff Sconyers asked.

"Yeah, just as soon as you boys give me the rest of the money your boss gave *you*. Ain't no use tryin' to hold out on me. My men got you covered." Now Cy noticed that another man had joined the fellow with the lantern. Both had drawn pistols. Did every white man in the world own a gun?

Jeff went to the wagon and returned with more coins. Cain took them, counted them, and seemed satisfied. "I reckon you two gentlemen got more stashed away, but, hell! I'm a fair man. Whoever sent you knows the cost of doin' business."

"So now will you take him?" Jeff asked.

"Yep. You can be on your way. My men and I can manage." Cain looked Cy full in the face. "What's your name, boy?"

"Cy, sir. Cy Williams."

"From now on, Cy'll be good enough. Ain't no place in this camp for the niceties of polite society." One of Cain's men chuckled. "Thanks, fellas, for the delivery. You can get on home now and tell your boss we'll take good care of his boy. He won't need to worry himself none about him anymore."

"Yes, sir," Jeff said. "Come on," he told Burwell. "Sooner we get goin', sooner we get home."

"Good luck, nigger," Burwell told Cy. "You sure as hell gonna need it!"

They climbed onto the wagon seat, backed up, and turned around in the road. Cy heard the gate swing shut and the lock click.

He felt like he'd been saved from drowning. No more sack, no more gag. No more hands tied. No more Sconyers brothers, who could be dying and begging for his help, and he'd spit on them and keep going.

Where was he now? Anyplace had to be better than that wagon bed, that sack, that gag.

Cain told his men to escort "the new boy" to a bunkhouse and get him settled for the night. They walked him to a door at the end of the nearer building, and one of the men unlocked it. Inside, he held the lantern high, and in the shadows, Cy saw them. Boys, all black. Some older than he was, others about the same age. And some young, just children, smaller than Travis. All lying side by side on a long, low wooden platform. All dressed alike in black-and-white-striped pants and jackets. All wearing ankle irons. All bound together by one long, thick chain. All pairs of eyes staring at him.

Horror washed over Cy. "What kind o' place is this?" he whispered.

One of the men laughed. "Ain't they got none o' these where you come from? Chain gang camp, some folks call it."

FIVE

CY BATTLED THE CRUELLY COLD WATER OF THE
Ogeechee. Something like the slimy mouth of a gigantic
fish kept pulling him under. He'd fight back to the surface,
his lungs bursting. On the far side of the river, his mother
and father stood together, calling to him to come on, to get
there so they could all go home. He swam hard but was
pulled under again. When he came up, he found himself
looking into the lifeless blue eyes of his friend Travis. The
corpse clutched him and dragged him down again.

"No!" he tried to scream, his lungs filling with water.

Cy jolted awake, gasping for air, at first grateful but
then disappointed to still be alive. The nightmare had
haunted him now for more than three years, but it never
grew less horrifying. Jess had promised him that prayer
would make his bad dreams go away, and for a while, Cy
had tried to pray. But prayer hadn't worked because the
"God of love" that Jess kept preaching about simply didn't
exist. Or if he did, he was busy with more important things

than the bad dreams of one black boy. Perhaps he simply didn't give a damn about black people. The world surely didn't, and hadn't God made the world, according to what Jess said? Or perhaps the white men who had taken charge of that sorry world were simply too strong for God. Even worse, maybe they worked for him.

Cy was sick of trying to figure it out. One thing he did know, though: any God worth believing in would have killed Mr. Dathan Cain and his men a long time ago and done something to save the boys who were their slaves. Or at least saved Cy. The others could look out for themselves.

He was desperate for more sleep, but he fought to stay awake. The dream was too much to face again. It was no comfort that some of the other boys were tormented by nightmares, too. Mouse would sometimes shout and wake up clawing at an invisible enemy. At first, Cy had felt sorry for him. Now Mouse and his dreams were just trespassing on Cy's sleep. You had to have rest after twelve-hour days breaking rocks or shoveling heavy, wet clay. You needed a small place of peace where you didn't have to deal with the nasty food, the reek of the outhouse, the stink of other boys who almost never got a bath. From the constant battles over the most ordinary things—an extra piece of cornpone, a blanket not yet infested with lice. From the need always to be looking over your shoulder, always to be protecting what few things you tried to pretend were your own. Rufus had pulled a knife—stolen from the kitchen—on High Boy in a fight over a worn-out cap. When it was over, High Boy had a three-inch slash across his left cheek, Rufus got twenty lashes, and the cap had been torn into worthless pieces.

Even though the air was cold, Cy's forehead and armpits were wet. He was glad no one near him was awake. You couldn't risk anyone seeing you were afraid. If you did, you were in danger of the stronger guys messing with you. Cy was glad he was one of the biggest in the camp, and he had a reputation now. It hadn't always been that way. When he first came to the camp, the older boys had beaten him, taken his boots, and mocked him for weeks after Bull found him crying. A year ago, Bull had picked on Cy one time too many and ended up with a broken arm. Cain got rid of him. Where he sent Bull and others who could no longer work, no one knew for sure. Cy hadn't much minded the light whipping he received for hurting Bull. He'd gotten rid of an enemy and made himself a boy to fear. Since then, no one had found the guts to try anything with him.

In the colorless shadows of dawn, Cy made out the gray shapes of sleeping boys stretched out on either side. Rain rattled against the roof and dripped through the holes in the rotting shakes. An icy drop hit his forehead.

Shit! Did he have to be wet from rain as well as his own sweat?

Cy tried to move out from under the leak, but there was nowhere to go. He and nineteen other boys were chained side by side on one long platform with only thin straw ticks between them and the wooden slats. Like everything else in the camp, there wasn't enough of the platform for everyone, so the boys slept jammed against one another. On Cy's left, Jess was dead asleep; he was big as a steer, and he took up a lot of room. More than his share. You could poke him, and he wouldn't budge. It was like sleeping next to a boulder. Next to Jess, the new kid, Billy, lay like a corpse, except that his chest rose and fell underneath his blanket. On Cy's right, Mouse pressed close, craving warmth.

Cy couldn't stand Mouse nestling against him. Sure, he made a little heat even though he was the smallest boy in camp, and yes, Jess kept preaching that they had to take care of him. Cy didn't see it that way. It didn't matter if you were huge, like Jess, or puny, like Mouse. When you got down to it, you had to take care of *yourself*, because no one else would. If you didn't—or couldn't—you were done for.

The way Jess babied the little guys got on Cy's nerves. Last night, it was all about Billy. He'd been brought to the camp after dark and sent into the kitchen where Cy, Jess, and a couple of other boys from their bunkhouse were scrubbing the pots. Billy was jabbering with fear, the way all the new ones did. Rosalee, the cook, got him some cold beans and cornpone, but Billy wouldn't eat. He couldn't do a thing except stand there, trembling.

"I get him calmed down, Mr. Cain, sir," Jess had said. "He be all right."

Don't bother, Cy thought.

"Do it, then," Cain told Jess. "He can sleep next to you tonight." He turned to Prescott. "Chain him. Sooner it's done, the better. Nigger looks like he's about to have a fit."

Prescott moved toward Billy, who backed away and bumped into Jess.

"It be all right," Jess assured him, his huge paw on the kid's shoulder. "He just got to chain you. It don't hurt."

Prescott brought out a set of leg irons. "Come here, you."

Billy didn't move.

"Go on," Jess said.

Billy took one step—stopped.

"I ain't got all night," Prescott growled.

"He too scared to move, sir."

"His feelings ain't my problem! Come on. Move!"

Do it! Cy yelled in his head. *Hangin' back ain't gonna get you nothin' but trouble. And, Jess, mind you own business. Let the boy find out for hisself what he got to look forward to. Sooner he understand how it is, the better.*

Jess nudged Billy toward the white man. Billy went, feet dragging across the wooden floor. Prescott squatted in front of him and snapped an iron ring on each ankle. A chain joined the two rings. Fixed to the middle was another piece of chain with a ring at the end. Billy would learn to tuck that into his belt so he wouldn't trip over it. But if he used his belt to try and hang himself, they'd take it away, and then he'd have to manage his chains as best he could. And he'd learn to shuffle. Playing tag, climbing a tree, walking somewhere in a hurry—no more of that stuff, not for a long time. Maybe never.

It all depended on how long Cain said you had to serve. Some of the boys claimed they'd been sentenced to a certain number of months or years by judges who'd tried them for stealing or other offenses. Other boys hadn't ever had a trial. Local sheriffs had picked them up as runaways or vagrants and delivered them to Cain without any kind of charges or formal hearing. Still others, like Cy, had been kidnapped. No trial, no sentence, no stated amount of time to serve.

In the three and a half years he'd been in Cain's camp, Cy had seen only a few boys leave. Some said if you were there more than five years, you wouldn't make it. No one could last more than five. By then, the boss men would have worked you to death, or starved you, or beaten the life out of you.

Prescott stood up, looking satisfied. "See, nigger? Nothin' to it."

That's when Billy puked all over Prescott's boots.

"God *damn* it!" Prescott cried. "Stupid little son of a bitch!"

Cain and Stryker laughed.

Cy wanted to laugh too—he hated Prescott worse than anyone else in his world—but he didn't want to risk having his face slapped or getting a whipping. Cain didn't put up with any crap from his "boys."

"What's so goddamn funny?" Prescott fumed.

"Stuff always happens to you, don't it?" Cain said dryly.

"What do you mean?"

"Seems like the world got it out for you, that's all."

"He didn't mean to do it, sir," Jess told Prescott.

"Shut up, you. My best boots! Damn it all to *hell*."

"We clean 'em up for you, sir."

Not me, Cy thought.

"You mean *he's* gonna clean 'em up. I don't care if it takes him all night to do it, either."

"Deal with it," Cain told him. "I got no more time for this mess."

Prescott ordered them to their bunkhouse, where he made Billy wash off his boots and polish them until they looked decent. The kid started crying in an annoying, whiny way once he began, and he didn't stop all the time he put on the black polish and buffed the boots with a rag. Cy felt like choking him, anything to make him shut up. Billy got quiet only when Prescott was satisfied and chained everyone for the night.

A raindrop hit Cy on the face, and then another. Damn! Couldn't the world leave him alone, for once? He wanted to pull the blanket over his face, but even doing that was difficult, what with Jess and Mouse lying so close by.

Somewhere down at the far end, in the gray gloom, cloth started to rustle. Someone playing with himself. All the boys who were old enough did it. Nobody minded, or at least nobody said anything. They all did whatever they could to feel good even for a few seconds, all without privacy. Everything without privacy. You pretended that no one saw you shitting in the five-hole outhouse or heard you crying for your mama in the night or playing with yourself when your body wouldn't give you any peace.

When he had first come to Cain's camp, Cy complained to Jess about having to do his business in the outhouse in front of other guys. "Pretend they ain't nobody there," Jess had told him, and Cy had learned to do just that. It didn't always work, of course, but you had to try. Otherwise you'd go loony, chained at night to the others, chained during the long marches to the woods, swamps, and fields where you worked—every day like the ones that went before it and no different from the ones that would come after it. For Cy, it had been three and a half years of those kinds of days, close as he could figure. Sooner or later, he'd die or get sent to the coal mines in Alabama. He couldn't make up his mind which would be worse. Maybe there wasn't much difference between the two.

SIX

BANGA-BANGA-BANGA-BANG! **THE SOUND OF** the wake-up gong shattered the silence. Cy knew he'd fallen asleep again, because daylight was filtering through the cracks in the doors. The rain had stopped, but he was still shivering. Another damn day, and still alive. He'd taken to hoping, halfheartedly, that he'd die in his sleep and be done with everything.

Mouse roused just enough to pull up his knees and burrow farther under his thin blanket. Cold weather hurt him because there wasn't a pinch of fat on him. His feet suffered the worst. When they touched Cy at night, they felt like fish pulled from a pond in January. The kid was no bigger than a child—*no bigger than Travis*—although Mouse swore he was thirteen. His arms and legs were little more than bones, and his voice hadn't begun to get deep. One night, Cy caught him sucking on his fist, just like a pup at its mama's tit, sound asleep.

Cy didn't move. Nobody did. Cain didn't mean that

first call. He complained that his boys were too lazy to get up when the gong sounded, and he'd have to get real tough on them one day soon unless they changed their ways. Cain hired out the boys in his camp to anyone who needed their labor. He made his money that way. It wasn't much, to hear Cain talk. He was always moaning how he was going broke running the camp when he could do much better up in Atlanta.

Cy closed his eyes again, and his mind went straight to where he didn't want it to go: visiting day. A visiting day was scheduled every three months, but it was a bad joke: nobody ever showed up. Many of the boys didn't have any family they remembered or wanted to remember. If they did have families, maybe their folks stayed too far away to make the trip or were glad to be rid of another mouth to feed. Maybe they just didn't care.

An image of Pete Williams, sweaty in work shirt and overalls, sloppy from too much moonshine, flashed into Cy's mind and stirred up the black hatred in his gut. Pete Williams had never come for his son. That was too much to forgive.

He dozed again. The second gong sounded. Now it *was* time to move. Jess opened his eyes, stretched, and said, like he always did, "Good day, gentlemen."

Cy poked Mouse. "Come on. We gotta go."

Mouse curled up even tighter.

Down the row, boys came awake. Groans, complaints, sounds of "Move it!" and "Wake up!" and "Lemme alone!"—all the usual morning noise.

"Mouse!" Cy shook him. "It time."

"Unnhh."

"*Now*. They gonna unlock us any minute."

Sure enough, from outside came the sound of Prescott opening the lock. At night, the chains with the ring at the end, the ones attached to the chain between the boys' ankles, were put down by their feet. Then Prescott and Stryker took another chain and passed it through the rings. This chain was pulled through a small hole in the far wall of the bunkhouse and attached to a post outside. After all the boys were secured, one of the white men fed the chain through a similar hole in the wall by the door and fastened it around another post. Any boy trying to escape would first have had to unlock the chain outside—but that was impossible. Cy sometimes worried what would happen should there be a fire at night. He and the others would be trapped unless someone from outside rescued them.

"Time to wake up, Billy," Jess said. "We got to get ready."

Billy opened his eyes, and Cy could tell he didn't know where he was. Then he remembered—and started to twitch.

Not another boy prone to fits, Cy hoped. They didn't need that mess.

"Hey, now." Jess put a gentle hand on Billy's chest. "No need for that. Jus' do what I do, and you be all right."

You be all right. Only Jess could make such a lie sound so true.

Billy got quiet.

"That better?"

"Yes, sir."

"Don't go callin' me sir. I ain't nobody special. Just 'nother dog like you." Jess looked down the line. "Y'all ready?"

The door was unlocked from the outside, and Prescott came in, tapping his straight stick against his palm, like he was itching to use it. The man was short, wiry, and bad-tempered as a cornered wildcat. Thick hair the color of dirt sprouted from his nostrils, crept up from his open shirt collar, and covered the backs of his hands. His teeth were brownish yellow from the chaw he worked all day long. More than one boy had gotten tobacco juice sprayed in his face when Prescott was mad about something, which was a lot of the time. He looked around to see that everything was in order, then called Stryker to pull the long chain. In a moment, the boys were free from one another, but it wasn't time to stand up—not yet.

Stryker came in. He was bigger and heavier than Prescott, with hair the color of coal. His right eye was blue, the left, milky white, the blind orb covered by some kind of thick film. Of the two men, Stryker was less vicious, the way a bigger dog is often calmer than the smaller one that's always trying to prove something by its constant growling and snapping. But Stryker could be dangerous, too.

"On yo' feet," Jess said.

Everyone lined up, backs straight, eyes on the dirt floor. The boys who slept with their caps on took them off now.

"Mornin', boys," Stryker said.

"Mornin', Mr. Stryker, sir!"

"How'd y'all sleep?"

"Fine, sir. Thank you, sir."

Prescott made his way down the line and came to a stop in front of Billy. "God damn! You done peed yourself last night, ain't you? Yer pants is soaked. Phew! Can you smell yerself, boy?"

Cy clenched his fist. Prescott was always on the prowl for someone to torment, and the new kid had given him more than enough excuse to have some fun.

Billy didn't look up.

"Answer me when I speak to you! You stink, don't you?"

"Yes, sir," Billy whispered.

"Just like a baby," Prescott declared. "See this, Dawson? Little baby Billy done peed hisself last night."

"What you expect, Onnie? They're just animals. It makes me despair. Yessir, that's what it makes me do: despair. Country give 'em their freedom, and see what happens without the forces of civilization to keep 'em in check? They go back to the animal state in less than one generation. That's what I heard a preacher say: less than one generation."

Prescott nodded, like he understood what Stryker was saying. He moved away from Billy and stopped in front of Mouse.

Not Mouse too! Cy thought. *Don't Prescott ever get tired o' playin' God?*

"Any critters on you this morning?" Prescott demanded. "Lizard in yer pocket? Little black snake in yer pants?" He laughed at his own bad joke.

Mouse knew to keep his eyes down. "Naw, sir."

"Aw, come on. You always got *somethin'* hid somewheres. You ain't got even *one* little bug or nothin'? Better tell the truth. If I find out you're lying to me, then—"

Mouse sighed and unbuttoned his jacket pocket. He reached inside and came up with a big black beetle.

"Glory be," Prescott said. "Look at the size of him! Lemme see. Hold him up."

Mouse opened his hand. The beetle twitched a little.

"I thought you said you didn't have nothing on you. You ain't nothing but a little liar."

Mouse was silent.

"Ain't you, boy?"

"Yessir."

"That's better. One thing I can't stand is a liar." Quick as a flash, he brought down his stick on Mouse's hand. The beetle fell to the ground, and Prescott crushed it with his boot.

Cy wished he could do that to Prescott.

"Piss-pants and liars in *this* group," he told Stryker. "That's what we got here this mornin'." He stepped in front of Jess. "Get these sorry niggers outta my sight. And try to get that baby's britches cleaned up before he stinks up the whole place."

"Yessir."

The white men went off to the other bunkhouse to unchain Jack and his gang. When they were out the door, everyone stirred. Jess had them line up, and they made their way outdoors.

Cy knew every boy in the gang: Jess, West, Mouse,

Ring, Oscar, Davy, High Boy, Darius, and all the rest. Knew their habits, the sound of their footsteps, the colors of their skin that ranged from darkest black and brown to copper, coffee and cream, yellow, all the way to near white. Ring was as white as any white man Cy had ever seen, but here he was anyway. He said one of his granddaddies was a light Negro, all his other grandparents white, but that one bit of Negro blood was all it took to land him here. That and threatening to hurt a white boy who'd stolen all of Ring's mama's chickens.

The air was chilly—an early cold snap. Fog lay on the ground and hid the trees on the other side of the camp fence. Soon Cain would give out winter clothes, maybe before Sunday. The few decent things they got from Cain— clean uniforms, secondhand boots, a regular hot meal— somehow always came just before a visiting day.

They marched toward the outhouse. Cy pushed his way to the front of the line, just behind Jess. No one dared try and stop him.

The outhouse stank bad, but not like in summer. Cy yanked down his pants and sat. He pissed and tried to shit even though he didn't feel the need. Sitting down was a lot better than squatting in the woods later on, like a lot of the boys did. One good thing about going outdoors, though: you could usually find some leaves. Better not use poison ivy, though, as West had done a while back. He never made that mistake again. Here in the outhouse there was nothing, not even corncobs.

"You gon' sit there all day?" Jess asked him. "Somethin' on your mind?"

"Naw. Just thinkin'. What's it to you?"

"Do yo' thinkin' somewhere else. They's a long line waitin' to get in."

Outside, boys were washing up by the pump. The boys from the other bunkhouse appeared, following Jack, their leader. They joined the line for the outhouse. Jess and Oscar poured water into a tub and stood by Billy while he stripped off his pants and started rinsing them, trying not to let anyone see his parts.

"Cy, see if you can get some clean britches for Billy, okay?"

It annoyed Cy when Jess asked him to do anything. Just because Jess was the head boy in their bunkhouse didn't give him the right to give orders. Whenever Cy was asked to do something, he told the next fellow to do it. He, in turn, would push the job off onto the next smaller boy. Everyone knew the order: Jess, Cy, Ring, Oscar, West, Davy, and so on all the way down to Mouse. Billy would quickly discover that his place was even below Mouse because he was the new kid. That's where he would stay, unless he could fight his way up the ladder and bully or bribe younger or weaker boys to do his bidding.

Cy cornered West, who had already found his place in the morning roll-call line and was standing, looking straight ahead at nothing in particular.

Cy poked his shoulder. "Jess say for you to go get the new kid some britches."

"You mean he told *you* to do it, and now you passin' it on to me."

"Could be. Don't matter, though. I's tellin' you to go. See if Rosalee got any."

West shrugged Cy's hand away and trudged toward the cookhouse, muttering to himself.

"You best watch yo' mouth," Cy called after him.

West knocked at the cookhouse door, and Rosalee answered. She looked annoyed—she didn't like to be disturbed when she was cooking, if that's what you'd call it. Like Ring, Rosalee was much more white than colored, but she too was doomed to live her life as a black person. She wasn't pretty, and she wasn't young. Sometimes she seemed in a fog, and certain mornings her speech was slurred and she was only half awake. "A drunk" was Oscar's verdict.

She might have been a drunk, but Rosalee wasn't a prisoner, even though she lived at the camp. She and her little boy, Pook, had a room behind the kitchen, but she clearly spent some of her nights with Cain, because Pook looked just like him: the same thin, wavy hair, gray eyes, small ears, and stocky build. Even so, Cain never let on the boy was his.

Sometimes Rosalee sneaked West some extra food when she thought no one was looking. Cy sometimes wondered why she would do that, but she had her favorites. No one minded West's luck, because he shared whatever he got. That made him popular, that plus his sassy mouth, which could make anyone laugh.

Rosalee disappeared and came back with a pair of uniform pants. They were dirt-stained and too big for Billy, but he wouldn't have to wear wet pants all day or go half naked.

As the boys finished in the outhouse, they lined up in their two gangs, Jess's boys facing Jack's across the small patch of red clay in the middle of the camp.

Jack strutted down the line of "his" boys, poking and threatening, trying to act like a big man. Prescott and Stryker didn't mind letting Jack do some of their dirty work, but Cy had seen him get cuffed when the white men thought he was being too big for his britches. That just made him meaner.

Prescott and Stryker stood by the cookhouse door, sipping coffee from tin cups. The aroma made Cy's mouth water. Of all the many things he missed about Aunt Dorcas's kitchen, her strong coffee was first. Inside the cookhouse, Rosalee was finishing getting breakfast. The smell of baking cornpone was in the air, and that made Cy think of Aunt Dorcas, too. Of home. But he blotted out those thoughts. If you let them get hold of you, you'd go crazy. Cy had seen it happen.

Rosalee appeared at the door of the cookhouse, Pook with her. He grabbed at her skirt with one hand while he chewed on the other. He looked even whiter than his mama did, with pasty skin, his gray eyes crusty at the corners, and his wispy hair uncombed. Pook never talked much, and some of the boys said he was simple-minded.

Rosalee folded her arms, waiting, frowning. Pook yanked her skirt. "Hungry, Mama."

"Shush. Can't do nothin' till Mist' Cain get here."

Cain made everyone wait to eat until he showed up. Sometimes that meant half an hour. It made Stryker and Prescott mad, but at least they had hot coffee. This morning he didn't take long. He came through the door of his cabin, his clothes buttoned up right and hair brushed back. West whispered that he must have run out of whiskey. The boys knew that was what made him late some mornings, sleeping off a bad drunk.

Cain took his place between the two lines. He was dressed like usual: riding boots, leather belt with a Confederate army buckle, worn-out gentleman's coat. Wide-brimmed hat stained dark with sweat. Clean and polished holster holding a Colt revolver.

"Good morning, boys," Cain said to Prescott and Stryker.

"Morning, Mr. Cain."

"Any problems?"

"Nothin' but the usual, sir," Prescott said. "Boys who pee their britches, lie to you for no reason."

"Stryker?"

"I got somethin' more serious than that, Cap'n. Seems like we still got thieves."

"What's missin' this time?"

"Rosalee says a slab of fatback's gone—'bout three pounds—plus a bottle of cane syrup, a bread knife, and some flour."

Cy knew Rosalee hadn't given those things to West. She wouldn't do that and then call attention to it. Besides, West would have shared anything he'd gotten. There was another thief in camp—or more than one.

Stuff was always going missing—food, tools, uniform shirts and pants, anything else Rosalee hung out to dry, even a little ball she managed to get for Pook. Just about whatever wasn't nailed down would disappear sooner or later.

"Damn it, Dawson! Ain't there anything you can do to keep these niggers from stealing us blind? Don't I pay you to keep an eye out?"

"With all due respect, Onnie and me keep careful watch, but you know how it is! Reckon some of them old-time niggers taught 'em. Back in the day, darkies'd steal a fried chicken leg out of a white man's mouth if he didn't watch out. Niggers used to think they had a right to anything they could lay their hands on. Nothin's changed."

"This will stop!" Cain cried. "Unless someone identifies the thief, I can make it plenty hot for *all* of you. They need miners over in Alabama. You boys wouldn't want to get sent over there, now, would you?"

He stopped right in front of Cy. "Would *you?*"

"Naw, sir, Mr. Cain. I's happy to be right here." Cy almost smiled at how sincere he sounded. He'd learned how to lie a long time ago, lie like he meant every word he said. Telling the truth—well, that was risky. Especially when the truth went something like this: "Naw, you dumbass cracker, I ain't happy to be here. Fact is, I wish I was in yo' place and you in mine. Then I'd lash you so long and hard you'd wish you was dead a hour 'fore I got through with you."

"I know you're happy to be here," Cain replied.

Could the man really be such a damn fool?

Cain looked over both lines. "I know y'*all* are, and you don't want to go to the coal mines, now, do you?"

"No, sir!"

"Then I better get the name of this thief—or thieves—before this day is over!"

No one said a thing. That was one of the boys' most important rules: no snitching. If any boy *did* snitch, he would pay. And when you were chained to other boys a lot of the time, you couldn't escape.

"You understand me?" Cain said.

"Yes, sir!" That would be the end of it. Cain was too lazy to do more.

"Let 'em eat," he told Stryker and Prescott. "But don't let 'em dawdle. We got a lot of work today."

SEVEN

Stryker and Prescott followed Cain into the cookhouse. Then Jack and his boys went in. Today was Jess's guys' turn to go last, so they waited outside.

Mouse was in an ugly mood.

"What's a matter?" Jess asked him.

"Nothin'."

"That ain't what yo' face be tellin' me."

"That stupid beetle," Cy suggested. "The one Prescott squashed, right?"

"I gon' kill that son'bitch one day," Mouse muttered. "Just you wait. I gon' *kill* him!"

"Don't you talk that way," Jess warned. "If Prescott ever find out, he kill you first."

"What I care? Dead be better'n this."

"It was only a beetle," Jess said. "You can find 'nother one."

"I don't want no other!" Mouse snapped. "'Sides, anything I get, he kill."

"Then don't get no more," Cy said. "Leave things alone if you wants 'em to live." He'd learned that the hard way, and paid for it every day.

"Shut up!"

Cy pushed him. "*You* shut up. You spend half the day pokin' 'round under logs and rocks 'stead o' workin'. I's sick of it."

"He do good as he can," Jess said. "You know that, Cy."

"Naw, I don't. When he gonna start doin' his share? He ain't nothin' but a baby."

"You got that right," Ring put in. He flicked Mouse on the ear.

"Quit it!" Mouse cried. "I ain't no baby!"

"Then quit actin' like one," Cy told him. "Forget about yo' damn lizards and frogs and do yo' job."

"Don't try an' tell me what to do!"

"Somebody got to," Ring said.

"Y'all quit," Jess warned. "You want 'em to hear you fussin'?"

Inside, they picked up tin cups, plates, and spoons. Rosalee and her helper, Sudie, a slovenly black girl, served up grits, fatback, and pone. There was water to drink—that was all there ever was. At the end of the room, Cain and his men sat at their own table, enjoying fried eggs and potatoes, real bacon with meat on it, and biscuits with honey.

To Cy, of all the thousand large and small punishments of this life, having to see and smell decent food he couldn't have himself was one of the worst. The grits on his own plate were watery, the chunks of fatback flabby, half cooked. He'd eat everything, though. Dinner was a long ways off.

Mouse wouldn't touch his food, and neither would Billy. Mouse was too angry, and Billy couldn't get anything down. He tried with the grits—gagged—and all he could do with the fatback was push it around with his spoon. West jumped on the cold grits before Davy could get at them, and Oscar wrestled the fatback from Darius. They'd learned you always ate anything you could get, no matter how nasty. Jess made Billy put his cornpone in his pocket, promising he'd be hungry later.

When breakfast was over, the boys loaded the wagons. Stryker and Prescott chained them in two long lines, and the trek to the work site began. It was a long hike, and while the leg irons were mostly an annoyance to the bigger boys, they tormented the smaller ones like Darius and Mouse. Today, Billy was the one having a bad time. He was trying, but he tripped and went down more than once. That stopped the line and brought a round of cussing from

Prescott, who got in Billy's face and tried to make him cry, but this time Billy kept still.

Finally they got to the place—an open pine wood with lots of saw palmetto under the tall trees. A road would soon be built through there, and the brush had to be cleared out. Cain's boys were moving fallen pine branches, taking down small trees, and chopping saw palmetto.

Saw palmetto was nasty stuff. Its roots were so dense and iron hard that they seemed to dare anyone to tear them out of the ground. The leaves spread out from thick stems like large ladies' fans. They got in your face as you worked, but the real problem was the stems, edged with needle-sharp teeth just the way a saw blade is, so even the hungriest animals avoided them. Unprotected by work gloves, the boys' hands stayed raw from trying to root up the palmetto.

They were unchained and put into groups. Cy was with Mouse, Jess, Billy, Ring, and West. Jess was boss.

Stryker and Prescott handed out the tools, which were nearly worthless. The hoe and shovel edges were dull, and the blades didn't fit the handles, which were always coming off. That got to Cy worse than anything else. All day long, Cain and his men complained that the work wasn't going fast enough, but they wouldn't come up with new, decent tools or pay to have these repaired.

Jess's group started where they had finished the day

before, at the end of a cleared space about two wagons wide, cut right through the woods. The palmetto came up on either side of the boys like walls.

If the living palmettos weren't bad enough, their dead stems and leaves carpeting the ground were bad news, too. Most of the boys were wearing tattered boots, and a couple were barefoot. Cain had been promising replacements, what with cold weather coming on, but so far, he'd done nothing. So while their hands got cut up by the live stems, their feet got the same punishment from the dead ones. Even worse, snakes loved the dense underbrush. Any step might land you on a copperhead or a pygmy rattler.

Prescott came up to Mouse. "Let me know if you find anything good today," he said. "I reckon they's lots of critters hiding in this brush."

"I gonna fix him one day," Mouse said after Prescott went away. "He be lyin' sleep under a tree, way he do, ugly mouth hangin' open, and I cut his throat!"

"Shut up with that talk," Cy warned. "That cracker hear you, we all gonna get it."

"Cy right," Jess said. "We can't afford to be fightin' each other. We's all we got."

Which is why we all gonna end up dead, Cy thought bitterly.

"Son'bitch Prescott," Mouse muttered.

Cain shot his rifle, the signal for the workday to begin. Square in front of Cy was a palmetto as tall as his shoulders. He wanted to dig it out without having to grab any of the stems, but the mass of leaves kept him from getting close enough to dig. A machete was what he needed—cut the stems down to the ground and then attack the roots—but naturally Cain wasn't going to hand out machetes.

Cy pushed a big stem away so he could move in with his dull-edged shovel, and right away, its teeth raked across his palm. "God damn it!" he cried.

"Takin' the Lord name in vain ain't gonna help you," Jess said.

"I can say what I want!"

"Jus' be careful 'bout what you ask the Lord to damn. That some serious business."

Cy was sick of such preacher talk, but there was no point answering back.

"Lemme see it," Jess said. "It deep?"

"Naw. Just sting like hell."

Jess reached into his jacket pocket and came up with a strip of rag. "Here. Use this."

"Where you get that?"

"West."

West looked their way, grinned, and went back to work. If anyone could lay his hands on anything useful, it was West. Maybe getting things from Rosalee didn't satisfy him. Maybe he *was* the thief who made things disappear. Cy thought about West having those three pounds of fatback all to himself and wondered if he had other goods he kept secret.

Jess wrapped the rag around Cy's hand and tied it. "Now, you be careful," he told Billy. "See what happen when you don't watch what you doin'?"

"I *was* bein' careful," Cy said.

"I see that."

Billy just stood there. He hadn't even picked up his shovel.

"I show you," Jess said. "It ain't hard. But we gotta get goin' 'fore Prescott notice." He grabbed the shovel and made Billy take it. "Come on, now."

"I don't want to."

"Neither do any o' the rest of us. But they ain't no choice."

EIGHT

WORK THAT MORNING WAS JUST LIKE ALWAYS:
difficult, dirty, and dull. Occasional cussing meant the palmetto had bloodied another hand or foot. A cry of pain
meant that Stryker or Prescott had decided someone wasn't
working hard enough and needed a taste of the whip.

The trick was not to attract attention to yourself. If
you did get cut, you tried not to shout "Son of a bitch!" or
"Damn it all to hell!" If you were so beat you felt like dropping your shovel and falling to the ground, you kept on
going. Anything to keep the boss men from messing with
you.

At first, Cy worried that Billy would attract attention
the way a lantern attracts moths. The kid couldn't seem to
figure out where he was or how he came to be there. When
Jess first gave him the shovel, he acted like he didn't know
what it was for. But then Billy surprised them all. Once
Jess got him started, he put his scrawny back into the work

and gave Prescott no excuse to use his whip, not even to cuss him out for slacking off.

At dinner, Prescott handed out the usual grub—cold sweet potatoes, cornpone, and water. Cain found a tree to lean against, took a long drink from his flask, pulled his hat down over his face, and fell asleep, just like he did every day.

Mouse stuffed his cornpone into his mouth, cramming it down his gullet the way a hog goes at a mess of slop. That kind of behavior used to bother Cy, but it was nothing compared to some of the other boys' nasty habits, so he didn't give it a second thought anymore. After the pone, Mouse took his own good time with the sweet potato. First, he put it in his lap. Then he used a thumbnail to slice it open, longways. Next he pulled the potato apart and pinched out some of the stringy orange meat. One strand at a time, the sweet potato went into his mouth. There it got chewed to a pulp, like a cow's cud. Mouse pulled pieces from the skin until it was empty. Then he tore the skin in pieces and put them in his jacket pocket.

Billy had watched the whole thing like it was a circus sideshow act. "What you gon' do with them peels?" he asked.

"Eat 'em. What you think?"

"He right," West added. "You best eat anything you can get."

West lived by that creed, and he'd proved it time and again. He was always on the lookout for something to put in his belly—wild grapes, blackberries, dandelion greens, even minnows and crawdaddies, raw. And then there was the extra food he managed to get from Rosalee.

Billy appeared to consider West's valuable advice, then retrieved the skin of his own potato from the ground and put it in his pocket.

It was time for the back-to-work gun to go off, but nothing happened. Cain was still asleep under his pine tree, and Prescott was nowhere to be seen. He often disappeared after he'd eaten: the boys figured it was to relieve himself. Stryker rolled a cigarette. He was never in a hurry to get back to work, if walking around making threats could be called work. All this meant some precious free time.

The day had faired off and gotten warmer. West found a sunny spot, lay down, and fell asleep almost instantly. That was an ability worth having. Cy often wished he could do the same, but getting his mind to stop racing was something he hadn't managed yet. He'd shut his eyes, try to sleep, and then the memories would come flooding back. So would the fear that when he finally did sleep, the nightmares would return to torment him.

Mouse started poking around in the brush and came up with a tiny orange lizard he called a salamander. He let it crawl over his fingers awhile, then popped it in his jacket pocket—right in with the sweet potato peel.

Cy closed his eyes and let the November sunshine soothe his skin. Maybe sleep would come . . . He had nearly fallen into a doze when Ring's voice roused him.

"So, Billy. How old are you?"

"Ten."

"And what you do to get sent here?"

Cy opened his eyes. New guys' stories were sometimes worth hearing.

"I didn't do nothin'!"

"Didn't think so. Nobody in here done nothin' wrong. Ain't that right, Cy?"

That was a joke in camp: no one ever admitted to breaking the law—or doing one thing to deserve the mess he was in.

"Right," Cy said. "We *all* innocent."

"I ain't done nothin'!" Billy repeated. "Honest."

"Course you ain't," said Ring patiently. "Cy and me is agreein' with you. So what happen? You didn't ask to come here."

"Mr. Talmadge Carter say I stole couple dollars from his store. Say I took it—all in silver—right off the counter."

"Why you get blamed?" Ring asked.

"I be workin' for Mr. Tal. Cleanin'—sweep the floor, empty the spittoons, slop his hogs. Stuff like that."

"And then you stole his money."

"*No!* How many times I got to say I didn't? It was Jenny."

Cy started to lose interest. He knew this story by heart. The names were always different, the crimes, petty or serious, sometimes different, too, but the claim never changed: *It wasn't me. It wasn't my fault.* How many times had he heard those same words from his own mouth?

"Who Jenny?" Jess asked.

"Mr. Tal daughter. *She* took the money and blame me—"

"Why she take money from her own daddy?" Jess wondered. "All she got to do was ask."

"Not *him.* That man never give nobody nothin'!"

"But you said he pay you," Ring pointed out.

"Sometimes, when he feel like it."

"So why you keep workin' for him?" Cy asked.

"How come y'all askin' me so many questions?" Billy cried. "I ain't got to say nothin' to anyone!" He got up and stomped away.

So the kid has some backbone after all, Cy thought. *He's gonna need it.*

"Come on, Billy," Jess said. "We didn't mean nothin' by it. We just interested in yo' story, that's all."

Billy came back and sat down. "Daddy made me keep workin'. Say we need all the money we can get. And if we didn't do what Mr. Tal say, maybe he kick us off his land. So when he miss the money—two dollar, like I said—and he ask if anybody seen it, we all say no—Sally, Joe, me—but he don't believe us. He make us come in his office one by one and ask us a lot o' questions. And when he done, he call the sheriff, and they take *me* to the jail."

"But you ain't done it."

"I swore I ain't! Next time the judge come around, he say I got to be here—do two years."

"Two years for stealin' two dollars." Jess shook his head.

At least you had a trial, Cy thought. Some of the other boys told similar stories, so he figured they were true. Having a trial and getting an "official" sentence still didn't mean you would ever go free. Oscar claimed the judge had sentenced him to ninety days for vagrancy. That was two years ago. Jess liked to preach to the other boys that they needed to believe in God so they wouldn't go to hell when they died. Once in hell, you could never get out. Cy had come to believe that the same was true about Cain's camp.

"I ain't worried, though." Billy sounded confident.

You was plenty worried last night, Cy thought, but didn't say so.

"My daddy gonna come get me. He promise. Say it only take a couple days, then he be here. Just a little mistake, is how he put it. He gonna get it worked out—then he get me. You'll see."

Cy had heard that kind of braggy talk before. They all had. Jess looked serious.

"Don't y'all believe me?" Billy asked. "Daddy be here. He promise!"

"Course he will," Jess assured him.

Another lie to make the kid feel better.

"Might take longer'n you think, though," Ring said. "Where you stay before here?"

"Over by Moultrie."

"Where that?"

"Cain't be too far. Daddy be here tomorrow."

So they were near a place called Moultrie. The name meant nothing to Cy. Was it near Davisville, where Warren Hall was? And where was that? Cy never could figure out how many miles the Sconyers boys had brought him during that terrible trip from his home to here. Fifty? A hundred? He wasn't even sure how long a mile was.

"What your daddy do?" Jess asked Billy.

"Sharecropper."

"Mine too," Cy said, then was sorry he'd opened his mouth. Now the questions would start.

"Yeah?" Billy asked. "What you do to get here?"

"Nothin'—same as you."

"Naw, really. What they *say* you done?"

"Cy don't like to talk about that," Jess said.

Cy stood up and walked away.

"I say somethin' wrong?" he heard Billy ask.

"Naw," Ring told him. "Just don't ask him about that stuff . . ."

Prescott emerged from the woods, his face white as paper. Everyone in camp knew he had bowel troubles, the dysentery, he called it. That explained why he'd drop everything and run off sometimes, and be gone a long time. He woke Cain, and the afternoon began.

It was a long one. Mouse swore he saw a copperhead, but no one else did. Everyone was nervous after that. Cy kept looking at the bare toes sticking out of his ragged right boot. Each step he took could bring those toes to the poisoned fangs of a lurking snake. When would Cain give them the promised new boots?

They were all glad when quitting time finally arrived. Billy had worked hard all day, so he had a bad time on the way back. He could hardly stay on his feet. But he'd caused no trouble, attracted no attention. That was more than Cy had expected.

In camp, Stryker ordered a bonfire built. And there was a surprise: supper was ready. Usually the half-starved boys had to wait, sometimes more than an hour, but tonight, Rosalee and Sudie had the watery rice all cooked. There was cornpone again and some mushy red beans. There were extra-big servings for everyone.

Cy knew why. Visiting day. Cain was feeding "his boys" extra well just in case somebody showed up and asked about the grub. The man seemed to think they were too stupid to remember farther back than one or two meals.

Cy ate, and for the first time in days, he had a full stomach. When supper was done, he joined the others by the fire. Soon, Cain appeared, with Prescott and Stryker in back, toting feed sacks.

"Get 'em to their feet," Cain ordered Jess and Jack. "Then line 'em up."

Stryker and Prescott dumped out the sacks.

"I got y'all new boots!" Cain announced.

Cy smiled to himself. He knew Cain so well. A decent

supper, a warm fire, boots they should have had weeks ago—all for visiting day.

"There's forty pair, and forty of y'all. I won't stand for any arguing over who gets what. This is gonna be done in decent order, not like dogs fighting over a bone. Take care of it," Cain ordered his men.

The boys stayed at attention while Prescott picked through the boots and handed them out. Even by firelight, it was obvious the boots weren't new. Wherever Cain had gotten them, he'd gotten them cheap. Soon, everyone had a pair.

Prescott's judgment about which boots would fit which boy was as bad as ever. Later, the boys would work it out on their own. The bigger and stronger would end up with the best ones, and the rest would make do with whatever was left.

"Yours all right?" Cy asked Jess.

"Too small. How 'bout yours?"

"No worse'n usual."

Mouse's boots were big for him—just as they had been last year. But his feet were so tiny that no boot fit right.

Next came the "new" blankets. Cain was right on schedule.

The boys got to use the latrine; then it was time for bed. Cy felt pretty good. His boots fit tolerably well, so maybe he wouldn't have to fight for a better pair. His blanket didn't have too many holes in it, and his stomach was full for once. Maybe tonight he'd sleep without the memories and dreams.

Everything was fine until Billy started to cry for his daddy. Not even Jess could comfort him.

NINE

THE BOYS WORKED PALMETTO AGAIN THE NEXT morning, but Cain called a halt at dinnertime and sent everyone back to camp. Baths and clean uniforms were the order of the afternoon. Stryker and Prescott oversaw the filling of the washtubs. As usual, there weren't enough tubs or pieces of soap for everyone to have his own, so the bigger guys pushed their way to the tubs first, before the water had become nasty from too many boys' accumulated dirt.

Cy welcomed bath days, not only because of the chance to scrub off the crusted filth from his feet and knees, but also because for once, he was free of his leg irons. After Stryker unlocked the metal rings, Cy sat down, pulled off his boots and pants, and looked at his legs. His ankles were rubbed raw in some places, scabbed over in others. Not even his pants or boots could keep the heavy, rough metal from eating at his skin. He touched the hurt places lightly. The open sores stung when he touched them, but he put his fingers on them anyway—as if by some magic he could make them disappear. He wished Cain and his men could find out what it felt like to be chained, to have the skin cut from their legs by rough iron rings and from their backs by leather whips.

He pulled off his jacket and stood up. The cool air felt good on his skin, and he let the sunshine warm his back. Already some of the biggest boys were washing themselves, lathering their heads with the soap, warning each other not to let the suds get into their eyes. It didn't take long for them to start a splashing game, laughing and playing jokes on each other. Stryker and Prescott stood at a distance, smoking. For once, they seemed not to care what the boys did.

Silly games weren't for Cy. He pushed his way to one of the tubs and grabbed a piece of soap. When he was done, he headed for a patch of sunshine, clean uniform in hand. Billy was sitting on the ground, still dressed, and Jess, naked like everyone else, was talking to him in a low voice.

"I don't want to!" Billy was saying.

"What now?" Cy asked Jess.

"He don't want to undress. You ain't got no choice," Jess told Billy. "Water feel good on you. Soap make you clean, and you get a fresh uniform."

"I ain't goin' to."

"Why not?" Cy asked.

"I don't know." Billy sounded like he was ready to cry.

"Come on," Jess said, trying to lift him.

"Lemme be!"

Cy looked to see if Stryker and Prescott had noticed them. They hadn't—so far. "If you don't undress yo'self, they gon' do it for you," Cy warned Billy. "And you won't like it. I seen 'em do it to other fellas."

"Naw!" Billy cried.

Jess said quietly, "You don't like for nobody to see you. That it?"

Billy hung his head. "Yeah."

"Ain't nobody gon' pay you no mind," Jess assured him. "They all be too busy scrubbin' theyselves. 'Sides, with everybody nekkid, nobody got an advantage."

"I don't want to," Billy repeated. "Mine ain't big. Joe say so. He say a boy my age oughtta have more'n I got. Say I'm a baby."

"Stuff like that ain't important here," Jess said. "Sooner or later, everybody gon' see you, so you might as well show 'em what you got right now."

"Naw, I ain't got to! I told you, Daddy comin' for me today, tomorrow at the latest. Ain't nobody have to see me—like you." Billy glanced up at them and then looked away.

"However God made you, it all right," Jess said. "Big, little, black, brown, whatever. Some dark as night, like High Boy and Oscar. Others got all sorts o' colors mixed up in 'em, like West. And they's Ring, almost pure white. We is what we is, and cain't none of us do nothin' about it. You know, one fellow here got six toes on each foot."

"Naw!"

"Cross my heart! See that big, high-yellow guy over there? Cornelius. You ask him to see them extra toes sometime, he show you. Ain't no big deal. Nobody pay him no mind, and nobody gon' pay you no mind neither."

Billy got up and removed his jacket. When his pants were off, he put his hands over his privates.

What a baby, Cy thought.

"Good boy," Jess told Billy. "Come on with me. I make sure nobody mess with you." Jess started toward the washtubs.

That's when Billy noticed Jess's back. "Why you all covered with them marks?"

Jess turned around. "From bein' whipped," he replied simply.

Billy's eyes got big. "Who done it?"

"You get washed up, and I tell you 'bout it later."

"You must of done somethin' real bad, get beat like that."

"He didn't do *nothin'* wrong," Cy retorted. "Sometimes you get whipped all the same."

"Let's get that bath," Jess suggested.

Billy relaxed and put down his hands, so Cy had a chance to look at him. That guy Joe was wrong about Billy. He had enough for a fellow his age. Maybe now he'd see that for himself.

After supper, generous by Cain's standards, there was another bonfire, and the boys were free to do as they liked until curfew. Cain was really laying on the soft touches: "new" boots, blankets, clean uniforms, decent meals, even free time. Was he really expecting visitors the next day?

Cain left Jess and Jack in charge, with the usual threats about what would happen if there was trouble. He and his men went into Cain's cabin.

Cy felt stirred up inside, just as he always did before a visiting day. He needed something to keep himself from wondering if maybe his father would show up tomorrow. If he didn't think about it, he wouldn't be so disappointed when Pete Williams didn't appear. He suggested that West tell some fortunes. He would do that every so often, and his mumbo-jumbo antics always made a big impression on the boys, especially the younger ones. Cy told himself he didn't hold with such stuff, but that was only half true.

Every older person he'd ever known had believed in all kinds of superstitions and hexes, so maybe there was something to it.

West agreed—after Cy gave him the extra piece of cornpone he'd lifted at supper. Besides getting some extra grub, West enjoyed being the center of attention, and he knew how to put on a good show. He retrieved his "hoodoo" bowl from its hiding place inside the sleeping shed and sat near the fire with the bowl in his lap. Cy, Mouse, Ring, and Billy joined him. Billy wanted West to ask the spirits when his father was coming to get him. Jess wouldn't have any part of it, insisting that telling fortunes was ungodly—devilish, even.

Mouse brought a dipper of water, and West poured some into the red clay bowl. There were strange, curling designs scratched on the bowl. Cy had asked what they meant, but West would never say. West dug into his jacket pocket and came up with a thorn that he used to prick his finger. Then he squeezed a drop of his blood into the bowl.

"Who first?" he asked.

"Me," Mouse said.

"Here." West handed the thorn to Mouse, who pricked his own finger and let a drop of blood fall into the water.

"Why y'all doin' that?" Billy asked.

"You want me to tell your fortune, you got to join your

spirit with mine. 'Less you do, I can't see nothin' 'bout you. 'Life be in the blood,' what the Bible say. So you got to mix your blood with mine."

Billy looked impressed.

"What you see?" Mouse asked West.

He stirred the water with his finger, held the bowl close to his face, and began singing softly. Whatever the words were, they weren't English.

Then West closed his eyes and the singing stopped. All the boys were silent, waiting. At last, he opened his eyes, but he seemed distant, off in some place that wasn't Cain's chain gang camp.

"What you see?" Mouse wanted to know.

"Two dark eyes, lookin' at me."

"Is that bad?"

West shook his head. "You gon' be free, Mouse. I seen that real plain."

Mouse smiled. "I knowed it! I been feelin' it for a long time now. Free!"

But West didn't look happy. "Anybody else?" he asked.

"Me," Billy said.

"You sure? I might not see what you want me to see."

"I bet you will. You gon' see my daddy comin' to get me!"

"Maybe. Ain't no way of knowin'."

"Come on," Billy urged.

West emptied the bowl, refilled it, and squeezed another drop of his blood into it. Billy couldn't make himself prick his finger, so Ring did it for him. West repeated the ritual. When he opened his eyes, he looked troubled.

"What's wrong?" Billy asked. "You saw Daddy, right?"

West shook his head. "I didn't see nothin' like that."

"What, then?"

"I seen—I seen you on a long, dark road. And you come to this river."

The word *river* jolted Cy. *River—Travis.*

"And?" Billy asked.

West closed his eyes again. The boys waited. Cy was eager to hear the rest, even if this wasn't about him.

West looked at Billy again. "You gon' get outta here, too. You gets your freedom."

"What about Daddy? He comin' tomorrow, right?"

"I didn't see that. But you gonna be free for sure."

"West don't always see everything," Mouse assured Billy.

"Daddy be here," Billy replied doggedly.

"Want me to look for you, Cy?" West asked.

Cy had never allowed West to read his fortune, even though he'd wanted to find out what West would tell the other boys. He reminded himself he didn't believe in hoodoo, but tonight he wasn't so sure. And he wouldn't let the others think he was afraid. He agreed.

West prepared the bowl, and Cy pierced his own finger. Three drops of blood fell into the water and West mixed them with his own. His weird, tuneless song went on and on, and Cy felt more and more uneasy. What was West seeing?

Finally, Cy had his answer.

"They's a lot gon' happen to you, Cy. I sees you walkin' along a long road, and eatin' good food again, and—" West looked back into the water. His head jerked back, and he looked away.

"And what?" Cy demanded. "What you see?"

"Somebody gonna put a knife in yo' back."

"Cy gonna be killed?" Billy asked.

"Naw," Ring said. "That's just a way of talkin'. Means somebody gonna do you wrong."

Cy didn't like what West had seen. Hadn't he had enough betrayal in his life already?

West looked into the water again. "That ain't all," he said. "You gon' be free, too, Cy. I sees that real plain."

Cy wanted to believe West, but he wouldn't get his hopes up.

"You okay, Cy?" Ring asked him. "You look strange."

"Course I is. Ain't nothin' to this stuff, anyway."

"Then why you ask West to do it?" Billy asked.

Cy felt like hitting him. "To keep you from cryin' for yo' daddy! You satisfied?"

Billy looked hurt. "You ever tell your own fortune, West?"

"Naw. It don't work that way. You try and tell your own, all you sees is what you wants to see."

"Can't somebody else see for you?"

"Maybe. If he got the gift."

"I think y'all done enough for one evenin'," Jess said. "West, put that bowl away and quit fillin' these boys' heads with nonsense."

West pouted. "It ain't nonsense. It real."

"I believe it," Billy said. "Tomorrow y'all gon' see West be right."

"I hope so," Jess said.

That night, after they were chained together for sleep, Billy chattered on and on about the next day and how his daddy would come and free him. He was long past being annoying.

"Can't we talk 'bout somethin' else?" Cy asked.

"All right," Billy agreed. "Who *you* fellows got comin' to see you tomorrow?"

No one replied.

Billy didn't understand. "Jess, you got somebody?"

"Naw."

"Not a mama or daddy?" Billy asked.

"Nope. Both dead."

"How they die?"

"Don't rightly know. They was both gone before I was big enough to remember 'em."

"What about you, Cy? You got a mama and daddy?"

"Only a daddy."

"Cy been here for a long time, and his daddy ain't never come see him," West added.

"Shut up!" Cy tried to poke West, but couldn't reach him.

"And your daddy ain't *never* been here?" Billy sounded shocked. "Why not?"

"How the hell should I know?" Cy snapped. "Ain't none o'your damn business, anyway."

"No more questions," Jess told Billy. "Some guys just don't like to talk about that stuff."

Mouse lay silent. Like Jess, he didn't have any folks to come visit.

"You still got your critter there?" Billy asked.

No answer.

"That orange lizard?"

"Salamander."

"You holdin' him?"

"Uh-huh."

"Better be careful," Jess cautioned. "You gon' lose him in the dark."

"No, I won't."

"You best let him go tomorrow. He got to eat. Besides, Prescott gonna find him."

"That ain't yo' problem."

"Suit yourself."

"How you get them marks on your back?" Billy asked Jess.

"Can't we just go to sleep?" Cy asked. He'd heard Jess's story plenty of times.

"Jess promised he tell me 'bout it if I got my bath. Remember, Jess?"

"I do."

"Then you got to tell it. Cy say you got beat a lot, Jess. That true?"

Jess replied softly, "Yeah. Man I lived with done it. He warn't my real daddy, thank God. He never got tired o' remindin' me about *that*."

"How you end up with him?"

"I dunno, and he never would tell me. His wife, neither. Mr. George and Miz Ada Prettyman. Sharecroppers over by Sparta. Long way from here."

"How come he beat you?"

"Dunno. He beat her just like he done me. Half the time he beatin' her, half the time he on her in the bed, tellin' her how much he love her, how she always gonna be his woman."

"You saw *that?*" Billy asked.

"Huh! You stay in a one-room shack with folks, you sees and hears lots o' stuff you rather not."

"Don't tell him that mess," Cy said. He remembered back before his mama left. Sometimes at night, when his parents thought he was asleep . . .

"He asked," Jess said. "You want to hear more, Billy?"

"Yeah."

"You guys hush," West complained from the other side of Billy. "I want to go to sleep."

"Ain't much more to tell," Jess said. "Mr. George used to beat me bad. Use a belt, razor strap, switch—whatever he could get his hands on. Say I was a sorry excuse for a boy. Accordin' to Mr. George, I couldn't never do *nothin'* right. Couldn't plow a straight furrow, couldn't chop cotton, couldn't even slop a hog the right way. Didn't matter what I done, Mr. George always find a reason to beat me."

"I'da run off from a man like him," Billy declared.

I'd of killed him, Cy thought.

"I thought about runnin', but I stayed for Miz Ada."

And see where it got you, Cy thought.

"Mr. George beat her like she was a dog. It hurt me deep down to see how he use her. Nothin' she did satisfy him, either. She and me tried to look out fo' one another.

"Miz Ada wanted a baby real bad—believed if she could give Mister George a son, maybe he love her and quit hittin' her. Long time went by, and nothin' happen, even though he on her all the time. Then she started to have a baby, and Mr. George soften up some, but she lost it, and he beat her again, like he blame her 'cause the baby born too soon—born dead.

"After that, Miz Ada kinda give up. One time Mr. George go after her—for burnin' the collards—and she tell him she pray he go ahead and kill her. She rather be dead and go see King Jesus in heaven than go on livin' in hell. That stop him fo' a while. But next time, he went at her like he planned to answer her prayer."

"And?"

"I tried to stop him," Jess said. "I was pretty big by then. When Mr. George got to hitting Miz Ada, I stepped in. 'Run 'way,' I told her. 'Go 'way, and don't never come back.' And she did."

"I bet you whipped his ass good then," Billy said.

"I tried, but he too much for me. He knocked me out cold, and when I come to, he had me stripped and tied, and then he beat me worse than he ever done before. He just kept on with that strap . . ."

Just like John Strong. The words hammered against Cy's brain.

"Mr. George kep' me tied all night, and next morning he took me to town—made me walk half naked behind his horse with a rope 'round my neck—and turned me over to the sheriff. He kept me in the jail until the next time the judge come to town, and he charge me with disorderly conduct and sentence me to ten years. Cain got his hands on me, and I been here 'bout four years. Longer'n Cy."

"How old are you?" Billy asked.

"Don't know for sure. Seventeen, maybe."

"Y'all quit now!" West said. "We don't want to hear no more about Jess and his hard times."

"Sorry," Jess told him. "We be quiet now."

"What happened to that Miz Ada?" Billy asked.

"Shut *up!*" West cried.

"Hold on," Jess told him. "Lemme finish all the way to the end, and then Billy won't have no more cause to ask any questions. Will you, Billy?"

"Naw. Sorry, West."

West turned over and put his hands over his ears.

"I don't know what happen to Miz Ada," Jess went on. "She was gone that next morning when I come to, and we didn't see her on the way to town, or in town, neither. Mr. George kept cussin' her, sayin' she was gon' get it good when he got his hands on her, and he had a good mind to bring her up before the judge fo' stealin' his horse. I pray she got clean away from that man. Let's go to sleep now. Big day tomorrow."

"Huh," Mouse muttered. "What so big about it?"

Then it was quiet. Soon, Jess started to breathe slow and deep, and Mouse curled into his little ball and slept too. But Cy couldn't sleep. Jess's story had worked on him the way it always did, put questions into his mind he couldn't answer.

On the other side of Jess, Billy wasn't asleep, either. "Cy, you awake?" he whispered.

"Yeah."

"My daddy *is* gonna be here tomorrow. Remember I told you."

"All right." There was no point arguing with the kid.

"He is."

"Sure he is."

"You don't believe me!"

"Course I do."

"Maybe your daddy'll come too. I want my daddy to meet him."

"Maybe he will."

"Good night," Billy said.

But sleep still wouldn't come. It wasn't just Jess's story that kept Cy awake. Jess had done something to help that woman. He, Cy, had tried to save Travis and failed.

At least the woman had gotten away.

Another sleepless night before visiting day. Every three months it was the same: some part of him still wanted to believe his daddy would finally come, the part that still held on to hope, and he had to fight it down.

Tonight was no different. In fact, it was worse, after all that crap West had fed them. Getting their hopes up like that. Let the others keep on believing. He was done with that nonsense. Free? It was a word, nothing more.

But maybe, just maybe, that hopeful voice said, tomorrow would be different. His father would come, would have figured out a way to take him home.

Home. His mama's pink bonnet . . .

TEN

NEXT MORNING, SUDIE, THE GIRL WHO HELPED in the cookhouse, had on a freshly washed apron. Pook, clinging to his mother's skirt as usual, had on a clean pair of pants and jacket. His hair was brushed, too. Rosalee herself was wearing a different dress—blue calico. Her hair was brushed back from her face and tied at the back with a piece of red ribbon. For once, she looked pretty.

"Somebody been extra nice to Cain lately," Cy remarked while the boys were waiting in line for grits and fried fatback.

"What that suppos' to mean?" West asked.

"New dress, pretty ribbon. Rosalee had to get 'em from somewhere, and Cain don't give out nothin' for free."

"Shut up!" West cried.

"What's eatin' you?"

"Cy didn't mean nothin' by it," Jess broke in.

"Then he can keep his stupid mouth shut," West said. "I's tired o' the way he always got to say somethin' low-down."

"Ain't nobody askin' you to listen," Cy shot back.

"It hard not to hear your big mouth."

Cy made a move toward West, but Jess stopped him. "Quit it!" he ordered.

Cy pushed Jess away. He felt like punching West, but there'd be another time to settle things.

After breakfast was done and cleaned up, Stryker and Prescott took off the boys' leg irons, and they were free for a while. Eager to stretch their legs, some boys got up a game of tag. West went off by himself to a sunny patch of ground, lay down, and went to sleep. Mouse walked around, searching the grass for critters.

Billy made his way to the front of the camp and stood gazing through the barbed wire in the direction the wagon had brought him from.

Cy wandered around wishing he had something to do. He felt irritable, the way Teufel used to get when he'd been cooped up in his stall too long. That was when he was likely to bite or kick, even though you were trying to bring him out for exercise. Strange that when he was allowed free time, Cy couldn't come up with a way to use it. Mess with West? That was tempting—the kid couldn't mouth off to him that way!—but Stryker or Prescott might notice.

Visiting day. Nothing more than a mean joke. Cy glanced at the gate where Billy had planted himself. Maybe his daddy *would* show up—most likely not. For a moment, Cy felt sorry for the kid.

He had wandered up near the cookhouse when Rosalee appeared at the door with Pook. "Go on, sugar," she told the child, gently removing his hand from her long skirt. "Let Mama see how fast you can run."

Pook stood still a moment, then looked up at Rosalee. She nodded and smiled at him. "Run, little man. Stretch them long legs."

Cy stopped and watched. The catch in his throat surprised him, but not as much as Pook did when the child ran right to him. Without stopping to think about it, Cy grabbed Pook under both arms, picked him up, and began to swing him around. The child squealed happily.

Cy put Pook down, but the boy wasn't satisfied. "Again!" he shouted.

So he did it again, and again. Pook kept laughing and asking for more.

"You havin' fun, sugar?" Rosalee called.

"Yeah!" he cried.

"I got to stop," Cy said. He was panting and dizzy, but happier than he could remember being in a long time.

"Let Cy be," Rosalee said. "He wore out from playin' with you. Tell him thank you."

Pook hugged Cy's knees. "T'ank you, Cy." He started back to his mother, then spotted something in the weeds. He squatted to look. Cy followed, and Mouse came over, too.

"Bood," Pook said.

"Dead bird," Mouse said, holding it up.

"Bood," Pook said again. Rosalee came and stood by him.

Mouse held the bird in his palm. It was small, with some yellow on its breast and throat, and white stripes on its wings. The back was darker, kind of dull green. "We got to bury him," Mouse declared.

"Bood," Pook repeated, staring at the pitiful thing.

"Just throw it over the fence," Cy suggested.

"We got to *bury* him," Mouse repeated. He laid the dead bird on the ground and began scrabbling in the dirt with both hands.

"Why? It only a bird."

Mouse didn't answer, just tore at the earth, digging his nails into the slimy red clay.

"Put him in," Mouse told Pook when the hole was dug.

"He don't understand."

"Course he do. Put him in."

Pook picked up the dead bird by one scrawny foot and carefully placed it in the hole.

Without warning, tears came to Cy's eyes. *Stop it!* he ordered himself. *You gonna cry over a dead bird?*

"Hey, you!" a voice shouted.

It took Cy a second to realize he was being called. It was Stryker, at the gate. "Get over here, boy! You got a visitor."

On the other side of the barbed wire, near where Billy waited, staring at the road, stood Pete Williams.

Stryker unlocked the gate and gestured for the man to step through. He carried a shabby carpetbag in one hand. His hair had started to go gray, and there was something wrong with his left leg.

Cy didn't move.

"What's wrong with you?" Stryker shouted across the yard. "Ain't you gonna come see your daddy?"

He started forward slowly. Many eyes were staring at him, and he didn't like it.

"Son?" Pete Williams limped toward him and looked into his eyes. "Ain't you glad to see me?"

Cy didn't answer.

"Oh, let me hug you! I didn't believe this day would ever arrive."

Cy let his father put his arms around him, hold him, but he himself made no move. This was the moment he'd thought about nearly every day for three and a half years, and he supposed he should feel glad, but all he felt was anger.

Stryker cleared his throat. "I got to see what's inside that carpetbag," he said.

Williams went back to the gate, where he'd left the bag. Cy and Stryker followed.

"I brought my boy a couple things he might be able to use."

"Like a file?" Stryker asked. He smiled as if he'd said something funny.

"Oh, no, suh. I sho' wouldn't never do nuthin' like that."

"So what *is* in there?"

He brought out a parcel wrapped in brown paper. "This is for *you*, suh. And for yo' helpers."

"*I* don't run this place," Stryker corrected him. "What is it?"

"Best quality tobacco. Some for smokin', some for chaw. I didn't know what y'all might like."

"You ain't put no poison in it?" It was impossible to tell if Stryker was serious or just making another bad joke.

"Oh, no, suh! Just wanted to bring you somethin' to show appreciation for how you takin' care o' my boy."

Cy felt disgusted by his father's lie. If Stryker believed it, he was as stupid as he was mean. But he had to pretend to believe the words, just as Pete Williams had to pretend he meant them.

Stryker took the tobacco. "What else you got?"

"Some sweet cakes—here's some for you, too—and some apples."

"And?"

"Stockin's, and some drawers and a undershirt."

"Nothin' else? No contraband?"

"I swear it, suh. Just these couple little things for Cy."

"All right, then. Y'all go on and visit." He walked away.

Pete Williams picked up the carpetbag. "Cy? Can we go somewhere quiet and talk?"

Cy was about to answer when he noticed Billy. He was still fixed in the same place, but now his eyes weren't on the road. They were riveted on Cy's father.

"Who that?" the man asked.

"Nobody. New kid. Name of Billy. Thinks his daddy gonna take him home today."

"That likely to happen?"

"Probably not. Folks never show up to take anyone away."

"I's here," Williams said.

"Took you long enough," Cy said.

"Let's go find someplace to talk," his father suggested again.

Cy led the way to a front corner of the camp, as far from everyone else as they could get.

They stopped, and Pete Williams put his hands on his son's shoulders. "Let me look at you. You mighty thin! They don't feed you much."

Cy stepped back and glared at his father. "Why you never come to see me?"

"Son—"

"Where you been all this time? You don't care nothin' 'bout me! Just go away and let me be."

Williams put his hand on Cy's shoulder again, but Cy brushed it off. "Don't touch me!"

"I can explain, if you give me a chance. Let's sit down. My leg hurts if I got to stand too long."

Cy didn't reply.

"Please, son! I tried to come right from the day them damn Sconyers boys snatched you away, but it done took me all this time to find you."

Cy still didn't move. Inside him, a battle had begun.

"Suit yourself," his father told him, "but I got to sit." Slowly, favoring his hurt leg, he eased himself onto the damp grass.

Cy wanted to turn his back and walk away—or part of him did. The other part wanted to fall to the ground, crawl into his father's lap, and cry his heart out. Instead, he simply sat down.

Pete Williams opened the carpetbag and brought out another parcel wrapped in brown paper. Inside were molasses cakes. "They's for you," he said, offering them. "Please, son. Have one."

The cakes looked just like the ones his mother used to make. They'd been his favorites. For a second, a crazy hope rose in him. Had she returned?

"Where you get these?"

"Bought 'em from a store up in a place called Tifton."

"Where that?"

"Little place 'bout ten miles north o' here. Ain't much to it—sawmill and a few businesses." He offered the molasses cakes again.

"You never come for me," Cy whispered. He could smell the spices and molasses in the cakes, and his mouth was watering. Something told him that if he took one bite, he wouldn't be able to stop until every one of them was stuffed into his belly. "What happen to your leg?"

"Please look at me, son. I *wanted* to get here! I been tryin' to get here for more'n three years now! You got to believe me."

Cy wanted to. "I thought—you didn't care. I thought—you forgot about me."

Pete Williams choked back a sob. "Forget you? Oh, son!" He dropped his molasses cake on the ground and tried to take Cy into his arms.

"You didn't forget me?"

"You all I got left in this world. I couldn't no more forget you than I could my own name."

Cy let his father put an arm around his shoulder. Then he let himself cry. When he was done, he wiped his eyes and runny nose. He grabbed one of the molasses cakes and took a bite. It tasted so good it startled him. All these years, he'd had no sugar, no syrup, no sweetening. He took another bite and had to keep himself from swallowing it whole. He didn't stop until he'd eaten four.

Pete Williams watched his son, a sad smile on his face. "You ain't had nothin' like them in a long time, right?"

Cy shook his head. "No, sir. No coffee, neither. No chicken, no ham, no biscuits, no food fit for a dog!" He had to wipe tears away again.

"I's so sorry," his father told him. "Sorry from the bottom o' my soul. But I found you at last. That the important thing now."

"Daddy, please get me outta here."

"I know. I got a plan. But first, I want to explain a couple things. Why it took all these years for me to find you."

"All right."

Williams looked at the sky, like he was trying to remember, or maybe because he didn't want to remember. "That day—the day Travis got drowned—Strong's men come for me in the field. They got hold of me and tied me, took me to a curing barn and locked me in."

"That's what they said," Cy remembered.

"Them Sconyers boys?"

"Yeah. They got me after they locked you up. Uncle Daniel tried to stop 'em, but they hit him, knocked him out, I guess, and took me away."

Cy's father's face showed that remembering was painful. "Strong didn't let me outta that barn till the next evening. By then, you was long gone."

Now Cy understood. "Bastard made sure you couldn't find me."

"Like I said. I's sorry, son. O' course Uncle Daniel told me who kidnapped you, but they didn't show up for almost two weeks. By that time . . ." He fell silent and fixed his eyes on the sky again.

"What, Daddy?"

"By that time, Strong was dead."

"Dead? How?"

"Two days after Travis drowned, Strong had that poor child buried in the graveyard next to his mama. Uncle Daniel said after all the folks left, Strong went into the barn and barred the doors from inside. Then he shot that black devil and turned the gun on hisself. They found him lyin' dead in Teufel's stall, right next to the horse. I dug his grave, and the white folks come and bury him next to Travis. So all them Strongs is together again, at last."

Cy wasn't sorry Strong was dead. But Travis? An old ache, one he thought he'd killed long ago, grabbed at his heart. And Teufel? Why?

"I got to piss," Cy said. He stood up, went to the corner of the camp, and relieved himself. When he returned, he found his father eating one of the molasses cakes.

"They mighty good. Have another."

Cy took one and chewed it slowly.

"After they bury Strong, his creditors come 'round right away, and 'fore we knew it, we was all kicked off the place. Daniel an' Dorcas had to leave. I don't even know where they is now."

"How you find me after all this time?" Cy asked.

"I went to them Sconyers boys and begged 'em to say where they took you. Jeff acted like he was halfway ready to, but that damn Burwell put in his two cents, and they made me a deal: for one hundred dollars, they agreed to tell me where they brung you. It taken me all this time to save up that much."

Was it possible? His father had had to work to earn the money to find out where he was? Cy looked at the man sitting opposite him and noticed things he'd missed earlier: how his father's hair had thinned, the deep lines of sadness around his eyes.

"Gettin' kicked off Strong's place didn't make it no easier, and then I hurt my leg," Williams went on.

"How that happen?"

"When Strong's creditors show up sayin' we had to leave, I took one o' the wagons and a mule and cleared out."

"You stole 'em?"

"Yep. Figured I had the right."

"You did." Cy's old familiar hatred of John Strong blazed up in him.

"I headed in the direction I thought they took you. Turns out I was goin' farther *away* from you, not closer. Anyways, I ended up near a place called Louisville, found a man what needed hands to work his place. Things went okay for a year or so, exceptin' I was mighty lonely. So many times I wanted to drink all my sorrows away, but somethin' inside stopped me. I ain't had a drop in two years, Cy."

"That's real good, Daddy."

"Then I was returnin' from town one Saturday afternoon, 'long a stretch o' road where they's deep gullies cut on either side, to keep the road from floodin'. Here come Rafe McReynolds, the son of Ol' Man Tucker McReynolds, the man I was workin' for, and a bunch o' his friends, ridin' hard toward me, side by side, all stretched out across the road. Prob'ly drunk as usual. I thought they'd slow down, give me room to pass, but they keep comin' on, at a full gallop, like they warn't gon' to stop. I had to get out they way fast, but the road drop off so steep there that I didn't know what to do. Then that mule Jupiter—you remember him— decide for me. He shied, and down we went, crashing down into that ditch. I got pitched off the seat, and here come the wagon down right on top of me. Broke my thighbone right in two. Jupiter broke a leg too, and they had to shoot him."

Cy did remember Jupiter. How many times had he helped Uncle Daniel hitch him up? How many times had he curried him? Jupiter wasn't like most mules, ornery and lazy. He'd been a good fellow. And now he was dead, like Teufel.

"Them boys stopped above me, laughin', and one of 'em shout, 'Why didn't you get out of the road, nigger?' Then they went. Reckon I passed out after that, 'cause next thing I know, some colored folks is pattin' me on the face, askin' me how I am.

"They was right kind, them folks. Got me back to McReynolds's place and told him what happen. Course he wouldn't speak nothin' bad 'bout his boy—they never do— but he did send for a doctor. He come right away, too, and set my leg. Hurt worse than anything I ever felt in my life. Took three men to hold me down. Leg healed up, sort of, but it ain't been right since then. I had to quit sharecroppin' and find some easier work in town. Done all sorts o' things, but finally earned that one hundred dollars. Then I made it back near Davisville and found the Sconyers boys. Paid 'em what they asked, and they told me how to find you."

"You trusted 'em to tell you the truth?"

"I thought about that, son. Sorry crackers like them be just as likely to tell me a lie. But what other choice did I have?"

"I *hate* white folks," Cy muttered.

Pete Williams spat in the grass. "We got plenty o' cause, don't we? I treated ol' Jupiter a hell of a lot better'n any white man ever treated me."

"Better than Cain and his men treat us."

"They rough on you fellows, ain't they?"

"You *got* to get me outta here, Daddy!"

The man glanced around to make sure no one was close enough to hear him. "That's why I's here. Listen to me now, Cy. Listen real careful. This is important. Listen and do just like I tell you, and be brave." He reached into the carpetbag and brought out an apple. "Have one. They's real good. Little sour, but good."

Cy took the apple and ran his fingers over its smooth green surface. He hadn't touched a piece of fresh fruit since the last time he and Travis had snitched peaches from the trees in Strong's orchard. Again, his mouth watered, even though he was stuffed with molasses cakes. The taste of that apple made him want to cry some more.

Cy could feel his heart beating. "What I got to do, Daddy?"

"I been 'round these parts a couple days, checkin' on things. I know where they got you boys workin', out in that pine wood. I even know how the day goes—at dinnertime, that Cain take a swig and gets in a nap, and them other sorry sons o' bitches tend to they own messes."

"How'd you find all that out?"

"No matter. Tomorrow, keep a sharp eye at dinner-time. When Cain go down for his nap and them others ain't payin' much mind, pretend you got the stomachache and got to go off and do your business."

"Okay."

"Go toward a place where six pines grow thick together, almost in a circle, like someone planted 'em that way. You know where I's talkin' about?"

"No, but I can find it."

"Go there. Then keep goin', quick as you can. You won't be missed right away. Past them pines, you come to a wet place where the palmetto is real thick. On the other side o' that, you gon' meet a colored man on a horse. Name's Arnold. You go with him. He gon' take you to a safe place off the main road toward Moultrie. You turn off to the right just past a little bridge over a creek, then keep goin' till you come to a dead oak tree, then take a right. That how you know Arnold be takin' you the right way. I be waitin' there for you. We can hide there a few days with the woman who own the place, name of Aunt Miriam. When they quit lookin' for you, she help us get away. You got all that?"

"What if this Arnold ain't there?"

"He be there. But if he ain't, you get on back to the

camp, act like you done your business and that's that. But he *is* gon' be there, Cy. He *got* to be! I already done give him ten dollar to help us out. He an honest man."

"Ten dollar? That ain't right! Why we got to pay for every damn thing?"

Pete Williams frowned. "Ain't *nothin'* free in this life, son. I know that now. Whatever you want, you got to pay for, one way or 'nother, 'specially if you a black man."

Cy realized he'd always known that too.

"Can you do it?" his father asked. "Find Arnold and trust him to bring you to Aunt Miriam's?"

Suddenly, Cy knew the plan was crazy. Too many things could go wrong. His heart was still beating fast, but not from excitement.

From fear.

Pete Williams looked at his son hard. "Can you do it?"

Folks said that no one could survive in Cain's camp more than five years. Cy had been there three, going on four.

"Yes, sir. I can."

Pete Williams held his son tight. "Then I'll see you at Aunt Miriam's. Tomorrow evenin', you gon' be free."

That's what West had seen in blood and water: Cy Williams, free.

ELEVEN

"HOW YOU GET HERE, DADDY?" CY ASKED, reaching for a second apple.

"Walked."

"*Walked?*"

"Surprised? You mean how I get here with a bum leg, right?"

Cy felt embarrassed. "Yes, sir," he answered, eyes on the ground.

"Man do what he got to do, I reckon. Good Lord gimme strength. Hitched some rides in wagons too. Folks is usually ready to help out a cripple' man."

It hurt to hear his father use that word. "You ain't crippled, Daddy!"

"Try tellin' that to this ol' leg. Many's the time I's had to give it a good talkin' to, remind it of its duty, to help me find my boy."

"How far you walk? I never could tell how long it was between Strong's place and here."

"'Bout hundred seventy miles, they tells me."

"That far? It a mighty long way." *Especially for a . . . cripple*, he found himself thinking.

Pete Williams smiled a little. "Ain't nothin' compared to what slaves done back in the old days. Some of 'em run hundreds o' miles, by night, with only the North Star to guide 'em. Shucks, Cy. Any daddy'd do what I done. Anything to find his son."

So his father hadn't forgotten him. Once again, white men were to blame for all the bad things that had happened. Cy felt the hatred rising up in him—hatred for John Strong, the Sconyers boys, Cain and his men. They could do whatever they wanted to black folks, and no one would stop them.

"Time's up," Prescott called from across the camp.

"So soon?" Pete Williams said.

More than anything in the world, Cy wanted to walk through the gate with his father, leave Cain's camp forever. Maybe Pete Williams could say something, ask, beg. Surely Cy had long since paid for whatever crime the white men thought he'd committed.

If he let such thoughts take over, he'd fall to the ground, wailing. That wouldn't help. No—he'd have to wait, follow the plan his father had made. It would work; it had to.

Cy went behind a tree and put on the drawers and

undershirt his father had brought him. They felt soft against his skin. Now the coarse material of his uniform wouldn't always be rubbing him wrong. Then he remembered: after tomorrow, he wouldn't have to wear that hated uniform ever again. If everything went the way his daddy promised it would . . .

Cy sat and put on the new stockings. He'd forgotten how it felt to have the soft padding of knitted cotton between the skin on his feet and cheap, brittle leather boots. "I's gonna need other pants and a jacket tomorrow," he said. "I can't wear this uniform once I get outta here."

"I thought o' that. I left some pants and a coat with Aunt Miriam."

"What about my chains?"

"Don't worry. Arnold get 'em off you."

"He don't have the key."

"No matter. I seen how you boys is chained up. Shucks! Them leg irons is right pitiful. Won't take but a couple licks with a good, strong hammer and chisel to get 'em off. Cain too cheap even to buy decent stuff."

"They ain't strong?"

"Hell, no! Any man who know what he doin' and what got a couple simple tools can get 'em off in a minute. And let's not even talk 'bout the sorry way you boys is bein' guarded. Three men for *forty* of y'all? When they take you out to work, at dinnertime Cain go to sleep, and them two sorry crackers use the time to slack off. Y'all could make a break for it then."

Cy and some of the others had talked about that lots of times. Had made plans even more outlandish than his father's. Such scheming had helped pass many a long evening. But despite all their big talk, they always came back to the same reality, which stopped them cold. "Cain and his men got guns."

"No matter. You think three men could stand up to forty? Make a plan, take a chance."

"They'd shoot us!"

"Maybe—couple of y'all, at most. But you really think they could stop you? You bigger fellows go for the guns, while some others hustle the smaller boys away. You got tools right there—after you take care o' Cain and his men, you break off the chains—"

"We couldn't ever do that."

"That way o' thinkin' is why y'all still here," Pete Williams said quietly.

His father's words stung. "We ain't yellow, Daddy."

But you ran from Strong that day at the river, said a voice in his head. *You're yellow, all right, and see where it landed you.*

Cy felt he had to defend himself and the others too. "If we got away from Cain, the sheriff would hunt us down! We couldn't never escape."

"You don't know till you try, son. Tomorrow you gon' be free, 'cause you got the courage. Maybe one day, them other boys'll find theirs, too."

Then Prescott reappeared and said Williams had to go. Father and son followed him toward the gate and found Billy, still standing, waiting. Cy had forgotten all about him.

"Your daddy ain't here yet?"

Billy looked like he didn't understand the question. Then he turned back toward the road and declared, "Any minute now."

Pete Williams walked Cy a few paces away from Prescott, hugged him hard, and whispered, "Be brave. Arnold bring you right to Aunt Miriam. I be waitin' there for you. Tomorrow evenin', you free."

Cy wanted to believe him. Saying goodbye was hard.

When Prescott unlocked the gate to let Williams out, Billy bolted through it and started racing down the road.

"Stop, you!" Prescott shouted.

Billy kept running.

Prescott yelled for Cain and Stryker. All the boys in

camp rushed toward the gate. They had a clear view of the road and Billy speeding away.

Prescott ran through the gate. "Stop, or I'll shoot!" he shouted. If Billy heard, he didn't respond. Just kept going.

As Prescott raised his rifle and took aim, Jess pushed through the crowd of boys, burst into the road, and grabbed Prescott's arm from behind. The rifle went off, and down the road, Billy dropped into the red mud. Cy couldn't tell if he'd been hit.

"Don't, Mr. Prescott!" Jess cried. "You don't got to kill him. He just upset 'cause his daddy ain't come to see him."

Prescott pushed Jess away and whirled around, pointing the rifle at Jess's chest. "Get back! I swear to God, I'll shoot you dead if you make another move."

Cain appeared, urging his horse forward. He galloped through the gate and down the road toward where Billy lay, unmoving.

Stryker hurried toward the gate, rifle in hand. Prescott kept his weapon trained on Jess. "Hands up," he ordered. "And back inside."

"I's sorry, Mr. Prescott," Jess said. "I didn't mean to make no trouble. I just didn't want you to shoot Billy."

Prescott gestured toward Pete Williams. "Get goin'," he said.

Williams squeezed Cy's shoulder and went through the gate. He stood in the road, looking back at Cy. Then he nodded. Cy understood what his father meant. Tomorrow . . .

"I told you to get!" Prescott shouted.

Cy watched Williams walk away until Prescott ordered everyone to form their lines. Cy half expected Cain to return with Billy's body, but before long, the man appeared, calmly sitting in the saddle. Behind his horse, a rope tied around his neck, stumbling, begging, was Billy.

Cain waited until dark. He had the boys build a bonfire by the whipping post and then lined everyone up to watch.

Billy had spent the afternoon locked with Jess in a tiny shed everyone called the icehouse. He didn't resist when Stryker led him to the post and pulled off his jacket. He let Stryker tie his hands to the post and stood there staring into space. Somehow, he wasn't there, even though his half-naked body was.

But he screamed when the whip hit him, and he kept it up the whole time Cain was lashing him.

Jess was standing between Stryker and Prescott, his hands tied behind his back. Cy stood with the other boys, Mouse on one side and West on the other. Rage boiled inside him. He remembered his father's words: *You think three men could stand up to forty?* Cy wanted to shout, urge the others to do something, anything, to stop the whipping.

What had Billy done to deserve this? He wanted what they all wanted: to go home. And he had been brave enough, or crazy enough, to make a break for it. "We ain't yellow," Cy had told his father. But he felt yellow now, compared to Billy. He felt yellow, saying and doing nothing to try and save the kid. Then he reminded himself it was Billy's own fault. If he hadn't run, he wouldn't be under the whip.

Mouse buried his face in Cy's side. Cy made a move to push him away, then changed his mind. If Mouse could find some comfort that way, let him. It didn't cost Cy a thing.

When Cain was done, Stryker untied Billy, and he collapsed onto the ground. Prescott dragged him back to the line and dropped his jacket on him.

Jess never made a sound when Cain whipped him. Then Cain stood aside and let Prescott get his licks, too. When it was over, they cut Jess loose. He picked up his jacket and walked slowly to the line. In the firelight, his face was resigned.

Cain had a little speech to make. "I run a tight camp,"

he began, "but I run a *fair* camp. State says I got to open the place to visitors, I obey the law. Give y'all clean uniforms, new boots, blankets, let you wash up, feed you as decent as I can—"

West whispered a filthy word. Cy poked him to keep quiet.

"—and this is what I get," Cain declared. He pointed at Billy, still lying in the dirt, and then at Jess. "And you! I put a lot of trust in you, makin' you leader of your gang, and this is how you repay me."

"I didn't want Mr. Prescott to hurt Billy."

"You ain't gang leader anymore. Cy, job's yours."

That took Cy by surprise. Once, the news would have pleased him. Jess was too soft, let the guys get away with too much. Cy would have gotten them in line and used his new power to make things easier on himself. Now this so-called honor didn't mean a thing. Tomorrow, he'd be long gone from here, and Cain could go to hell.

Cain turned back to Jess. "You ever cross me again, it's Alabama and the mines. Understand?"

"Yessir."

"Chains in ten minutes," Cain told Stryker and Prescott. "If anybody gives you a lick of trouble, come get me. My arm was just gettin' warmed up good."

Cain walked into the darkness.

"You heard him," Stryker shouted.

Jess helped Billy up and took him away. Then Cy led the gang—*his* gang, for a few hours, at least—to water, the outhouse, their bunk, and chains.

TWELVE

THE BOYS WERE ALREADY ON THEIR PALLETS
when Prescott brought in Jess and Billy. "I ain't gonna
put up with no mess from y'all tonight," he warned. "I'm
gonna check on you, and if I hear so much as a peep, y'all
gonna get it."

Billy was chained next to Cy. Jess was on Billy's other
side, and Billy lay down facing him. He couldn't be on his
back—not the way it was all cut up.

"You all right?" West asked from beyond Cy.

No answer.

"Billy, you all right?" West repeated.

"He hurtin' bad," Jess said quietly. "I look after him."

"Daddy didn't come," Billy whispered.

"He be here," Jess promised.

When will Jess quit lyin'? Cy wondered.

"They say you stop Prescott from shootin' me," Billy
said.

"I had to do somethin'."

"And they whipped you."

"Yeah, they did."

"You saved my life."

"I don't know 'bout that. Prescott can't shoot worth a damn, and you was way down that road."

"You saved me." Billy moved closer to Jess, whose big arm came around and held him.

"Did what I had to do," Jess said. "Now, you try to get some sleep—"

Cy lay on his back, staring into the darkness. Through a chink in the roof, he thought he could see a star. He pulled his blanket up to his chin. The night was cold, but his new shirt and stockings offered some extra, welcome warmth. Of course he wouldn't sleep; he could think only about the coming day. Time after time, he imagined how he would play it:

"Mr. Prescott, I gotta go bad. My bowels is all water today."

"Go on," Prescott would say. *"Just hurry it up, hear?"*

He would already have found the place where the six pines grew in a circle. Beyond that, the wet place where the palmetto was thick. And beyond that—

"You awake, Cy?" whispered Jess.

"Uh-huh."

"How it go between you and yo' daddy today?"

That was just like Jess, to worry about another guy after he himself had been whipped. But Cy didn't want to answer. All afternoon he'd been turning back questions about his father's visit. When Mouse asked him, he got choked up. He had too much on his mind to dwell on all that, and he had to think straight.

"Okay," Cy told Jess.

Jess sighed. "I guess it hurt too much to talk about."

"Yeah."

"Maybe in a couple days, when you feel better."

"Uh-huh." *You liar*, said a voice in his head. *In a couple days you won't be here.*

Cy put that out of his mind. "How's Billy?"

"Sleepin'. Po' kid. He too small to take a whippin' like Cain give him."

"All them should burn in hell."

Now Jess would deliver a little sermon about forgiveness and not hating your enemies. But what he said surprised Cy.

"You right. They *oughtta* burn. And they will, too, one day. I don't mind what they done to me. But Billy—he didn't mean nothin'. Just wanted his daddy."

"We *got* to get out of here," Cy whispered fiercely. He

was on the edge of saying that tomorrow, they could all be free.

"Ain't no way *we* gonna get ourselves outta here," Jess said. "What with they guns, and dogs, and how they can call in folks from all over to track us—ain't no way."

Cy didn't want to hear about swarms of white men with rifles and bloodhounds closing in on a few black boys who didn't have a chance.

"Cy?" Jess whispered.

"Yeah?"

"You know I's right."

"I *don't* know that. What I know is, it only a matter of time till Cain pick up his whip again."

"We got to face what *is*, not what *might* be! We got to keep goin', one day at a time, lookin' out for each other best ways we know how, and trust in God. He the one gonna come set us free, jus' like he done freed the people o' Israel from ol' Pharaoh."

"Would you stop with that stuff?" Cy whispered. "Billy trusted God to bring his daddy, and look at what happened. Got the shit beat outta him."

"Billy daddy ain't God, and God ain't through yet. Look what he done for us black folks. We ain't slaves no more."

Cy rattled his leg irons. "The hell we ain't."

. . .

It was dark when the wake-up gong sounded—like always. No one moved—like always. Cy had slept, after all. Stryker burst through the door, shouting at everyone to get up.

This was how Cy's day of freedom started.

Jess had a hard time getting Billy going. Even Mouse was ready before him. Jess put his hand on Billy's forehead and said he had the fever. In the cold morning air, Billy was shivering.

"He can't stay in the bed," Jess warned. "Stryker ain't in no mood for excuses this morning."

Together, they got Billy to his feet.

"I's cold," he kept saying.

Cy's new shirt felt soft and warm. "Here," he said, unbuttoning his jacket and pulling off the shirt. "Put this on. It'll help you."

Cy could feel Jess's eyes on him. "If he can't make it, they's gonna be more trouble," he said. He was feeling irritated with Billy, and with Jess.

"I can't take that," Billy murmured.

Cy pulled the shirt over his head. The air was chilly on his body. "No matter. You have it." *I won't need it anyway,* he thought. *I'm gettin' all new clothes today.*

"Naw, Cy, it ain't right," Billy objected.

"Go on. Take it," Jess urged.

"Thanks, Cy."

Jess helped Billy take off his jacket, and Cy saw Billy's back—a tangle of raw welts.

Breakfast was little dabs of cold mush, half-cooked hunks of fatback, and water. Sudie's eyes were red—she was softhearted, if simple-minded—but Rosalee's face was blank.

As gang leader, Cy got to issue orders, see that everyone was there, that everyone worked to load the wagons and was ready to leave camp. No one gave him any back talk. Stryker and Prescott seemed to be everywhere, shouting, poking at boys with their sticks, making threats.

Black night was just giving way to gray dawn when they started the long march to the palmetto woods.

Cy turned back for one last look at the camp. He didn't believe in praying, but he found himself wishing that the place would come crashing down to the ground, that the men who ran it would be swallowed up and dragged down to burn in hell forever.

Stryker and Prescott kept the boys at a trot. After the first mile, Jess was half carrying Billy. Mouse stumbled, but Cy helped him. Why not? After today, he'd never see Mouse again.

Then it began to rain—icy rain, mixed with sleet.

At the palmetto woods, Cy located the six pine trees his father had told him about. The palmetto did grow thick there. Other small trees and bushes crowded in, tall enough to hide a man—even a man on horseback.

His mind went back and forth about the plan all morning. One moment, he knew it would happen. Arnold would be there. The next second, he realized it was just plain crazy. Arnold *wouldn't* be there. Even if he did show up, Cain and his men would quickly see what was happening. The plan was impossible. But maybe . . .

Cold rain kept coming down hard. In this kind of weather, sometimes Cain would call off work, let everyone go back to camp, mostly because he and his men didn't want to stand outside in that mess. Not today. Everyone was being punished for what Billy and Jess had done yesterday. Even Stryker and Prescott. They'd be in an ugly mood later on. But Cy wouldn't be there to see it, he kept telling himself.

As he worked, Cy wondered what Cain would do to the others once he realized Cy had escaped. He didn't like to think about it. But he told himself it wasn't his problem. The others had to look out for themselves. He'd tried to explain that they had to get free, not wait for Jess's God to swoop down and rescue them, and Jess had disagreed. Sure, he felt bad for Jess and the other guys, but he had to take the chance he was being given.

The boys hacked at the palmetto as hard as they could,

not just to avoid the white men's beatings, but also to keep warm. Mouse took to shivering anyway. Billy tried to work, but he wasn't up to much. Prescott was all for messing with him, but Stryker told him to back off. West cussed Cain, Prescott, Stryker, the world. Jess tried to help the others and do his own job too.

Finally Cain called the break for dinner. The rain had let up, but Cy was shivering, and not just from the cold. He couldn't eat his cornpone and sweet potato.

"What's with you?" Jess asked. "You jumpy as a squirrel."

"My stomach," Cy lied. But it wasn't really a lie. He felt ready to vomit.

"Yo' body here, but yo' mind somewhere a million miles off," Jess added.

"I ain't the only one. Everybody tryin' to pretend they ain't here. Look."

Mouse was poking in the muck with a stick, always looking for some little critter to befriend. West had folded himself up under a palmetto bush and gone to sleep. Ring was braiding long strands of pine straw together and dropping them into a pile between his feet. Sitting by himself, Billy picked at his food.

Jess nodded at him. "He bad off. Unless his daddy come, he might not make it."

It was now or never. Cy clutched his belly.

"What is it?"

"Been hurtin' all morning. Like a knife cuttin' me."

"Dysentery. You got the runs?"

Cy shook his head. "Not yet. But I got to go real bad. Right now." He jumped up and hurried toward where the white men were huddled together by the wagons, passing a flask.

"What you want?" Stryker asked.

"I got to go real bad," he gasped. "I think I got the dysentery."

"That's all we need," Cain grumbled.

"Let him go. He ain't never given you any trouble," Stryker said.

"One of the 'good' ones?" Prescott shot back. "Like any of 'em is worth a pile of horseshit."

"Please, sir," Cy cried. "I got to go right now."

"Then git!" Stryker said. "Five minutes. And don't forget, we got an eye on you."

Cy went straight toward the six pine trees. The ground got soggy, and he stumbled in a shallow pool where the water came up over his boots. He pushed his way through the thick palmetto that seemed to go on forever, and at last he came into a clearing. Gasping for breath, he stared around him.

No Arnold. His father was wrong. The idea of going back was more than Cy could stand. Dying would be better. Even without Arnold, he would keep going. That would give him a chance. Back at camp, there was no chance, no hope.

Anyone would be hard to spot among these palmetto thickets. That was the thing to do: hide in the underbrush. No one would find him, not if he concealed himself well enough. When they went to fetch the dogs, he'd go deep into the swamp beyond the woods, through water, so that the dogs couldn't follow him. Somehow, he'd—

"Boy!"

He jumped.

"You Cy Williams?"

A black face was looking at him through a gap in the wall of leaves at the far side of the clearing.

Cy couldn't speak. He nodded.

"I's Arnold. Been waitin' for you all morning."

Cy wanted to shout for pure joy. His father hadn't failed him.

"Come on." Arnold's face disappeared in among the leaves, and Cy followed. The palmetto thinned out, and Cy saw a black horse tied to a pine tree.

"Let's go!" Arnold whispered. "Ain't no time to lose."

Arnold untied the horse and helped Cy get on. It wasn't

easy, not with his legs in chains. He sat sideways on the horse, just behind the saddle. Arnold climbed up and took the reins. "Put yo' arms 'round me and hold on. Soon as we get clear o' here, I stop and get them irons off you."

With the horse at a walk, they moved quietly away. "Road about half mile straight on," Arnold whispered over his shoulder. "We got to follow it but not be on it. Too risky."

The journey to the road seemed to take an hour. Cy kept looking back, certain they were being followed. Every second, he expected to hear the shouts of the white men, the sound of gunshots. His heart did a fearful dance inside his chest. But there was nothing, no sound of pursuit. Why? By now, he must have been missed. It was all too easy.

When at last they came to the road, Arnold turned left and made the horse trot.

"I thought we was gonna stay in the woods," Cy said.

"Soon. Just hold on."

"If you take off my leg irons, I can ride the right way."

"We's almost there."

Almost where? His father had said Aunt Miriam's place was miles away. Something was wrong.

Soon they came to a turnoff. Cy recognized the path back to where they were clearing palmetto.

"No!" he cried. He let go of Arnold and threw himself face forward off the horse, into darkness.

When he opened his eyes, he was lying on the ground. On his neck was an iron ring attached to a chain that ended in Arnold's hand.

Arnold looked down at him. "You gonna come along quiet?"

Cy looked into the man's eyes, trying to read the mind behind them.

"I said, is you gonna come along quiet?" Arnold repeated.

Cy nodded.

"Then git up."

Cy took his time. He was shaky from the shock of his fall, from fear, and from the hatred he felt for this man who had betrayed him.

When he got to his feet, he hurled himself at Arnold. But Arnold was no fool, and he was fast. His right fist caught Cy square on the chin, and Cy went down again. Arnold pulled out a pistol and pointed it in Cy's face.

"Now get up and let's go."

Cy fought back tears of rage and fear. *"Why you doin' this?"*

"Hard times, boy. I got a family to feed."

You don't know what hard times is, Cy thought bitterly. "You gonna pay!" he cried.

Arnold chuckled. "That's where you's wrong. I already *been* paid. Your daddy give me ten dollar up front and promise me ten more when I deliver you safe. Twenty bucks ain't bad for a few hours' work. But if I take you back to Cain—"

"No! You can't—"

"*When* I take you back to Cain, he pay me at least ten dollar for your return, maybe more. Then I go back to your daddy and collect again."

"How? He won't pay you a cent more if you don't take me to him."

"I just tell your daddy that it didn't work out, but he still owe me the other ten for my trouble. If he *don't* pay me, I might have to come back and inform Mr. Cain the exact location of Aunt Miriam place. It worth your daddy's money for me *not* to go back to Cain. Who knows? Maybe that Aunt Miriam can find some extra cash lyin' around too. Anything to keep Sam Arnold quiet."

"I hope you burn in hell!"

"Don't make me laugh! God, hell, the devil—any black man who believe in God and all that nonsense is a fool."

"I don't care about nothin' you got to say!" Cy was desperate to get his hands around Arnold's neck.

"You got spunk," Arnold went on. "Gotta give you that. Tell you what. I ain't really a bad fellow, and I know you's in a tight spot. When we get back to the camp, I can throw Cain off the scent. I'll say your daddy waitin' for you in just the opposite direction of where he really at. That way, I got time to collect my thank-you money, and your daddy won't get caught. With any luck, he get clean away. All you got to do is cooperate, and you can give your daddy a fightin' chance."

Cy was done for, and suddenly he knew it. Arnold had the gun. *The bad guy always had the gun.* All Cy had was an iron ring around his neck and chains on his feet. And the end of a cruel dream of freedom.

"All right," Cy said.

"Good boy! I knew you'd see it my way. Sure, you'll get a whippin', but hell, a whippin' ain't nothin'. I done had more'n my share of 'em in my day, and look at me. No harm done. I's tough, and that's what you gotta be, if you gonna survive in this stinkin' world. Tough son of a bitch like me. Now come on."

Arnold climbed back into the saddle and told his black horse to walk on. Cy had to follow on foot. Arnold kept hold of the chain and his reins with one hand, and his pistol with the other.

As Cy trudged along, he found himself thinking of Teufel. Teufel, who could run faster than any other horse he'd ever seen. Who had made the fatal mistake of losing the big race and was shot in his own stall. Cy wondered if the men who buried John Strong did the same for the big stallion, or if the horse's body was left to rot where it lay.

Cy thought of trying to break free. He could pull the chain from Arnold's hand and run for it. The man would shoot him, and it would be over. But then Arnold would tell Cain where his father was and Pete Williams would end up dead too.

Cy owed him the chance to escape.

THIRTEEN

AS THEY NEARED THE WORK SITE, PANIC ROSE
in Cy's throat. The iron ring was choking him. He clawed
at it. "It ain't too late," he pleaded. "Please don't take me
back there."

Arnold didn't bother to answer him.

In the clearing, Arnold brought his horse to a stop. All
the boys stood in their two rows, long chains in place, as if
ready for the trek back to camp.

Cain stood between the rows, his back to Arnold.

"Hey, look there!" one of the boys shouted, pointing
their way.

Cain spun around, and all the boys started talking. Cy
could hear his name repeated. He scanned the crowd and
caught Jess looking at him with solemn eyes.

Cain pointed his rifle at Arnold, sitting calmly in his
saddle. "Well, what have we here?" he asked.

Arnold removed his hat. "Sam Arnold, Mr. Cain. You
don't know me, but I knows you. You got a powerful

reputation in these parts. I brung you somethin'. Don't want no trouble."

"Where'd you find *him?*"

"I can explain, sir, you give me a chance."

"Start talking."

Cy looked around. Familiar faces were staring at him—West, Mouse, Ring, Billy. He felt ashamed that they should see him like this.

"How'd you get him?" Cain repeated. "My men are off searchin' for him right now." Cain fired into the air. He came toward Cy and nudged the iron ring with the rifle barrel. "You didn't just run across him by accident," he told Arnold. "Or do you always ride around with a chain and collar?"

"You got a sharp eye, Mr. Cain," Arnold said humbly. "Truth is, I was expectin' to meet this boy this mornin', and I was ready for him."

"How so?"

"Well, sir, his daddy—the one come visit him yesterday—he showed up in Colored Town a few days ago, askin' around to see if he could work up a deal with somebody to make a plan to free his boy. I got wind of it and met up with him."

"Why didn't you go straight to the sheriff?"

Arnold dropped his eyes. "Aw, shucks, Mr. Cain, you

knows how complicated all that can get! I didn't see no reason to involve the law when you and me can work out this thing between us."

"Oh?"

"I made arrangements to pick up this boy in the woods this mornin'. Him and his daddy made plans for him to pretend to be sick—to go off and relieve hisself. I was waitin' for him, and I was suppos' to carry him to a place where his daddy would meet him and take him away."

Cain came in close to Cy's face. "Is that true? You and your daddy in this together?"

Cy stared at the ground and said nothing.

"Is it *true*, or am I gonna have to beat the answer out of you?"

Stryker and Prescott emerged from the dense stand of pine and palmetto. "What the hell?" Prescott asked.

"Seems like Cy worked up a little scheme with his daddy yesterday. Only they didn't figure that one o' their own kind would turn 'em in." Cain grabbed Cy's jacket collar. "Boy, you ain't answered my question yet. Your daddy put you up to this?"

Cy couldn't figure how to keep his father out of it. Cain would realize there was no way Cy could have contacted Arnold on his own. He nodded.

"And this boy was supposed to whisk you away and deliver you safely somewhere?"

"Yes, sir."

"And your daddy was gonna take you back to home, sweet home?"

Cy nodded. He wondered if Cain had any idea of how bitterly he hated him.

"How much did he pay you to help?" Cain asked Arnold.

"Ten dollar, sir."

Cain whistled. "That's a little steep for a nigger. I can get all I want for free."

"Yes, sir," Arnold agreed. "Reckon the boy's daddy see some value in him."

"How much *you* want for him?" Cain asked.

"Ten dollar. That how much more his daddy promise me. I don't reckon he gonna pay me *now!*"

Cain chuckled. "I reckon not. Ten dollars, eh? A lot of money. More than this boy is worth. You know what I *should* pay you?"

"Can't rightly say."

"Thirty pieces o' silver."

"Sir?"

"Forget it. So you want ten dollars?"

"I got six chillun to feed."

"Tell you what. You tell me where to find this boy's daddy, and I'll give you two dollars."

"Aw, shucks, Mr. Cain. No wonder they all say you drive a hard bargain."

"That's right, *nigger*. Tell me where to find this boy's daddy so we can finish this deal. The sight of you makes me want to puke."

"North o' here, 'bout five miles. Back off the road, they's a place yo' men might be familiar with. Got some real pretty high-yaller gals. His daddy puttin' up there. He reckon nobody come lookin' for a respectable man in a whorehouse."

Cy felt relief wash over him. He was in terrible trouble, but Arnold had kept his promise so far.

"Respectable?" Prescott said. "Ain't no such thing as a respectable nigger."

"You two know the place?" Cain asked.

"Heard tell of it, Cap'n," Prescott replied.

Stryker pushed him. "I reckon you have. They got a room with your name on it!"

"That's enough," Cain ordered. He turned to Arnold. "Here's your money," he said, dropping two bills into the mud. "Take it and get out before I decide to call the sheriff on you."

Arnold got down from his horse and took his money from the muck.

"Now the boy."

All this time Arnold hadn't let go the chain. "I can unlock his collar," he offered.

"Just give me the key."

"That my chain."

"It *was* your chain. The key." Cain put out his hand, waiting.

Arnold dug in his pocket and dropped a key on Cain's palm.

"Now *git*," Cain commanded.

Arnold went to his horse. As he passed Cy, he winked.

When he was gone, Cain gave orders to head back to camp. "We got more important things to tend to," he said.

They tied Cy to the first wagon. Prescott kept up a fast pace, so he had to run to keep from falling and being dragged.

When they got to camp, Prescott led him to the icehouse and shoved him in. He looked down to where Cy lay, sprawled on the dirt floor.

"I feel sorry for you, boy. You gonna get the livin' Jesus beat out of you later on! I ain't never seen Cain as riled as he is right now. You dumb niggers just never learn."

He slammed the door. The key turned in the lock.

Cy sat in the darkness, trying to keep his hands from tearing themselves to pieces against the rough metal of the strangling iron ring. He couldn't stop the sobs that rose in his throat.

At dusk, Cain unlocked the door and peered into the darkness. "You really thought you could get away with a damn-fool thing like that?"

Cy didn't speak.

"Stryker went for the sheriff, and they rode down to Lily's—uh, the place Arnold said your daddy would meet you. He was right there, too, just like y'all planned it. Stryker said he was one surprised nigger when he showed up with the law, instead of you."

You goddamn liar, Cy thought.

"So tonight, your daddy is in the county jail. I reckon he'll end up on a chain gang too—followin' in his boy's footsteps, as they say."

It was all a lie. Cy believed his father was safe. He had to believe it: that was all he had left. Aunt Miriam would hide him, help him get safely away.

"But we got other things to tend to. Prescott!"

Cy was dragged to the whipping post. Another bonfire had been lit nearby. All the boys were there.

Prescott yanked Cy's jacket from his back, popping some buttons. Cy's hands were tied to the top of the pole.

Cain started in on one of his speeches. He made a big point about the boys' lack of gratitude and how Cy's foolish plan showed that trying to escape their just punishment could never work. Then he started in on how niggers were untrustworthy, that they couldn't even count on one another. Sam Arnold was proof of that. Cain said that to his mind, the worst nigger is one who turns against his own kind. Arnold was just like Judas in the Bible, a Jew who betrayed Jesus, a fellow Jew, for thirty pieces of silver. Even animals didn't go against their own the way Arnold had gone against Cy—for two stinking dollars. But then what did you expect, seeing that niggers couldn't be civilized . . .

Cy tried not to listen. His mind searched for something else to focus on, a place of escape from what was about to happen.

Then came the bite of Cain's whip. It struck again and again, cutting, burning. He clenched his jaw, then bit his lip until blood came. He would not scream.

At last, Cain was done. "Cut him down and put him back in the icehouse," he ordered. "And take that goddamn ring off his neck. Thing makes me sick. I ain't a cruel man." He addressed the other boys. "Let's see how Cy here likes bein' by himself for a night or two. Give him some time to think things over. Help him realize how good he had it."

After the door was locked behind him, Cy's legs wouldn't hold him any longer. He fell down and passed out.

The sound of creaking hinges woke him. Outside it was still dark. Cy pushed himself back toward the wall and pulled his knees up. Instinct told him to be on his guard.

"So you're awake." He couldn't see Prescott, but he felt the man standing over him, and he smelled whiskey.

"Answer me!"

"I's awake."

"How'd you like your little lesson?"

"I didn't, sir."

"I didn't think you would. You sure had it comin', though. Now I got a lesson for you, too. Stand up!"

As he struggled to his feet, Cy heard the click of a knife blade springing from its holder.

"I wouldn't want to have to cut your pretty black throat," Prescott whispered, "but if you give me any trouble, that's what I'll do. All I'd have to tell Cain is that I come here to check up on you and you jumped me. Then I had to fight back. You don't want to die tonight, do you?" He pressed the blade against Cy's neck.

"No, sir. Please, sir!"

"You say a word to anyone, I'll tear out your heart. Understand?"

"Yes, sir."

"You gonna cooperate?"

Cy nodded.

"Good. Then I won't have to use this."

The knife blade snapped shut.

"Now drop them pants and turn around."

FOURTEEN

THINGS HE WANTED:

Something—anything—to drink. He'd emptied the small water bucket long ago.

To wash himself all over.

His father.

His mother.

To die.

To forget.

To destroy Prescott. He dreamed . . .

"Tie him."

Ring and Billy put the ropes around Prescott's wrists.

"Tighter!"

Ring pulled until the ropes cut deep into the white skin.

"On the ground," Cy commanded.

Billy shoved Prescott off his feet. He fell backwards and landed with a thud.

"You boys better quit right now!" Prescott shouted. "It ain't too late. You let me go, I won't say nothing to Cain."

"Down!" Cy ordered.

Prescott obeyed.

"His arms."

Ring and Billy yanked the man's arms out from his sides and tied the ropes to the stakes in the ground.

"Now his legs."

"You niggers are crazy!" Prescott cried.

"Bring it!"

Mouse came forward, a cloth sack in his hands.

Ring tore open Prescott's shirt, baring his scrawny, hairy chest.

"Now."

Mouse got down beside Prescott, opened the sack, and pulled out the snake. Eastern diamondback rattler. Big one, five foot long, at least.

"Jesus God!" Prescott cried.

"One bite kill you dead," Mouse intoned.

"Do it!" Cy ordered.

Mouse lowered the snake onto Prescott's body. The man began to scream. "No! Oh, God, help me! Help me!"

"They ain't no God," Cy informed him, "and the sooner you get that through your dumb cracker head, the better off you gonna be—"

Cy roused.

Somewhere outside in the darkness, Prescott and

Stryker were laughing. Cy put his hands over his ears. He slept again.

When he woke next, light was filtering through the cracks in the wooden walls of the icehouse. Cy pushed himself to his feet. He groaned. His back was on fire from the beating Cain had given him. His body ached where Prescott had torn him. He had to piss, but where? A corner was the only place, and he used it.

A spider hung from its web in the corner above his head, lit by a bar of yellow light. Cy went to touch it, make it move—something alive to keep him company. It fell from the web and dropped onto the dirt floor.

Dead . . .

He crumpled into the corner, and sobbing took him, until sleep blessed him again.

Someone was knocking on the door. It was daylight, but which day?

"Cy? You all right in there?" Rosalee.

Cain's woman.

He didn't answer.

"Cy?"

"Lemme alone."

"I got to tell you somethin'."

"How long I been in here?" Cy croaked.

"Two days. Cain say he gonna let you out tonight. You all right?"

"What you think?"

"I got to tell you somethin'."

"What?"

"That man—the one what brung you back to camp—"

"What about him?"

"I hear Cain tell Stryker that he dead. Shot. Cain laugh and say somethin' 'bout gettin' his two dollar back. Thought you want to know."

That made him glad. He was only sorry he hadn't had a chance to kill Arnold himself.

He wanted to ask Rosalee if she knew anything about his father. He almost spoke, then shut his mouth. Why should he trust this woman?

"What time is it?" he asked instead.

"After dinner. They all gone. Only Sudie and me here."

"I got to have water."

"I know. You hungry too, I reckon."

Tears flooded his eyes. "Please bring me some water!"

"They ain't no way to get it to you. Cain got the key, and they ain't no room to get a cup under this door."

"Please!"

"Hold on. I be right back."

In a couple minutes, she returned. "I got water and a cloth. I gon' wet the cloth and push it under the door."

Cy pulled the cloth through the crack and twisted it over his mouth. Several drops dripped down. He swallowed them, then began to suck on the cloth.

"Send it back," Rosalee told him.

After she'd wet the cloth many times, Rosalee pushed some slices of bread under the door, and Cy gobbled them. Then Rosalee left him in the shadows of the icehouse, sucking on a ragged piece of feed sack and wishing for his own mother.

Rosalee was right: that evening, Cain appeared at the icehouse. It was dark, but he held a lantern.

"Ready to get outta here and behave yourself?" he asked.

Cy kept his eyes fixed on the dirt. "Yes, sir."

"You'd die in here if I wanted you to. You know that."

"Yes, sir."

"Or I could bring you out in front of them others and whip you to death."

"Yes, sir."

"But I ain't gonna do that," Cain assured him. "You never gave me no trouble before, so I've decided to show you mercy."

Cy knew all about that kind of mercy now. "Thank you, sir."

There was a sound behind Cain, and the lantern light showed Prescott.

Cy pushed himself farther back into the corner.

"Is he tamed?" Prescott asked.

"Appears so. Never can tell with 'em, though. Look at me," Cain ordered.

Cy raised his eyes.

"You got two choices. Mind yourself from now on, let the others know how sorry you are for what you done, warn 'em about tryin' any such foolishness themselves, and you'll be all right. No more whippings. Maybe even be a leader again one day. I got Jess to take charge in your bunk again, since you let me down. And that was after *he* messed up. I'm all for giving folks a second chance. You'd like another chance, wouldn't you?"

"Yes, sir," Cy lied.

"Or you can be a troublemaker. Let the other boys look up to you like some kind of martyr."

He didn't know what Cain meant.

"If that's what you choose, you're gonna find yourself digging coal before you know what hit you. Understand?"

"Yes, sir."

"Have him wash up, and get him a clean uniform," Cain told Prescott.

"What gang you want him with?"

"Same one."

"With his pals? You think that's a good idea?"

Cain turned on him. "You let me do the thinking, Onnie. Hell, yes, it's a good idea! Give him a chance to show if he can keep his word. If he's tempted to get sympathy, it'll be from his buddies—Jess, Mouse, that idiot Billy."

"Right, Cap'n."

"Let him clean up and get to bed." Cain walked off.

Prescott smirked. "You smell like just what you are. Remember what I told you the other night. You ever say one word, I'll kill you if it's the last thing I do."

You wrong, Cy thought. *You the one gonna die.*

Prescott took him to the washtubs. Cy hated undressing in front of him. If Prescott said one more word, he'd go for him, no matter what. But his tormentor was silent.

Things in camp looked the same, but Cy was seeing through different eyes. It was between supper and bedtime, and the boys were spending the time like they usually did—some standing and talking, a few gambling for pebbles with dice they had made from bits of wood. The whipping post was gone.

"Cain says for you to eat," Prescott said. "Rosalee got somethin' for you. Then you're free until bedtime."

Free.

"Cain wasn't jokin' about what he said. You've had your last chance."

"Yes, sir."

"You don't want no more nights in the icehouse."

"No, sir."

"Remember, I got my eye on you."

At the kitchen, Rosalee handed him a plate of cold rice and neck bones and a slice of bread. She filled a cup with water and waited while he drank it dry three times.

"Thanks for comin' to help me," Cy told her.

"I didn't mind."

"Pook all right?" Not that he cared. It was something to say, nothing more.

"He okay. Good as he *can* be in a place like this."

Cy wasn't sure why he asked the next question. "Why you stay here, Miss Rosalee?"

"That ain't none of yo' business. Now, go and behave yo'self."

"Yes, ma'am."

"Don't say ma'am to me! I ain't yo' mama."

"Thank you for the food."

"I tell you to git!"

He did.

Cy wandered away from the kitchen. He desperately wanted sleep, but for some reason he wanted to see Jess too.

Something touched him, and he jumped. Mouse took his hand, but Cy pulled away. "Where Jess?" he asked.

"With Billy. I show you."

Mouse led him to the fire where Jess and Billy sat. Jess's arm lay over Billy's shoulder.

Cy sat down next to Jess, who glanced at him, then looked away. If Billy realized Cy was there, he gave no sign.

"What's with him?" Cy asked, gesturing toward Billy.

"He gone away for a while."

"What you talkin' about?"

"In his mind. He ain't spoke much since Cain whip you." Jess kept his eyes on the fire.

"They let me out of the icehouse."

"So I see."

"Thought you be happy to see me."

"Should I be?"

Cy didn't expect the cold shoulder—especially not from

Jess. It hurt. He realized he'd come looking for sympathy. "If I could of got away, would you be glad?"

"Glad that you tried to escape without botherin' to tell yo' friends goodbye, without carin' how Cain would take it out on the rest of us?"

"That ain't the way it was! I can explain—"

"They ain't no point goin' over all that mess now," Jess said. "Maybe you should go somewheres else. Billy an' me don't want no more trouble."

So that was how it was. Cy started to get up. He didn't need Jess to feel sorry for him. But then he sat down again. There was something he had to talk about, something more important than his hurt feelings. Could he trust Jess not to betray him, the way Arnold had?

"Jess?"

"What?"

"We *got* to get out of here."

Jess moved to get up. "Come on, Billy."

"No, wait. Just listen, all right?"

Jess sat down again. "I told you, Cy. They ain't no way. And I don't want to hear nothin' more about it. Understand? You keep bringin' this up to me, I won't be able to talk to you no more."

"Don't say that! We *got* to talk about it. Gettin' away'd

be easy, only we can't see it! Daddy say Cain run a sorry operation. Our chains ain't strong. We could get 'em off easy."

Jess started to his feet again, but Cy grabbed his arm and pulled him back. "Three men ain't enough to stop us. We got to try! If we don't, we all gonna end up dead."

Jess looked him in the eyes. "You wrong. You think Cain and his men gonna stand by while we try and break these chains? They gonna give us nice new clothes, hand us some fried chicken and biscuits, and wave goodbye as we head down the road, singin'? We'd have to kill 'em first, and I don't want nothin' to do with that mess."

Billy must have heard, but he didn't move. Jess was right. He'd gone far away, somewhere deep into his own mind.

"Killin' ain't a bad idea," Cy told Jess. "Question is, do we got the guts to try it?"

"You don't mean that. Bible say the one who live by the sword, die by the sword. One day, I got to stand before the judgment throne o' God, an' I rather not have the blood o' any man, black or white, on me. I come too close to killin' once before, and I ain't takin' no more risks."

"The man who beat you so bad?"

Jess nodded. "Prettyman. I tried to kill him. I *wanted* to kill him. Would have, but he too strong for me."

"That's why you here! If you'd of killed him, you could of got away."

"Maybe. Maybe I could of escaped, gone up north or somethin'. But I didn't. So I's here, and I know it ain't fair. But my hands is clean, and I won't dirty 'em with no man's blood. I got to be ready to meet God when that day come."

"Please, Jess!"

"If we *could* get outta here, what then? What about the sheriff? And men on horses with dogs? Where you think forty runaway black boys gon' go and *be* safe? The whole world against us."

Maybe Jess was right, but Cy didn't want to hear it, and he didn't like being talked to as if he were a child. "I don't care," he shot back. "What you rather do—stay here and wait to die?"

"Naw—stay here and pray to God to free us."

"Any black man who believes in God is a fool!" Cy was shocked to hear Arnold's words come out of his own mouth, but they were true.

"You really believe what you said?" Jess asked.

"Yeah! Way I figures it, they ain't no heaven, and hell is right here on earth."

Jess looked pained. "It natural you so bitter. I know what Prescott done to you."

Shame swept over him. "How?"

"Ain't important how."

"Everybody in on it?" He hated the thought that others knew.

"Naw. And I ain't gonna tell. Nothin' like that oughtta happen to nobody. Prescott is one evil man. He gonna have a bad time come judgment day."

"Maybe you don't care 'bout yourself, but what about all the others?" Cy insisted. "Mouse, Ring, Billy. Next time it could be any of 'em. We got to protect 'em. We *got* to do somethin'!"

"I told you. I *is* doin' somethin'. Lookin' after my boys. And prayin'."

Wastin' your time, Cy thought. "So you won't help me?"

"Help sentence all these boys to somethin' worse'n what they got here? Have 'em shot down in the woods? Tore up by dogs? No, sir. You best forget the whole idea."

"I can't."

"Then don't say nothin' more to me."

So that was the end of it. Jess would sit back and wait for the next disaster to happen. This time it had been three whippings and—no, he refused to think about the other thing. Next time, someone would die.

You all alone, he told himself. *Best face it. You don't need Jess. You don't need nobody.*

Then Cy realized Billy wasn't staring into the fire. The

boy's eyes were fixed on him. How much had he heard? How much had he understood? Cy looked into Billy's eyes and wished he could read what he saw there. But everything in those depths was black—blacker than night in the icehouse.

FIFTEEN

WHAT NOW? CY WONDERED, LYING AWAKE after the others had drifted into sleep. Trust in Jess's God? He wanted to laugh. That was like trusting in the wind. The only thing left to trust in was himself. If he wanted freedom, he'd have to find it on his own. When Mouse tried to snuggle next to him that night, Cy pushed him away.

Before he fell asleep, Cy promised himself that starting the next day, he'd be looking for his chance. And when it came, he'd take it and run with it as far as he could go. Until he found his way to freedom or they killed him for trying.

The weather turned bitter cold. Cain was forced to bring wood stoves into both bunkhouses and cut holes in the walls for the pipes to vent the smoke outside. He grumbled about the cost and the extra mess, and he made his men responsible for keeping wood on hand and the fires going.

Stryker and Prescott just as quickly pushed that responsibility off onto the boys. The older, bigger boys made the younger ones do the hard work of lugging the wood into the buildings and the hot, dirty work of cleaning out the stoves. At least they could all sleep a little better, until the fires died out sometime in the night.

Most of the boys were huddled around the stove one night before bedtime when Cy persuaded West to tell fortunes again. West retrieved his pottery hoodoo bowl from its hiding place and filled it from the small barrel that held drinking water. He pricked his finger with a needle he said he'd found in the cookhouse and squeezed some drops of blood into the water.

"Why you askin' to know yo' fortune?" West asked Cy. "I already done it for you a while back. Man's fortune don't change. What's set out for him is gon' happen, sooner or later."

"You saw freedom for all of us," Cy replied. "Billy, me, Mouse. But ain't none of us free yet."

"It didn't say *when*," West replied.

Cy noticed Billy standing in the shadows behind Mouse. Bit by bit, he'd returned to the world. As his back healed up, so did his mind, and now, most of the time, he was all right. Never said a lot, cowered when the white men came around, and stuck to Jess like a sand burr to a pant leg.

"You can tell my fortune," Billy said.

"Come on, then. Hold out your finger." He poked Billy's finger, and the red blood dropped into the water. Then West closed his eyes and began humming. He peered into the water, holding the bowl close to his face to see better in the flickering light from the open door of the stove.

"What you see?" Billy asked.

"Same as before. You gon' get free. It ain't gon' be easy, though. I still sees water ahead o' you. And—I hear shots."

"Guns?"

"Reckon so. You gonna have to be brave. Braver than you ever been. Do that, and you be free."

Billy stared at West. "You ain't messin' with me?"

West shook his head. "I never do when it come to this. This is serious."

"You see my daddy there?"

West gazed into the bloody water again. "Don't see no black man. I sees—"

West put the bowl down on the ground so hard that some water spilled.

"What is it?" Cy demanded. "What you see?" A creepy feeling had been coming over him ever since West had begun. He was starting to regret asking for this. Now he felt sure West had seen something he didn't want to share.

"Nothin'," West answered. "I didn't see nothin'."

"You did! You just don't want to tell it."

But West couldn't be persuaded to change his mind. "Who next?" he asked.

Mouse volunteered. West told him the same thing: he'd be free. Mouse allowed that he knew it, had always known it, and one day he was going back to the Okefenokee and find Tiberius, the old man who had taught him all about wild critters and their ways.

"My turn," Cy said. West took his blood and held the bowl close to his face.

"What you see?' Cy asked.

West stared at him. "Freedom. First one kind, then another."

"What that mean?"

"Don't know. But that what I heard. The voice say, 'First one kind, then another.'"

"Nothin' else?"

West shook his head.

Cy felt annoyed. He didn't like West's riddles. They could mean anything or nothing. Maybe he was just making everything up.

"You ever look for yourself?" Billy asked.

"I done told you once, no!" West's voice was shrill.

"Why you so bothered?" Cy wanted to know.

"I ain't!"

"I bet you *have* looked for yourself before," Mouse said. "Ain't that so?"

West dumped the water into the dirt and threw the bowl against the wall, where it broke into pieces. Boys warming themselves at the stove looked up.

"Why you so mad?" Cy asked. "Is Mouse right?"

"What if he is? Ain't no concern o' yours."

"If that how you want it," Cy agreed.

"You can tell us what you seen for yourself," Billy told West, drawing up close to him. "Somethin' bad?"

West pulled himself together. "Naw. Nothin' like that."

"Then why you break yo' bowl?"

"I dunno. Guess I's just tired o' messin' with it. Nothin' to it, anyway."

Christmas came and went. Cy wouldn't have known, but West noticed that Pook had some new clothes and a little wooden horse that rolled on wheels. He asked Rosalee about it, and she let it slip that it was Christmas. As she dished up breakfast that morning, her eyes had a dreamy expression and she seemed only half awake. Christmas also explained why Cain and Stryker didn't show up for breakfast that day, and why Prescott was badly hung over and in an evil mood. They'd celebrated way too much the night before.

Cy had never enjoyed much of a Christmas growing up. The Williams family had never earned enough extra for store-bought gifts. But his mama had always tried to make something nice for him, even if it was only a new shirt made of cheap cotton cloth. And Pete Williams always found a way to get hold of penny candy. Christmas dinner had been special—a chicken, maybe, or fried catfish if luck was on the side of the fishermen.

In Cain's camp, Christmas meant nothing except that the boys didn't have to work palmetto. A free day, but the weather was cold and rainy, so everyone stayed inside, trying to keep close to the wood stoves that offered the only relief from the chilly, damp air.

That night, Mouse developed a cough and a fever. Jess reported to Cain that he was sick, but Cain brushed it off as nothing more than a cold. What did anyone expect, given the weather?

The days went by, and Mouse didn't get better. Instead, a lot of the other boys caught the same thing. Coughing, sneezing, fever. Some days, the sickest boys couldn't go to work, and Stryker or Prescott had to stay in camp to keep an eye on them. Cy almost wished he would come down sick, too, and spend his days lying in bed instead of cutting his hands to pieces on the biting teeth of the palmetto plants.

One night, about two weeks after Mouse first took ill, he woke up the boys near him with his coughing. The coughing got worse and worse until it turned into a regular fit. His entire body shook with it.

"Hey, Mouse, take it easy! Lemme help you," Jess offered. He tried to slap Mouse on the back, but Mouse pushed him away. He doubled over, head between his knees, coughing as if his lungs would burst.

"He bad off," Jess declared. "Y'all make some racket, get Stryker or Prescott in here."

The boys, all awake now, obliged by shouting and clanking their leg irons as loudly as they could. The fit kept its grip on Mouse's tiny body as he coughed, choked, gasped for breath. Finally, it stopped. Mouse tried to suck in a big gulp of air, and he made an awful, high-pitched whistling sound when he did. Then he vomited all over himself.

"Aw, shit," West cried from his place on Mouse's other side.

Mouse started to cry.

"Mouse!" Jess said. "Take it easy. It gonna be all right. Somebody be in here in a minute, take care o' you."

And who would that be? Cy wondered. Jess just couldn't stop himself from trying to make things better.

"I's sick," Mouse whimpered. "Bad sick. Help me, Jess."

"Keep up that ruckus," Jess told everyone. "We *got* to get somebody in here."

Then another fit took Mouse. Runny snot poured out of his nose, slid over his mouth, and ran down his chin. When the attack stopped, the whistling noise came again. Mouse fell backwards, worn out from the fit.

But it came on him yet again.

At last, Stryker appeared at the door. "What's goin' on in here? What y'all think you're doing, making all this fuss? Shut up and go back to sleep."

"Please, sir," Jess implored. "Mouse is real sick, and he done puked all over hisself."

"I can smell it," Stryker said.

Just at the moment, another attack seized the boy. Stryker came in close and held his lantern overhead. "Jesus Christ," he exclaimed. "This is all we need."

"What is it, Mr. Stryker?" Jess asked.

"Hoopin' cough."

"What that?"

"Don't ask a stupid question. It's just what you see. You get it, your lungs fill up with that slime, you try and cough it up so you don't strangle to death, and then you make that noise when you try and catch your breath back."

"Mouse got it bad."

"You think I can't see that? Christ, what do we do now?"

"Give him some medicine," Billy suggested.

"Did I ask for your advice?" Stryker snarled. "There *ain't* no medicine for it! You got to let it take its course. And now *all* y'all are gonna get it."

A pang of fear shot through Cy. He looked at Mouse, covered in puke, and tried not to imagine himself in the same trouble.

"How come we all gon' get it?" Jess asked.

"'Cause that's the way it works! It's *contagious,* if you dummies know what that means. Once one of you comes down with it, y'all will, too. Just a matter of time. It ain't gonna be pretty, I promise you that. Shit! This is really gonna fry Cain's eggs. That's what he gets," Stryker said to himself.

Another fit began, and Stryker moved away. "I'll be back," he said.

He returned with Cain, Prescott, and Rosalee, who was moving slowly and seemed to be half asleep. Mouse started coughing again, and everyone waited until the fit passed, ending with the awful sound of his gasping for air.

"Told you," Stryker said to Cain.

"You sure it's hoopin' cough? I ain't ever seen it before."

"Then you're lucky. Trust me. That's what it is."

"So what do we do?"

"Nothing *to* do but let it be."

"How long will it take?"

"Long time. Couple weeks once it gets to this stage. Maybe more. And it's gonna seem like a year before it's all over."

Cain looked weary. "A doctor couldn't help?"

"From what I know, most likely not. And if we tell him the truth about what we got on our hands, he might not even come out and have a look. This stuff is mighty catchin'."

"No way to stop it from spreading?" Cain asked.

"Quarantine. You got to separate the sick boys from the healthy ones, and pray that every single one of 'em don't come down with it."

"Separate 'em?"

Stryker sighed, then went on, like he was trying to explain something to a child. "We got to keep these boys away from the other gang, starting tomorrow. Nobody in that other bunk has it yet, far as I know. But the minute anyone from over there starts actin' sick, we move him here. The sick and the healthy—they got to eat separate, shit separate—everything."

"Damn it!" Cain exclaimed. "I reckon they can't work when they got it." He sounded disappointed.

You son of a bitch, Cy thought bitterly. *Only worried about how much work you can squeeze outta us.*

"No, they can't *work* when they got it!" Stryker shot back at Cain. "The ones that get it bad ain't gonna be able to do *anything*. And the sickest ones . . ."

Cy could guess what was in his mind. The sickest ones might die.

Cain looked down at Mouse, slumped forward, his head down, covered in his vomit. "Get him cleaned up," he ordered.

"You want all of 'em unchained, or just clean him up where he is?"

"Unchain 'em all. Kid needs to be washed off and put in another uniform. Looks like he needs a new blanket, too."

"He needs a couple of blankets, at least," Stryker declared. "Chances are he's gonna have more spells before the night is out. Then we'll just have to clean him up again."

"You two and Rosalee can handle it. Lemme know the situation in the morning. I'm going back to bed."

A look of disgust flickered across Stryker's face. He waited until his boss was gone before he cursed. Prescott looked just as unhappy. Rosalee stood like a figure carved in wood, gazing off into the dark corners of the bunkhouse. But she obeyed Stryker when he told her to go fetch a water bucket, towels, and a clean uniform. Stryker and

Prescott unlocked everyone and got Mouse separated so he could be cleaned up.

Rosalee returned with the water and the clean clothes. Mouse didn't protest as she undressed him and got him to his feet. In the dim light of the lantern, his body looked as fragile as a tiny scarecrow, one the slightest wind could push into the dust. His ribs showed through the skin of his chest. Rosalee washed him and held a basin under his chin during the next attack of vomiting.

At last he was cleaned up. Stryker moved him to the end of the sleeping platform and let Jess take the place next to him. Rosalee gave Jess the basin and a towel.

"If he has more fits, y'all are gonna have to take care of it," Stryker announced. "I can't lose a night's sleep over a sick nig—a sick kid."

Stryker and Rosalee left the building and closed the door. At least they had put fresh wood on the fire, and the stove gave off enough heat that Cy could feel it on his feet.

No one could sleep. Cy kept waiting for Mouse's next fit. Already he hated the attacks: the coughing, the gagging, the gulping for air. The final sound, the high-pitched whistle at the end, was the worst. Stryker said it took a long time for the sickness to end, maybe weeks. And if he was right, all the rest of them would get it, too. Cy thought for a moment about what it would be like if they were all coughing, gagging, vomiting. And what if some of them died? Maybe Stryker was hiding the truth. Maybe Mouse *would* die. Maybe everyone who got this cough died.

There were more attacks that night, but no more vomiting. Mouse's stomach was empty. Finally, before dawn, he fell asleep. He slept through both morning gongs, and he was deeply asleep when Prescott came in and the boys got to their feet.

Stryker appeared with a pitcher and a tin cup. He went right to Mouse and roused him.

"How you doin'?" he asked.

Mouse was too weak to answer. He just moaned. Stryker called Prescott to come close. "See," he said, pulling Mouse's left eyelid down. "His eyes."

"Glory be!" Prescott exclaimed. "The whites ain't white."

"God, you're a smart man, Onnie," Stryker said. "No, they ain't white. Red."

"Why?"

"Boy coughed so hard he broke some of the vessels in his eyes."

"Sure 'nough? I didn't think nobody could cough that hard."

"That's 'cause you ain't never had hoopin' cough," Stryker said.

"And I suppose you have?"

"Matter of fact, yeah."

These two men, Cy had come to realize, shared a habit with other whites he'd known: they would talk to each other as if the black folks nearby didn't exist or couldn't understand. Sometimes you could gather useful information from whites when they didn't stop to think you had ears.

"When you get the cough?" Prescott asked.

"When I was a kid."

"You have it bad?"

Stryker didn't answer that right away. Instead, he filled the cup from the pitcher and held it in front of Mouse. "Drink it," he ordered.

Mouse turned his head away. "I can't."

Stryker seized his head and turned his face back to the cup. "You sure as hell can, and you're goin' to. And when you're done, you're gonna drink some more, and more after that. You're gonna drink this pitcher dry, and then another one."

Mouse gave in. He began to sip from the cup.

"All of it," Stryker commanded.

"So you had it yourself when you was young?" Prescott persisted.

"Said so, didn't I? Got it when I was about his age," he said, nodding at Billy. "Whole family got it."

"And . . . ?"

"We recovered. All except for Mary Elizabeth. She didn't make it."

"But *you* got over it," Prescott said helpfully. "That's somethin', at least."

"Yeah, I got all the luck. I recovered, after a trip through hell."

"What about him?" Prescott nodded at Mouse. He was talking about Mouse like he was a piece of damaged furniture.

"Who knows? We gotta keep puttin' water into him, food, too, if he can stand it. Let him have a chance to rest. Hope he don't die of dehydration, or choke to death, or die from sheer exhaustion."

So Mouse *could* die. And if Mouse could, others probably could, too. Anyone who got sick could die.

"Can I look after him?" Jess asked. "Please, sir?"

"Why not? In a couple days, y'all are gonna have to be lookin' after each other. Cain's got no idea what he's in for. Y'all, either." Stryker was quiet a moment, and an expression something like pity came over his face. "The rest of you who ain't sick, get on with your day. You can eat after the other gang gets finished. Jess, see to it he drinks that pitcher dry. Then get a refill. He got to eat if he can.

Rosalee can make him some thin grits. Anything to help keep his strength up."

He and Prescott left. Jess held the cup up to Mouse's lips again, but the boy refused to drink.

"You got to," Jess urged him.

"I can't. It don't make no difference, noways. I's gonna die, so what do it matter?"

"Don't you listen to that ignorant cracker talk," Jess told him. "But do what Stryker say. He been through this hisself, and he know that this is important. And don't worry none: I's gonna be right here with you, takin' care o' you. You think I's gonna let Ol' Man Death stop by here? Not while I can fight him."

Brave words, but Cy wondered if Jess was that strong.

SIXTEEN

THE QUARANTINE BEGAN THAT MORNING. CAIN made the other gang dig an open-air latrine at the far corner of the camp. Then Cain and Prescott took that gang to the palmetto woods, leaving Stryker in charge of Cy's group. He put everyone to work except Mouse and Jess. Mouse was just too sick, and Stryker knew that if anyone could keep Mouse alive, it was Jess.

Stryker found many things for the boys to do: mend some fence, replace some shakes on the roofs of the bunkhouses so they wouldn't leak so bad, air out all their straw ticks. Cy felt all right except for a runny nose, but he tried to ignore it. So far, only Mouse was truly sick. He spent the day shivering under blankets, drinking all the water Jess could get down him, and then throwing it up again when the coughing spells came.

After dinner, Stryker gave the boys a break. Some played dice, and others slept. They acted like a day in camp was all a game, with them the winners. The others had to work palmetto, while the boys in quarantine had it a lot easier. *Maybe they right to enjoy themselves*, Cy thought. *Maybe no one else gonna get sick. Maybe Stryker wrong.*

But the fun didn't last long. When the other guys got back that evening, Cain made the quarantined boys go inside their shed and wouldn't let them out except to use the latrine. Dinner was brought to them, but they had to eat sitting on the dirt floor. That night, Mouse had more fits that made it hard for the others to sleep.

The next day was the same, and the day after. Cain grumbled and said something about losing a heap of money and called Stryker an alarmist. Soon, quarantine just felt like a different kind of prison. There was little to do. Fights broke out. They all got sick of being cooped up, waiting for something to happen.

And Mouse got no better.

Cy was nervous, on edge. He picked on the other boys. The sound of Mouse's spells made him want to choke the life out of the kid. Anything to shut him up.

On the fourth night, Davy had a coughing fit. Next morning, Billy did, too. That afternoon, Ring and two other boys had it. Stryker had been right.

The fifth morning Billy huddled near Jess, coughing, puking, gasping for air between his attacks. "We ain't never gon' get well," he said. "We all gon' die."

"No, you ain't," Jess insisted. "Stryker had it when he was our age, and he made it."

"He said that girl didn't."

"You will, though."

Cy had had enough. "Why you keep on lyin' to everyone? How you know he gonna get well?"

"You ever heard of a thing called hope?"

"Don't preach at me!"

"I ain't tryin' to do that, Cy. Just tryin' to give you—and all these boys—somethin' to hold on to."

"You can keep it," Cy told him. "Hope ain't never done one thing for any of us."

Jess started to respond, but Billy broke in. "He gonna make it?" Billy asked, his eyes on Mouse, who was lost in fitful sleep.

"Him too," Jess assured him.

Billy already looked worn out, and his fits had only just begun. *You oughtta have your mind on yourself*, Cy thought. *Worry if you gonna make it, not Mouse.*

Oscar came into the bunkhouse, his hands cupped. "I got somethin' for Mouse. Found it stuck to a tree outside."

He held a giant dead moth. It was brown with little

white dots on each of its upper wings, and two big dark spots on the lower ones.

"He 'sleep?" Oscar asked.

"Yeah," Jess said.

"Hey, Mouse," Oscar called. "Got somethin' for you."

Mouse roused. His breathing was gurgly and shallow. He looked pinched all over, like his skin was stretched too tight over his bones.

"What is it?" he asked.

"Big ol' moth. Biggest I ever seen. Sorry he dead, but I thought you want to have him."

He gave the moth to Mouse, who held it up close to his face. "Thanks, Oscar." He lay down again. "I's gon' to sleep now. He keep me company." Mouse held the moth to his chest.

West nudged Cy and whispered to him. "The eyes, remember?"

"Eyes?"

"What I seen that first time I told Mouse fortune. You know."

Cy did remember. West had seen a pair of dark eyes. The spots on the moth were like two eyes, looking at you. Dead eyes. He shivered.

Mouse shouldn't have the moth. It was bad luck, like

a bird in the house. That always meant Death wasn't far behind. But before Cy could say so, Billy had a coughing attack. Later, when Cy looked for the moth in the sleeping Mouse's hands, it wasn't there.

That night, Cy had his first attack. One moment, he was drifting to sleep, then he was coughing like he'd never coughed before. It felt like something the size of an egg was stuck in his windpipe. He had to get it out.

The fit woke Billy and Jess. "Easy, now," Jess said. "It be over soon."

That was no help. Cy knew he was choking to death. Panic took him, and he began to shake. He tried to get up, get outside, get some air. He coughed as hard as he could—the thing in his throat *had* to come out, or he'd die.

Finally the fit ended. He gulped air, and now *he* was the one making those high-pitched whooping sounds.

Mouse didn't even move.

"I's real sorry, Cy," Billy told him. "I prayed you wasn't gonna get sick."

That night was the worst he'd ever lived through.

In the morning, Mouse was a little better, but more boys were sick. "Damn it!" Stryker exclaimed when he came in, a bandanna over his mouth. "How many boys down with it now?"

"'Bout half," Jess told him. "Cy got it last night."

Cy raised his head. The sour smell of vomit revolted him. He needed a clean uniform. He needed to relieve himself. But he felt too weak to move. Then an attack took him.

"Christ, what a mess!" Stryker looked worried. "Cain's *got* to get a doctor over here. Maybe they have new treatments since I was a kid."

"That be a good thing," Jess told him. "Please help us, Mr. Stryker."

"I'll do what I can."

In the afternoon, Cain showed up. Stryker and Prescott were with him, so all the boys were in camp, even though it was a regular workday. Three other white men were there, too, all with handkerchiefs over their noses and mouths.

Cy had been dozing since morning, waking up only when the fits seized him. But seeing strange white men brought him wide awake. Up and down the line, other boys were sitting up. A crazy idea came into Cy's mind. *They here to set us free.*

Cain led the way down the line of sick boys. The men stared over the tops of their handkerchiefs. Billy got a coughing fit just then, and they gathered around him to see the show.

"No question about it," one of the white men declared. "Full-blown whooping cough."

"I told you, Doc," Stryker put in. "Regular epidemic."

"We've been doin' everything we can for 'em," Cain added. "Extra food and water, lettin' 'em rest up, not makin' 'em go off the place to work. Anything else we can do?"

The doctor kept looking at Billy. "How long have you been sick, boy?"

"Few days, sir."

"Are you feeling any better?"

Billy didn't seem sure what to say.

"Answer when you're spoken to!" Cain growled.

"I reckon so," Billy said.

"That's good," the doctor replied.

"This here boy," Cain said, pointing at Mouse, "had it real bad, but he's a lot better now. On the mend, ain't you, Mouse?"

"Yessir."

"And you?" the man asked Cy.

He felt Cain's eyes on him. "I's better, sir," he lied.

"Take care of yourself," the man said. "Get your rest. Soon you'll be able to go back to work."

"Yes, sir."

"Do you want to examine any of 'em?" Stryker asked.

"I don't believe that will be necessary," the doctor replied. He put his hands in his coat pockets. "No point in taking the risk of spreading the contagion."

"We're gonna keep on doin' all we can for 'em," Cain promised. "They'll soon be back on the job."

Suddenly Billy jumped off his bed and ran at the doctor. He threw himself on the ground and grabbed him by the legs. "Please, sir!" he cried. "I ain't suppos' to be here! I didn't do nothin'! My daddy say he come an' get me after he make it all right with the judge. But that been a long time ago. You got to help me! Please, mister!"

The doctor stepped back, trying to shake Billy off without touching him.

"Dawson!" Cain cried.

Stryker moved in. He grabbed Billy and pulled him off the doctor. Billy fought back, but a coughing spell came on him, and he fell onto the hard-packed dirt floor.

"Get him out of here!" Cain ordered. Stryker and Prescott took hold of Billy and dragged him away.

"Sorry," Cain said to the doctor. "That one's a little crazy. Been like that since the first day. Got some wild notion that his daddy is gonna come for him. Ain't even got a father, from what they told me when they brought him in. None of 'em do, for that matter. They ain't like us, Doctor.

Got no concept of family the way the good Lord revealed it to us in his Holy Scriptures."

"Indeed?" The doctor seemed unimpressed.

Cain chuckled. "Course, they all claim to be innocent."

The doctor gave him a look.

The men started for the door. "Do you have time to see the child?" Cain asked.

"Certainly. How old is he?"

"About four."

They were at the door.

"And how long has he been ill?"

"Fits started last night."

So Pook had it too.

Cy got deathly sick. They told him later he had it worse than any other boy, even Mouse. The coughing spells exhausted him. One was so bad he broke a rib. He found that out when he roused from a feverish sleep to feel someone poking at his chest. He nearly jumped out of his skin when he realized it was Stryker.

"Yeah, it's a rib," he heard the man say through the haze of his fever. "Can't bind him, though, not with that sickness in his lungs. He's just gonna have to live with the pain."

Later, he woke again after what seemed days, only to

hear Stryker say, "Pneumonia, Cap'n. Not much hope for this one."

Other times, Cy would find Jess beside him, holding a water cup, insisting he drink. Sometimes it was Billy. Once, Cy stayed awake long enough to realize he had on a clean cotton shirt under his jacket. He recognized it as the one his father had brought him, the one he'd made Billy take when he thought he wouldn't be needing it any longer. When he thought he'd be free.

While he was lying awake, too weak and sick to get up but not needing to sleep, Cy wondered why Jess and Billy had taken care of him. Jess never did come down with the sickness, but Billy had had it bad. Even so, he'd done what he could to help the others. Cy knew he wouldn't have done as much for Billy. Why had they looked after him so kindly, even cleaning him up when he was no better than a baby too small and helpless to wipe off his own puke?

Slowly, he began to get better. His fever broke, and he slept easier as the coughing attacks subsided. Then one morning he overheard Stryker tell Cain that the epidemic seemed to be over. No boys in the other gang had come down with it, and all the sick boys had recovered. It was a miracle, actually, Stryker had said. A miracle that only one boy had died. But the disease claimed most of its victims among the youngest and weakest, so it was surprising that Mouse had survived. And it wasn't surprising that Pook had not. The little fellow had died and been buried during the empty days and nights Cy had been so sick. So Death had perched above the camp, claimed one life, and then moved on.

SEVENTEEN

LOSING POOK HIT ROSALEE HARD. SOMETIMES
Cy could tell she'd been crying. Other days, in the mornings especially, she simply looked empty, her dark eyes strangely unfocused, the black pupils just pinpoints. Mostly silent before, she was mute now. Often, her face looked unwashed, her hair unkempt. At some meals, she was absent, and Sudie had all she could do to serve up the sloppy food by herself.

No one knew where Cain had buried Pook. The boy was his son, too, but he gave no sign that he missed the child or grieved his loss. Maybe he was just as glad that now no one could claim he'd lain with a black woman.

Jess felt sorry for Rosalee. No woman should lose a child, he said. Cy allowed that it was too bad Pook died, but he didn't feel sad. Still, Rosalee had helped him that one time when he'd been locked in the icehouse. That made her worth some sympathy, but he didn't have much to spare.

The whooping cough had done something to West, too. His case had been mild, compared to what Mouse, Billy, and Cy had been through. But when it was all over and life got back to what passed for normal in Cain's camp, West was different, changed. Before, he'd kept the other boys laughing with his jokes and mocking imitations of the white men. Now, like Rosalee, he was silent most of the time. He had always been on the lookout for extra things to eat, but now he had no appetite and often gave away half his meals. Instead of being in the middle of every game, he kept to himself, slept more than ever, and didn't seem to notice most of what was going on around him. Jess fretted over him, the way he did over any boy who was having a hard time. Cy tried not to care. It wasn't his problem. Still, he missed West's jokes.

Then West started doing dangerous things. He talked ugly about the white men, cursing them openly, sometimes when they were close enough to hear his tone of voice, if not his exact words. He talked freely about how much he hated Cain and his slaves, which is how he referred to Stryker and Prescott. He did this even in front of some boys that Cy and others suspected of being snitches, ready to inform on other boys in hopes that Cain would grant them favors.

When Jess tried to warn West, he was told to mind his own business, and what did it matter now, anyway? Jess tried to get West to explain what he meant by those words and got a cussing for his trouble.

One morning in late January, Prescott and Stryker both came into the bunkhouse smelling of stale cigars. Stryker's neck was marked with purple bruises, and West muttered that last night must have cost him a lot of money.

Prescott was in a black mood. He went up and down the line yelling at everyone, and even started giving Jess a hard time for playing "Mammy" to the other boys. Jess took it like he always did: eyes on the ground, answering every one of Prescott's ugly questions with polite *yessir*s and *nosir*s.

"Cracker must not o' got hisself none last night," West muttered, loud enough for Cy and Mouse to hear him. Cy managed to keep from laughing, but Mouse giggled.

That was a mistake.

Like lightning, Prescott was on him. "What's so goddamn funny, you ugly little toad?"

"Nothin', Mr. Prescott, sir."

Prescott slapped Mouse across the mouth. "Don't you know better than to lie to me? I asked you what's so funny."

"Nothin'. I just laughed, that's all."

Prescott hit him again. Mouse hadn't died of the whooping cough, but he hadn't recovered any strength, either, and weighed not much more than sixty pounds. Mouse fell against Cy, who caught him before he hit the ground. Jess was standing at rigid attention but breathing hard.

"Easy there, Onnie," Stryker said. "Maybe the kid wasn't laughing at you."

"Like hell! That's *all* these niggers do—laugh at us behind our backs. Or ain't you noticed?" He took Mouse by the collar of his jacket. "Tell me what you was laughing at!"

"At somethin' I said," West announced.

Prescott released Mouse and went for West. "And what was it? Tell us so we can all enjoy it."

West hung his head, pretending to be sorry. Cy could tell he wasn't, though. He was never sorry for talking ugly about the white men. "I don't reckon you think it be funny, Mr. Prescott."

"That's for me to decide! Now spill it, unless you want a dose of what your friend here got."

West kept his eyes fixed to the ground. The bunkhouse had gotten quiet except for the sound of Jess's breathing. Prescott glanced in his direction. "Shut up, you!"

Jess took one deep breath and was silent.

"Now tell us what's so funny. I could use a good laugh."

"Well, sir, I just wonder if you in a bad mood this mornin' 'cause you didn't get none at the whorehouse last night."

All the boys except Jess started to laugh.

"Kid got *you* pegged," Stryker commented. He was trying not to laugh, too. "Didn't get none last night. It wasn't for lack of trying, though, was it?"

Prescott grabbed West and slapped him across the face. Stryker let Prescott get in three or four licks, then grabbed his arm. "That's enough, Onnie. Let it go. You made your point."

"I hate you all," Prescott panted. "I wish you was all dead. I wish *all* niggers was dead! You're a plague on the nation. A scourge! A curse!"

"Calm down," Stryker soothed. "You been listening to too many speeches."

Prescott shook him off. He got in West's face again. "Apologize," he demanded.

"I's sorry, sir."

"If you disrespect me again, I'll kill you." He turned on his heel and stalked out of the building.

The minute the white men were gone, everyone started talking at once. Cy was all over West. "You got a smart mouth! Quit causin' trouble."

"Leave him alone," Jess said. "He done had enough already."

"Stop makin' excuses for him! And for everything. He got to learn to keep quiet."

"I's tired o' keepin' quiet," West said.

"We got to go," Jess said. "If we late for lineup, it only give Prescott more reason to mess with us. And I don't feel like puttin' up with no more o' that kind o' stuff. Already had more'n enough for the day."

Cain had a surprise for them that morning. Instead of clearing palmetto, the boys were going to help on a stretch of railroad a couple miles in the other direction from camp. He made it sound like he was doing everyone a favor, giving them a change of work. He said there would be another gang there, all grown men, and the boys were to stay clear of them. They were hardened, desperate criminals, Cain warned, ready to cut a boy's throat if he did or said something he shouldn't.

Cy remembered the feel of Prescott's knife against his own throat. He glanced down the line at West, wondering if Cain's words were meant especially for him.

While they were loading up for the trip to the railroad line, Jess kept wiping his eyes with his sleeve.

"What's a matter?" Cy asked.

"I failed."

"Failed how?"

"When Prescott was beatin' on West, I shoulda done somethin'. Stopped him. I wanted to, but I didn't."

"If you did anything, you be on your way to Alabama by now."

"That don't matter. We should of done somethin' to help West, but we didn't. Prescott could of killed him, and the rest of us just be standin' there watchin'."

"West needs to learn to shut up."

"I promised God I look after all the ones what couldn't help theyselves, and when it come down to it, I just stood there like a coward. That's all I is—a yellow coward."

"Don't talk like that. What could you do?"

"Somethin'."

"What happen to all that stuff about prayin', waitin' for God to take care o' things?"

Jess was clearly troubled. "I dunno, Cy. That use to make sense to me, but now—I dunno."

"I been tellin' you we got to do somethin'!"

"Maybe."

A faint hope stirred in Cy. Perhaps he could get Jess to come around to his side, after all. He'd wait until the right moment and make his case again.

■ ■ ■

When they got to the railroad site, the chain gang men were already hard at work. It was open country, big fields all around. Standing water filled the low places, so the ground was soft and wet, but a railroad needed solid ground so the tracks wouldn't sink when the heavy trains came along. The men worked in two long lines facing each other, everybody shoveling dirt toward the middle to build up the bed.

The men from the other chain gang didn't look dangerous, and they didn't act dangerous. Cy had seen chain gangs of grown men before he ended up on a gang himself, and he remembered how the men laughed and joked, even sang as they worked. But these men were different—lifeless. They were heavily chained on their ankles and waists. And silent. No songs, no jokes.

Guards stood along both lines, rifles ready. One had a whip.

The faces of the chained men bothered Cy the most. They had dark, dead eyes. When Cain's boys approached them, not one even glanced their way.

After talking with the boss man, Cain came back and said the boys would be divided into two groups, one on each side of the railroad bed. They would be chained, and there was to be no talk. He unchained all the boys, mixed them up so friends wouldn't be together, and had the chains put back on. Jess, Billy, Ring, and Davy were assigned to the other team, just not side by side. Cy, West, and Mouse were on the same gang, but not next to each other, either.

There was trouble with Cy's team right away. Prescott wasn't finished with West for embarrassing him earlier that morning. He was on West from the start, calling him names, accusing him of not working hard. Finally, West dropped his shovel, stared Prescott in the face, and seemed to be waiting for everyone to look his way. Then he said, loud and clear, "I know why you didn't get none last night. You didn't *want* none. Everybody know you likes boys better'n girls any day."

Cy was shocked to hear that spoken aloud.

Prescott stood stunned for a second, then went nuts. He grabbed West's shovel and swung it so that its edge caught West on the side of his head. The force broke his neck, and the boy dropped like a stone. He must have been dead before he hit the ground.

The boys chained on either side of West pulled away from the body. Everyone began shouting. Some boys were crying. Mouse dropped to his knees and wailed. The boys working on the other side of the embankment appeared at its top to see what had happened. Stryker was with them. Cain and the other boss man were running to where Prescott stood over West's body, the shovel still in his hands. He looked at it like he didn't recognize it, then let it drop.

From the top of the embankment, Billy began shrieking. Jess put his hand over his mouth and tried to shush him.

Cy felt dazed, trying to make sense of it. Part of him wanted to get to Mouse, comfort him. But he didn't move.

Cain knelt by West and put a finger on his neck, feeling for a heartbeat, but one look at his head, bent at a crazy angle to his shoulders, told the story. West's brown eyes, open wide, stared into blue sky.

Just the way Travis's eyes had done on that day so long ago . . .

Cy wanted to look away, but he couldn't.

"He's dead," Cain declared, getting to his feet. "What the hell, Onnie?"

"I warned him! No *white* man could say that to me and get away with it, let alone a nigger! I warned him!"

The men in the other gang, at a word from their boss, went back to work.

"He told a lie on me! A goddamn lie!" Prescott cried.

"What was it?" Cain asked.

Prescott whispered something to him.

Cain stepped away, like Prescott smelled bad. "And you killed him for that?"

"He didn't have no right to tell a lie like that on me! I warned him."

Cain looked at Stryker and the rest of his boys standing atop the embankment. "Dawson, get down here. Day's over."

Stryker ordered everyone to stay put and slid down the embankment. He huddled with Cain and the other boss man, then unchained the boys in both gangs. Those who had been working near West backed farther away from his body, which still lay crumpled where it had fallen.

Cain called out, "Y'all get your tools and head to the wagons."

Cy heard a snarl of fury and turned to see Jess charging down the embankment, straight at Prescott. Jess tackled the white man and took him down. Sobbing, shouting curses, he pinned Prescott's shoulders to the ground with his knees and started beating his face.

"Hey!" Cain shouted, and rushed at Jess. Stryker and the other boss man were right behind him. Together, the three of them managed to pull Jess off of Prescott. Still on his back, Prescott scuttled away as fast as he could. Stryker punched Jess full in the face, and he collapsed.

Cy stood with the others, struck dumb. Jess had finally done something, but Cy understood that Jess would now pay a huge price.

The white men ordered Jess to his feet. He obeyed without question, and he didn't object when he was told to put his hands behind his back for the handcuffs.

Prescott stayed where he was in the dirt. "The nigger made me!" he shouted suddenly. "He didn't have no right to say a lie about me in front of everybody!"

Stryker stalked over to him. "Shut up!" he commanded. "You're the biggest goddamn fool I ever met, you know that, Onnie? You make me ashamed to be a man. Now get your sorry ass up off the ground. We got work to do."

Cy had always hated Stryker, just as he hated all white men, but at this moment, he could have shaken Stryker's hand.

Prescott got to his feet. His nose was running blood, and when he wiped it on his sleeve, he winced. "Nigger broke my nose!"

"Didn't I tell you to shut up?" Stryker said. "Get over here and help me." He went to West and began pulling the long chain through the ring in the middle of his leg irons. In a moment, the boy's body was free.

"Onnie, right now!" Stryker cried. "Help me pick him up."

"Not me!" Prescott shouted back. "Not after—"

"Damn it!" Stryker growled. "I said to help me!"

"I won't. You can't make me. I'm never gonna touch a nigger again. I'm done with all this." Prescott turned his back and limped toward the line of chained men, some of whom hadn't even bothered to glance up from their toil.

Stryker made a move toward him.

"Let him go," Cain said. Then he looked at the boys, some huddled away from West's body, others still lining the top of the embankment. "Didn't I tell y'all to move?"

They loaded the equipment onto the wagons and waited. By now, many of the boys were crying. Billy, empty-eyed, had retreated back into his own safe place. Mouse found Cy, and this time Cy didn't brush him away.

Finally, Stryker approached the wagons, bearing West's body in his arms. Behind him trudged Jess, head bowed, Cain holding a pistol on him. Stryker placed the body in one of the wagon beds. Chained again, Cy and the others started their march back to camp.

Stryker drove the wagon holding West's body, his eyes straight ahead. Cain had the reins of the other wagon, his horse tied to one side, Jess tied to the back.

As they shuffled along, no one spoke a word. No one stumbled or broke stride. All the smaller boys kept pace.

Cy tried to make sense of all that had changed so quickly. It didn't feel real that West could be dead. One moment alive, shoveling dirt a few feet away from him, and then—a thing lying in the wagon bed up ahead, covered in a piece of oilskin. Just that morning, Cy had hoped Jess might help him plan their escape before it was too late. Now this horror. West dead. And Jess—done for too. Cy was back where he'd started: alone.

EIGHTEEN

IT WAS ONLY MIDDAY WHEN THEY CAME INTO the camp. Rosalee appeared from the cookhouse.

"Mr. Cain, why y'all back so soon?" she asked. "What'sa matter?"

"There was an accident. One of the boys got hurt bad. He's dead."

"Which boy?"

"West."

Rosalee screamed and started to crumple. When Cain grabbed her, she shook him off and cried, "West? Oh, no! Sweet Jesus, not my *child*. Not him! Not my boy!"

Cain shook her. "Get hold of yourself! He ain't your boy."

Rosalee rushed to the wagon and pulled the oilskin away. She screamed again. And again—and again. She scrambled into the wagon bed and knelt beside the body, lifted it, and cradled it in her arms.

Cain was right behind her. "Get down from there! Get

hold of yourself. You've seen boys die before. This one wasn't no different."

"No different? He was my *son!* My own flesh and blood."

A hush fell over the camp, as if everyone had stopped breathing.

West, Rosalee's son? How is it possible? Cy wondered. How could a mother and son live so close to each other and keep it a secret? But one thing made sense now. Rosalee had kept giving West extra food not because he was her favorite, as everyone had thought, but because he was her *son*.

Rosalee clutched West's body to her bosom. "Why you think I ever come to this hellhole in the first place?" she shouted at Cain. "To be near my *child!* They made up some lie 'bout him, lookin' for an excuse to punish him for sassin' some ol' white lady what cheated him out of a dime. My little boy, not ten years old, got *seven* years hard labor. You hear me?" she shouted at the chained black boys all around her. "He just like you! All o' you—forced here on some lyin' charges 'cause men like him"—she gestured at Cain—"can't figure no honest way to make a livin'!"

"Shut your mouth, girl, before you regret it! You're beside yourself," Cain exclaimed, hoisting himself into the wagon bed. "Hush, now! Come down, and I'll get you your medicine."

"I don't want no more o' your dope!" she shouted at him. "I don't want no more of that poison! I already done sold my soul for it, done everything you wanted, so's I could have it."

So it wasn't liquor, Cy thought. Sorrow for Rosalee welled up in his chest, and this time he didn't try to stop it.

"She's insane," Cain told Stryker. "She doesn't know what she's saying."

"I *do* know what I's sayin'," Rosalee cried. "I found out where my boy been sent, and I come 'round, lookin' for work so's I could be near him. You was only too glad to hire me. I'd of done anything, *anything* to stay. And look what it got me! My baby dead from the hoopin' cough 'cause you too stingy to send for the doctor. And now West! Who kill him?"

"It was an accident," Cain told her. "Nobody meant for it to happen."

She turned to Stryker. "You? You kill my baby?"

"Never touched him."

"Prescott? Where he?"

"Prescott the one done it," Mouse called out. He moved toward the wagon, pulling Cy and the others with him.

"West say somethin' Prescott didn't like, and he took a shovel and smash West upside the head. I saw everything."

"Shut him up!" Cain shouted to Stryker.

"Where Prescott?" Rosalee cried out. "Where the man who murdered my baby?"

"Gone," Cain assured her. "Up and gone. You won't see him again."

"Sheriff got him, then?"

Cain was silent.

"No, ma'am, sheriff ain't got him," Jess said. All eyes turned on him. "Prescott keep sayin' West have it comin'. When Mr. Cain tell him to help pick up West body, he wouldn't. Just walk off. Mr. Cain didn't do nothin' to stop him."

"He do murder in front o' all these boys, and you let him go *free?*" Rosalee cried.

Cain climbed down from the wagon. "I'll explain later. This ain't the time."

"How you gon' *explain* lettin' the man what murdered my child go free?" She began to weep again, holding West's head in her lap and rocking back and forth.

Cain found Cy in the crowd. "You're in charge of your gang. Get 'em to their bunkhouse and keep 'em there. Jack, you know what to do with yours."

The moment Cy had heard the crack of the shovel against West's head, he'd fallen into a kind of daze, a distorted dream where things felt both familiar and strange. Now his mind cleared, and he found himself thinking about something that made him sick with disappointment. If he'd been able to convince Jess to make a plan, they might be making a break for freedom this very minute. Prescott was gone, Cain distracted—who could make the boys go to their bunkhouses? Who could keep them from having their way? Forty—no, thirty-nine—boys could take two men whose guard was down, who would never expect a revolt today of all days.

But there was no plan. Jess had tried the way of prayer, of patient waiting for God to reach down from heaven and set things right. But his God hadn't shown up, and his rage took over. Cy realized that Jess would have killed Prescott if he'd had the chance. And now he would pay.

No, there was no plan, but Pete Williams had been right. Fear was the master, not white men with whips, horses, packs of bloodhounds, guns. Get past the fear, and Cy and the others could be free. Or die trying to be.

Shortly before dark, Stryker came into the bunkhouse and said it was suppertime. In the kitchen, Sudie dished up the food, her eyes and nose dripping. Jess was missing, and Cy guessed he was locked in the icehouse until Cain decided what to do with him.

After the meal was cleaned up, the boys were ordered to bed. The minute Cy lay down and pulled his blanket over himself, he was asleep.

The next morning at lineup, a strange white man stood near Cain and Stryker by the cookhouse door. There was no sign of Rosalee. Cain was hollow-eyed and haggard.

"What happened yesterday ought never to have been," he began. "That boy should of known better than to sass Mr. Prescott. He was already in trouble yesterday morning, and ought not to have said anything else, no matter how bad he was provoked. So West is partly to blame for what happened to him."

Cy wanted to shout that Prescott was nothing but a killer and Cain had let him go scot-free. No one said a word, but all around him, Cy could feel the others' fury. He glanced at Ring, who had his eyes fixed straight ahead, looking at nothing.

"That don't mean that I excuse Mr. Prescott for what he did," Cain went on. "He let his temper get the better of him. Nobody likes other folks to tell lies on them, but Mr. Prescott lost his self-control. And now he's payin'. He lost his job because he let his feelings get the better of him."

Cy didn't care a mouthful of spit for Prescott's feelings.

Cain looked uneasily down the two lines of boys, almost as if he were expecting some protest. "Mr. Stryker and me buried West last night, so y'all don't need to worry about that." He gestured toward the strange man. "This here is Mr. Love Davis. He's gonna take Mr. Prescott's place."

The man was heavily built, shorter than Stryker and maybe younger, with a bushy black beard. Where had Cain come up with him so quickly?

"Mr. Davis is a fair man, like me. And he got a more even . . . *temperament* than Mr. Prescott. So as long as y'all mind yourselves, you won't have no trouble with him."

Davis nodded.

"In light of recent events, I've decided to give y'all a day off," Cain went on. "You can wash uniforms if you want to or just take it easy. If any of y'all want to get together and have a little service for West, you can. So after you eat, you got the day to yourselves. Can't any man say I ain't fair, and more than fair."

Midmorning, a few of the boys had their service for West, even though there was no body, no coffin, no preacher, no nothing. Stryker showed up and stood to one side. Cy figured Cain had told him to keep an eye on things, make sure no one "lost his self-control." *Can't have that in camp*, Cy thought bitterly.

He found himself wishing Jess could be there. *He* would have the right words to make them feel better, even if those words might not be—exactly true. But Jess was still in the icehouse.

Cy felt the other boys' eyes on him. Wouldn't they be shocked to learn what was really in his mind? But a glance at Stryker, casually rolling a cigarette, told him now wasn't the time. Still, he had to say something. He was the leader again.

"We sure gon' miss West," he began. "Warn't no boy in camp could make us laugh like he could. Always had somethin' funny to say. Always in a good mood. And could that boy eat? I seen him put stuff in his mouth didn't even *look* like food—"

Oscar and Davy laughed, remembering.

"West was always gnawin' on some sort o' root or leaf or berry, or somethin'. And I know some of y'all remember the time he ate them minnows—"

"Raw," Oscar said. "And them little clams he found in the creek—made a mess tryin' to break 'em open with a rock."

"And all kind o' mushrooms," Mouse added.

"Miracle he didn't poison hisself," Ring said. "He was always lookin' for somethin' good to eat—"

"Because he was always hungry," Cy said quietly. The second the words were out, he felt nervous. What if Stryker had heard? But the man wasn't even looking in their direction.

Cy glanced at the other guys and realized that they agreed with what he had said.

"Yeah, he was always hungry," Ring said. "Just like the rest of us. You tell it, Cy."

"I still can't figure what went wrong with West," Oscar said. "I know *somethin'* bad happen to him after he sick. He warn't never the same after that hoopin' cough."

"It warn't the sickness that change him," Ring replied. "It was Pook dyin'."

"Yeah, that's it," Cy said.

"'Cause Pook his brother?" Oscar asked.

"Yeah. Rosalee was West mama, so that made Pook his brother—"

"Half brother," Ring corrected.

"Half brother," Cy went on. "I reckon Rosalee planned on stayin' 'round here till West seven years be up, then she could go away, take her boys with her. When Pook die, all that fell apart. West just give up."

"Maybe he saw some o' that stuff when he told his own fortune," Billy put in. "You know, in the bowl with the blood and water. Scared him, so he wouldn't tell us 'bout it."

Oscar shook his head. "None o' us ever gon' know the answers, not till we get up there and be with West on them streets o' gold."

"Yes, Jesus," Davy agreed.

"West gone to a better place," Billy declared.

Cy wanted to tell them they were wrong. There was no better place, no city called heaven with streets of gold and gates of pearl.

"Gone right up to the golden throne where Father be sittin', sendin' his angels down to bring the dyin' home to him," Ring exclaimed.

"Tell it!" Davy said.

"Yes, Lord!" Billy shouted.

They were making too much noise. Cy looked toward Stryker, sure that he would come over and break up their meeting. But Stryker had wandered away.

Billy's eyes were shining. "West done gone up to that throne, and bow low before Father God, and he see the four livin' creatures and the burnin' seraphim. And there, next to Father, on his own throne, he see Jesus!"

"Yes, Lord," Cy heard himself cry with the others. Why? He'd just reminded himself he didn't believe any of that stuff. He looked into the happy faces of the others and, for a moment, wished that he had what they seemed to have, something to make this hell more bearable.

"And Father gon' wipe away all the tears from every eye," Billy continued, his voice rising. "So I reckon West ain't cryin' none now—he ain't never gon' cry no more. He lookin' all around at them green pastures—"

"That's enough," Stryker broke in. They hadn't noticed his return. "Y'all have had your time, so get back to whatever it is you were doing."

Why did the white men always get the last word?

The next morning before breakfast, Cain had the boys stand in two lines at attention while Stryker brought Jess from the icehouse. His hands weren't cuffed now, but tied in front. Cain made him stand before them all. Cy had expected that Jess would be whipped again, but the post was not in sight.

As always, Cain had a speech to make. "Like I said yesterday, while we all regret Mr. Prescott's losing his temper the other day, we got to keep in mind that West ought not have provoked him. And neither should Jess, here, have taken it into his own hands to *judge* Mr. Prescott's behavior."

Cain was just getting warmed up. He rocked back on his heels. "I reckon y'all understand a basic principle of incarceration."

Mouse whispered at Cy, "What that mean?"

"Prison," he whispered back.

"In a prison environment," Cain went on, "the prisoners do not correct the officials placed in authority over them. The authorities are mandated by the state to impose correction on those who have broken the law. In other words, Jess had no right to go after Prescott, no matter how he felt about things. We ain't concerned here with how any of you feel! Y'all got that?"

A chorus of *yessir*s.

Cain looked satisfied. "Two times in recent memory, Jess has showed us all that he don't like how things are run in my camp. First, he interfered with Mr. Prescott, who was capably handling a runaway state prisoner by the name of Billy. Then, a couple days ago, he showed his displeasure with Mr. Prescott by trying to—inflict pain on him. First offense, Jess got the whippin' he deserved and my stern warning. Second offense, no more warnings. I can't and won't tolerate a boy in my camp who won't obey the rules.

Therefore"—he turned to look at Jess—"this fellow gets to learn for himself how they dig coal over in Alabama. That oughtta keep him too busy to mess in things he got no business with."

Love Davis came from the horse barn, driving one of the wagons. He stopped next to Cain.

"Say goodbye to Jess, boys," Cain directed. "You want to see him again, just do the kind o' foolish stuff he did, and you can get yourselves a free ride over to Birmingham too."

Davis jumped down from the wagon and approached Jess. "Let's go," he ordered.

This whole time, Jess had been calm, his face sad. He moved toward the wagon. Suddenly, Billy raced to Jess and grabbed on to his arm.

Not again, Cy thought. Billy had already acted crazy twice before, trying to escape on visiting day and then throwing himself at the doctor's feet when they were sick with whooping cough. Given Cain's mood, Billy might find himself getting his wish and going with Jess to the mines.

Screeching, kicking, biting, Billy hung on. Above the racket, Cy heard Jess calling his name. They locked eyes, and Jess called, "Look after Billy, and Mouse too."

It took all three white men working together to finally pull Billy off Jess. "Throw this brat in the icehouse!" Cain ordered, and Stryker took Billy away.

Cain and Davis restored order. Jess climbed into the wagon and sat down. He gazed out sadly at the faces of the other boys.

Why don't you fight? Cy wanted to shout. *Don't make it easy for 'em!*

Davis climbed onto the wagon seat and told the horse to go. The wagon went through the gate and down the road. All the boys watched until it was gone. No one besides Billy had protested. All the other boys had allowed the white men to send Jess away to the mines and to death.

Cy hated them for that. He hated himself just as much. *You're still yellow*, he thought. *A kid like Billy got more guts than you.*

Cy took a step back out of his line. He waited for Cain or Stryker to tell him to get back in place, but neither one did. Cy looked at the others. They were all still boys. That was their problem. They thought like boys, acted like boys. Were scared like boys.

And boys weren't ever going to get free, no matter how old they got.

I's so sick o' bein' a boy, Cy thought. *Of lettin' Cain and his men treat me like dirt under they feet.*

A resolve formed in the back of his mind. Small at first, it grew quickly, and it grew so large that it filled his thoughts. This new determination frightened him, but excited him too.

From now on, Cy Williams promised himself, he would do everything in his power to escape the hell of Cain's camp. If others wanted to risk it with him, they were welcome.

Starting now, he was no longer a boy.

He was a man.

NINETEEN

IN MARCH, THE TIPS OF TREE BRANCHES BEGAN to show deep red and yellowish green as new leaves sprouted. The first fiddlehead ferns poked through dry leaves on the forest floor. Flocks of robins, passing through to their northern nesting grounds, searched for bugs and worms after early morning rain showers.

Billy stuck to Cy like tar. He wanted to sleep next to him, work at his side when they went to shovel dirt at the railroad bed, sit next to him at meals. At first, Cy didn't want Billy hanging around him like a puppy. He wasn't interested in being a replacement for Jess. But it came to him that Billy's devotion might be useful when the moment came to escape. What he would need Billy to do—that he couldn't say. Hell, he didn't even have a plan yet, so how could he know what part Billy, or any of the other boys, would play in it? Still, it didn't cost anything to let the kid hang around. Even a puppy has sharp teeth, and it knows how to use them in a pinch.

Mouse had survived the whooping cough, but what little strength he'd had before was gone. For a while Cain sent him with the road gangs, only to have him collapse after an hour during which he hadn't accomplished anything. Threats made no difference. Mouse simply couldn't do hard labor, and Cain finally accepted that. Instead of sending Mouse away, Cain assigned him to help Rosalee and Sudie in the cookhouse.

Rosalee was in a bad way. Cy knew now that she was drugged. He guessed that Cain kept her doped up so she wouldn't carry on about losing both her sons. Or maybe she did whatever he wanted in exchange for the next dose of her "medicine." Maybe that was why she stayed around.

Cy bided his time, waiting for a plan to come to him.

Day followed day as the springtime advanced. Dogwood and redbud frosted the woods white and pink. Climbing wisteria covered the tall pines in purple. And life dragged on, dull, hard, unchanging.

Then a boy in Cy's gang died—simply died. Darius. Quiet boy, no trouble, did his work without complaining. One morning he refused to get up, even when Stryker and Davis came in and promised a whipping. "I's done" is all he would say. He wouldn't leave his bed, eat, or drink. Just lay on his straw tick looking up at the roof of the bunkhouse. Three days later, he was gone.

A boy didn't have to come down with a sickness like whooping cough in order to end up dead. Or provoke a white man to kill him. Cy saw that he—any one of them—could die just by deciding that he'd had enough. The longer the boys were Cain's prisoners, the greater the chance that more of them would give up the way Darius had done.

In the cookhouse one morning, Cy glanced at Rosalee. All the boys had gone through the line, so she had a moment to herself. Standing over the empty pots of food, Rosalee had fixed her eyes on the table where Cain and his men were enjoying their fried eggs, potatoes, and coffee. Cy saw on her face an expression of such deep, bitter hatred that it startled him. And planted an idea in his brain.

So Rosalee hated Cain. Of course she did, after what he'd done to her children. The thought grew. Maybe Cy could make her hatred part of his plan.

The next afternoon at the railroad bed, as Cain was sauntering down the line of chained boys, laughing with the boss man of the other gang, Cy noticed two things: Cain's pistol and the keys that hung from a metal ring attached to his belt. Cy had been aware of the gun and the key ring every day for as long as he'd been at the camp, but it was as if he were seeing them today for the first time.

Cain's pistol. The keys. He had to have them. How to get them?

Rosalee.

Cy lay awake that night, and by dawn, he'd decided what to do. The plan sounded crazy, but he couldn't come up with anything better, and he'd decided that doing something, *anything*, was better than doing nothing.

He began the day pretending to have twisted his left ankle so badly that he could hardly walk. Cy put on such a good show that Cain said he could stay in camp and work in the cookhouse with Mouse and the two women. Davis would stay too, to make sure Cy and Mouse didn't "try anything." But Cy already knew Davis well enough to be sure the white man would spend the day sitting in the sun whittling and depositing tobacco juice in his spit cup. He wouldn't show up in the cookhouse until it was time for dinner.

At breakfast, Rosalee didn't look drugged, which Cy took as a sign that things would go his way. After the others had left, she put him and Mouse to work scrubbing pots. When they were done, Rosalee told Mouse to go back to the bunkhouse and get some rest. Sudie tidied up around the stove and didn't even look up when Cy asked Rosalee if he could talk to her outside for a minute.

The morning was bright with spring sunshine that felt good in the cool air. Over the camp, a turkey buzzard scouted for something to eat.

They stood beside the door to the cookhouse. "What you want?" she asked him. "I got work to do."

Cy had planned his opening. "I's sorry 'bout Pook and West."

"That's it? I don't want to think about all that mess, and I *don't* need no sympathy from you."

Keep going, Cy told himself. "Remember the day Pook let me swing him around? That was fun."

Her face softened. "He liked that. You about the only one ever show interest in him."

Now Cy realized how to reach her. "I miss West too. He always could make us laugh. He was a good friend, always shared the extra food you give him. We others wasn't sure where that grub come from, but we was mighty thankful."

"Huh! Didn't make no difference in the end."

"Must o' been right hard for him to see you every day and not be able to let on you his mama," Cy went on. "I think about that, and it make me miss my own mama. At least West had you close by."

"Lot o' good it done him! Prescott kill him just the same. And Cain let my little Pook die."

Cy did his best to look sympathetic. In truth, his heart

was racing with excitement. Here was the test: everything depended on his choosing every word carefully.

Across the yard, he noticed a spot of gold in the middle of the trampled grass. "Hold on a minute," he said. He walked over to the place and quickly returned with a brilliant yellow dandelion on a long stem. He handed it to the woman. "Pretty, ain't it?"

Rosalee held the flower in her palm.

It was time to take the lead again. "Mr. Cain didn't do nothin' for us when we got the hoopin' cough. I thought he might take better care o' Pook."

She crushed the dandelion in her fist. "His own flesh and blood! Let him die like a dog."

"Miss Rosalee, I got to tell you somethin'." Cy lowered his eyes and tried to look pitiful.

"What is it?"

"I's real scared."

"We *all* scared. Every black man, woman, child—we scared all the time."

"I's scared all us boys is gonna die just like Pook and West, or get sent to the mines like Jess, 'less we can get outta here. I thought the hoopin' cough was gonna get a bunch more of us, but by the mercy o' God, we still here." Cy was grateful he'd learned to lie as if he meant what he said.

"Oh, yeah! God sho' done *poured* out his mercy on y'all!" Rosalee said it like it was a curse.

Cy pressed onward, testing her. "*You* can leave."

"No, I can't! I need my dope, and that devil Cain give it to me! You know about laudanum? You start off takin' jus' a little, it make you feel good. Help you forget you's nothin' but a whore. Then you need a little more, an' more—"

"Aw, Miss Rosalee, don't talk like that. You ain't a—"

"Don't be sorry for me! I knows what I is, and I got jus' what I deserve."

"Naw, you didn't! You come here to help West. You can get off that stuff. You don't got to stay here."

The woman looked into Cy's eyes. "I stay here to get even with Cain! There! I said it! You satisfied?"

Cy could have shouted. He'd been ready to suggest that very thing, and here she had said it for him.

"What?" she asked him. "Why you lookin' at me that-away? You gon' turn me in to Cain now?"

"Naw! Course not. I feels bad for you. I won't say nothin', I promise."

Cy glanced around. Sudie wasn't in sight. He spotted Davis across the yard, sitting in a rickety chair against a pine tree. Sure enough, his whittling knife was out and he was contentedly making a pile of shavings. His jaw worked away at his plug.

Cy lowered his voice and spoke urgently. "I need to tell you somethin', but first you got to swear you won't tell nobody."

Rosalee threw him a sharp look. "You tryin' to trick me? If you is, you better know Cain'd believe my word over yours. I's still his woman."

"It ain't a trick, I swear! God is my witness."

"Since when you believe in God?"

Cy looked up into the blue sky, dotted with drifting white clouds. "Since Jess talk to me about him," he lied. "And Jesus, too."

"If you say so."

"I swear, I ain't tryin' to get you in no trouble. Truth is, you could get *me* in a heap o' trouble if you let on to Cain what I's gonna tell you."

Rosalee sighed. "It don't matter. All right. I ain't gonna tell nobody. Go 'head and say what you got to say. I swear to keep quiet, if that what you need."

His heart beat wildly. "Okay. I got a plan to help us boys escape, 'cause if we stay here, we all gonna end up dead or sent off to Alabama and the mines. But to do that, I got to have Cain's keys."

"And—"

"I need you to get 'em for me without Cain knowin'."

"And why would I want to do that?"

"Like you said. To get even with him! To get . . . revenge."

"I might do somethin' like that just for *myself*. Why should I help y'all?"

"Because we all black! So you can do for us what you couldn't do for West!"

Rosalee let the crushed flower drop onto the hard-packed earth. She faced Cy, her hands in front of her chest, palms toward him, as if she were trying to push him away. "They's only one way to get them keys from Cain."

Cy lowered his eyes. "I know," he murmured. "Kill him." A trickle of sweat ran down his forehead.

"Stryker and Davis, too," she said.

Suddenly everything felt wrong. Here they were, talking about murdering three men. Three *white* men. It was like a nightmare Cy wanted to escape, make himself wake from. But this was no dream. It was real, and it felt terrible. The only way to freedom was to go through that feeling, no matter how it sickened him.

"I know they got to die," Cy said.

"And who's gonna do all that killin'?"

Cy wanted to stop everything this second, go away and pretend it hadn't happened. But he made himself keep going. "I ain't got no way to get to Cain. You do. You take care o' him, I take care of them others."

"*How?*"

He hadn't thought of these things, and now wished he had. He made up the plan as he went along. "You and Cain—sleep together sometimes, right?"

"Yeah. What of it?"

"One night, while he sleepin', you can do it."

"Kill him?"

Cy nodded.

"How?" Rosalee asked again.

"Knife. Pistol make too much noise."

Rosalee's head drooped. "I always knew my life would end up like this! Hooked on dope, white man's whore, and . . . a killer."

Cy couldn't let her think of those things, not yet. "Kill him, take his keys, and come get me. Unlock me, and I go take care of Stryker and Davis. They be 'sleep too, and I sneak in and finish 'em with Cain's pistol 'fore they knows what hit 'em."

"I never figured you for a murderer!" Rosalee looked toward the green pine woods. "You just never know what a man might do."

Yeah, a man. "I don't wanna be no murderer," Cy said, "but I can't figure no other way."

"Say we do manage it. What then? How you gonna get all them boys away from here? Where y'all gonna go? How far you think you make it in them uniforms? They'd get every one of you in a day or less."

He *had* thought about that during his long, sleepless night. "Cain got regular clothes stashed away somewhere. Get the fellows into ordinary pants and shirts, divide 'em into groups, send 'em different directions, tell 'em to find some colored folks to help 'em. At least some of 'em would have a fightin' chance to get away." He paused, determined to make himself look both sad and serious. "Anyway, I rather be dead tryin' to get away from here than stay and die for sure."

"What about me? After I kill a white man, where can *I* go? They get me too, and then you gon' see me hangin' from the end of a rope!"

"We got to take the chance. Somebody could hide you—help you get far away from here."

"I ain't got no friends. I ain't got—nobody."

"When my daddy was here, he tell me about a woman—Aunt Miriam. You know her?"

"Heard tell of her."

"Where she live?"

"Why you want to know?"

"'Cause when we escape, that's where I's going."

"*You?* How 'bout all them others?"

"I don't know."

"You *better* know! You got to do more than unlock them boys' chains. Most of 'em be as helpless as chickens outside the coop."

She was right, but he didn't want to think about that. "We can get it figured out."

"I bet."

Cy studied the ground, where green grass shoots poked through the red soil, despite being trampled by many feet. "Will you do it?"

This was the most important question he would ever ask anyone in his life. He was halfway hoping Rosalee would laugh in his face and tell him to forget all about it.

"It ain't much of a chance," Rosalee said.

"I know. But it *is* a chance."

"Maybe you right. When I think of what Cain did to my babies . . ."

"So?"

She nodded, and Cy's knees felt like jelly.

"When?"

"Sooner the better, 'fore I lose my nerve."

"Tonight?"

"You crazy? Naw, I got to have time to think. Tomorrow."

"All right."

Rosalee glanced around the camp. "We best get back to work."

Work didn't seem important anymore, but Cy helped her sweep the cookhouse. Then Rosalee sent him to "take care o' his twisted ankle."

He limped past Davis, who glanced up at him, then sent a stream of tobacco juice flying onto the grass. His knife never stopped scraping the pine stick he held in his thick fist. Was it possible that sometime soon, Cy would put a bullet through his brain?

Of course it wasn't. *It ain't gonna work*, Cy thought as he headed into the bunkhouse. He would find Rosalee later and tell her to forget it.

She'd have changed her mind by then anyway. No one in their right mind would think seriously about trying to carry out such a hopeless plan.

TWENTY

FROM THE SECOND CY ENTERED THE BUNK-
house and found Mouse asleep, time slowed way down. Cy
lay down beside Mouse and wished he could sleep, too, but
that was impossible. When he closed his eyes, he saw foul
images of blood and spattered brains. He fought them off
by remembering all that Cain and his henchmen had done.
He thought of the starvation, whippings, and backbreaking
work. The humiliation. The sentence of death in the coal
mines. Murder. Now the white men would pay, and he, Cy,
a black man, would collect.

He lay there until Davis stuck his head in and said that
dinner was ready. Cy woke Mouse, and they went to eat,
but when the food was put in front of him, he couldn't
swallow even a mouthful. Rosalee served up the beans and
potatoes impassively. The blacks of her eyes were as small
as pinpoints.

That afternoon, Cy did sleep, deeply and dreamlessly

at first, but he woke in a panic, his heart thudding. To his disgust, he realized he'd wet himself a little.

The other boys returned from their day of labor. Everything was the same; nothing was the same. Billy had had a rough day, and he wanted to stay close to Cy, who let him. If things worked out, he might need the kid's help soon. Best to treat him well until then.

Cy slept fitfully that night. He dozed, woke to find himself aroused, and jerked off, seeking relief for his body. But he could not find the restfulness that usually came over him after the act.

He was awake at dawn, his nerves stretched as tight as barbed wire on a new fence. Rather than pretend to have a bad leg again, he decided to go to the railroad site. Being with people and using his muscles would be better than staying in camp alone all day, waiting for a word from Rosalee.

She wouldn't look at him during breakfast, and he had to leave the camp not knowing what, if anything, she had decided. That day, he worked like a machine, striving to exhaust himself, trying to find distraction from the uproar in his brain. Nothing helped. As they trudged home, Cy decided he would find Rosalee and call off the whole thing. He couldn't stand any more of this tension.

But after supper, Rosalee pulled him aside. "Tonight," she told him.

He wanted to tell her no, that he'd changed his mind. But he heard himself saying, "You mean it?"

"It was your idea! Now, is you in it or not?"

He nodded. "In." A thought struck him. "What about Sudie? She'll hear everything! She'll know!"

"Today Saturday, remember? She gone till Monday morning."

He hadn't thought of that. It was good news, but it put him in a panic. Maybe there were lots of other things he hadn't thought of. . . .

"After I do it, I's gonna unlock the chain outside and come in and get you. Then you finish the job. Understand?"

"You gonna have the pistol?"

"Yeah."

"When?"

"Probably after midnight, when I knows they all asleep."

"All right."

Rosalee looked into his eyes. "We both gonna die tonight. You know that, don't you?"

Her words pierced him. The woman was most likely

right. But if he died—that would at least end this hell. And if she was wrong . . .

Cy managed to have himself chained at the end of the row of boys that night, Billy next to him. He lay motionless, terrified of what lay ahead, but desperate for it to happen.

After hours, he heard what he'd been both wanting and dreading to hear: the sound of the chain being unlocked outside. A minute later, Rosalee crept through the bunk-house door and found him in the darkness.

"You do it?" Cy whispered.

"Yeah." Although they did not touch, Cy could feel her trembling. "I's gonna pull the chain through the wall, then you get free of it. We gotta put it back through, though, keep the rest of 'em here till you done."

She went to the wall and began to pull the chain. It scraped, but Cy was surprised how silently Rosalee did it. He kept glancing down the row of sleeping boys, dread-ing that someone would wake up and cause trouble. When the chain was pulled all the way through, Cy eased off the sleeping platform and freed himself.

That's when Billy woke up. "Cy?" he asked. "What's goin' on?"

In a second, Cy was at Billy's side, his hand over his

mouth. "Shhh!" he warned. "Cain sent Rosalee to get me. Somethin' important at his cabin. I be back soon."

Billy tried to push Cy's hand away.

"You got to trust me," Cy whispered fiercely. "Don't wake up the others. I be back soon. I promise. All right?"

Billy nodded.

"Now, lay back down and wait. If anybody else wakes up, you tell 'em everything all right."

Rosalee went back outside and Cy fed the chain to her. Then he went outside too. They relocked the chain, and then Rosalee unlocked Cy's leg irons.

Overhead, the night sky was clear, and the stars glittered. They moved away from the bunkhouse. Every second, Cy expected to see Stryker and Davis headed their way, rifles in hand. But there was nothing. The camp was dark and silent.

"You sure Cain dead?" Cy asked.

"Would I be here if he warn't?"

He wanted to ask her how she'd done it, where she'd stabbed him. But this wasn't the time. "You got his pistol?"

Without a word, she handed it to him. It was heavier than he expected, and he almost dropped it. His hand was shaking.

"How many bullets?"

"Six. I counted 'em. Checked out the whole thing. It ready to go. You do know how to use it, don't you?"

"Yeah. Daddy had one, and he use to let me shoot."

"All right. Once you do it, then what?"

"No time now. Let me go."

Together, they made their way to the cabin where Stryker and Davis slept. At the door, Cy listened. The sound of snoring came even through the wooden door. A good sign. He peered through the front window. An oil lamp was glowing dimly on a table. Another good sign: he'd be able to see once he got inside.

"They beds is to the right," Rosalee told him, "by the back corner."

He nodded. In his right hand, the pistol felt heavy, its metal cool in the night air.

"You best hurry," she told him. "Ain't no goin' back now." She moved off into the darkness.

Around him, all was silence, but in his head, Cy seemed to hear a horrible mixture of sounds that grew louder and louder. Cain's voice intoning his endless speeches. Billy screaming when they took Jess away. Prescott saying, "Drop them pants and turn around." And beneath the rising shriek of voices, the never-ending clanking of chains.

He stood, panting, struggling to clear his mind. To make himself take the next step.

Please let the door not be locked, Cy thought as he put his hand on the latch. It lifted, and the door yielded to his pressure. The hinges didn't creak, and Cy eased himself into the room. His heart was pounding so violently that he almost believed he could hear it. Any second, the white men would wake up. Surely they slept with pistols under their pillows. They'd grab them and shoot him dead.

But there was no movement, only the sound of two men snoring.

Cy's eyes adjusted to the gloom. Yes, in the far corner were two beds, pushed together so that their heads touched. He cocked the pistol; its click sounded like a scream in the silence. Still the sleeping men did not move.

Cy took a silent step forward, then another. His right hand would not stop shaking, so he pulled the pistol toward himself and steadied it against his chest.

Another step forward, and now he could see the shapes of the men. They were sprawled on their beds, Stryker fully clothed, Davis stark naked.

Another step, then another, and Cy stood directly above Stryker. For a moment, he felt something like pity for the sleeping man. Stryker had been the best of them all, had even shown moments of concern when they were so sick with the whooping cough. He hadn't agreed with what

Prescott had done, murdering West that way. He'd lost the girl he called Mary Elizabeth—his sister?—when he was just a kid himself.

None of that mattered now.

All at once, the coiled tension in Cy's body was released. He knelt down, shoved the barrel of the pistol against the side of Stryker's head, and pulled the trigger. The noise was like a clap of thunder. Cy jumped to his feet. Davis jerked awake and turned toward him just in time to take a bullet in the forehead. He collapsed back on his pillow as blood began pouring from the hole above his eyes.

Cy gripped the pistol in both hands now. He felt certain both men were alive; it had been too easy to destroy each one with a single bullet. But there was no movement, and the only sound was the hiss of the breath emptying out of Stryker's lungs.

Cy moved back, waiting. Nothing. He lowered the pistol and let it drop on the table. Then he began to sob. It had all happened in a moment, like a dream. Surely *he* had not done this thing. No, he had stood back, watching someone like himself, but *not* himself, send bullets into the brains of two white men, bringing their lives crashing down in the mess of blood that had darkened his imagination.

With a shaking hand, he picked up the lamp, turned its wick higher, and approached the beds again. Were they truly dead? He held up the light above them. Stryker's wound oozed dark blood. Davis's eyes were open in surprise, and blood was running down his forehead and pooling in the left eye before continuing its way down into his beard.

They *were* dead. He, Cy, had killed them. On impulse, he grabbed Davis's bedsheet and pulled it over him, hiding his nakedness.

A sound behind him made him jump. It was Rosalee at the door. "They dead?"

"Yeah." Another wave of panic surged over him, and he dropped onto a chair by the table, his head touching his knees.

"No time for that," Rosalee said. "Whatever else you got in mind, you got to do it *now*."

Now. He could grab different clothes, some food, whatever money he could find, bullets, and leave with Rosalee.

He heard shouting. Rosalee went to the door and listened. "Boys in the bunkhouses. They done heard the shots and is wonderin' what's goin' on."

Grab what you can and run, Cy thought. *The others ain't your concern*.

"Cy!" Rosalee exclaimed. "Tell me yo' plan."

He jumped up, his decision made. "Come on," he told her.

She followed him to the bunkhouse. The boys were gabbling with fright, but silence fell when they walked in.

"Cy!" Billy cried. "What's happenin'?"

He held the lamp high. "Y'all hush, now! I got somethin' to say. Somethin' important."

Cy could feel many eyes on him. A sense of his own power ran through him, and he felt brave. Strong as Teufel.

"Listen to me, and listen good. After you hear what I got to say, be steady, 'cause they's a lot to do."

Murmured questions hummed in the air until Cy silenced them again. "Okay, here it is: Cain and his men is all dead."

The murmurs turned to shouts.

"Quiet!" Cy yelled. "I's tellin' you the truth. They's dead. Rosalee and me got the keys. Any o' you who wants to get outta here, now's the time. We gonna find the regular clothes Cain got stashed, get all the food and stuff we can carry, and head out. We got to go in small groups, go in different directions, stay off the roads, try and find black folks to help us. Then maybe we got a chance."

Shouted questions and protests answered him. A couple of boys started to cry. In the middle of everything, Cy noticed Billy staring at him with adoring eyes.

"I got to go tell the other guys what I just told you," he finished. "I be back soon."

"Unlock us!" someone shouted.

"Not yet," Rosalee told Cy quietly. "Not till we get charge o' the whole thing."

They left the boys chained up and went to the other bunk. Cy told the same story, met with the same reactions, and explained the same plan of escape.

Leaving them chained too, Cy and Rosalee headed to Cain's cabin. Rosalee spat on Cain's body as she passed the bed. She went to a cupboard and started emptying its contents into a saddlebag. She took bottles of liquid, which Cy figured to be her dope. She came up with a second pistol and bullets and a large wad of cash, which she split with Cy. Then she went to the cookhouse to finish gathering her things.

Cy was eager to search Cain's cabin, but to his surprise, he couldn't stand the sight of Cain, no matter how often he'd wished him dead.

He grabbed a quilt and covered the body. Once again, horror swept over him at what he and Rosalee had done, even as he ransacked the cabin. He found some of Cain's shirts and pants, which he thought might fit some of the bigger boys.

Cy went to the cookhouse next. He had to find where Cain kept the boys' other clothes, the ones they had when they first came to his camp. Rosalee led him to a locked room. She found the right key, and inside they discovered what they were looking for: all kinds and sizes of clothing. Pants, shirts, jackets, boots. Even stockings and drawers.

Cy began rooting through the clothing. Somehow, it seemed utterly necessary to find his own things, even if it took time to locate them. Then he remembered he'd been delivered to Cain wearing only drawers and a pair of overalls. On a day so long ago, John Strong had grabbed Cy's shirt to cover Travis's body, and Cy had never gotten it back.

I gotta find them overalls, he thought. Would he even recognize them? Yes. He had patched the right knee himself, using scraps of feed sack. Sewing on that patch had taken him a long time. He'd know it anywhere.

And suddenly, at the bottom of a pile of pants, he found what he was looking for. Not caring that Rosalee was in the room, he pulled off his uniform pants and stepped into the overalls. They were so small that he couldn't get the straps over his shoulders to fasten them to the bib.

A wave of disappointment washed over him. So much had happened since the last time he wore that tattered and faded garment. So much had happened, almost all of it bad.

"Run back and get some o' Cain's things," Rosalee told him. "And quit wastin' time!"

Cy hurried back to the cabin and grabbed trousers, a shirt, and a jacket. They all fit him tolerably well, although the touch of Cain's clothes made his skin crawl.

He had lost track of time. How long had it been since they'd killed the white men, and how long was it until dawn? They had to be scattered and making their various ways through the woods well before then.

Cy pulled on Cain's boots, which fit him, too. He went back to the cookhouse and helped Rosalee finish scavenging. Then they went to Cy's bunkhouse. Rosalee held the lamp high, and Cy did the same with Cain's pistol. "We found clothes and food for everyone," he began. "We gonna unlock you, and then we gonna find different stuff for y'all to wear. Then hand out what food they is and send y'all on your ways. They ain't gonna be no trouble, understand? No runnin' every which way. Not while I got this." He brandished the pistol. "Y'all give me your word?"

Many voices agreed.

"After we take off yo' chains, meet us outside and we get rid of these goddamn leg irons once and for all."

That brought a cheer.

Billy grabbed Cy's sleeve. "I's comin' with you, right?"

"Me too," Mouse added.

Cy pulled himself free of Billy's grasp. "I dunno, Billy . . ."

"We can go to Moultrie!" Billy went on. "It ain't far. Daddy an' them can help us."

"We'll see," Cy said, heading for the door. "Let's get outta here first."

He hadn't planned to take anyone with him. While he'd never allowed himself to decide that for sure, now he admitted that's what had been in his mind all along. Alone, he had a better chance. No one to slow him down, no one to look after. He would make his way to the woman called Aunt Miriam. She would hide him, like she'd promised to hide his father and him before. Then he'd find his way back home. Wherever that was.

Cy repeated his speech in the other bunkhouse, and soon all the boys were gathered in the yard. One by one, Rosalee unlocked their leg irons. Cy had anticipated trouble, especially from Jack, but the sight of Cain's pistol and Cy's promise to use it if necessary made everyone obey him.

Then Ring stepped forward. "I ain't in this," he declared. "Ain't no way we can escape from here. Only take 'em a day or two to round up anybody try an' escape. Then they gonna be hell to pay."

Ring's words took Cy by surprise. He had to stop this now, before other boys agreed.

"I thought you be glad for what I done," Cy told him. "I figured you want us to do anything to get outta here. And you got the best chance to escape."

"How so?"

"Look at yo'self. You as white as Cain or any of 'em. Get into some different clothes and ain't nobody gon' suspect you. By tomorrow, you be long gone."

Ring shook his head. "You gone crazy, Cy. Do what you want, but I's staying right here."

Some boys muttered their agreement. Cy could sense their uncertainty, their fear. He felt those things, too, but there was no time for feelings now.

"Okay," he shouted to everyone. "I ain't forcin' nobody to come with us. All I's sayin' is that if you stay here, chances are you gonna die here. Look at Pook and West. Look at what happen to Jess. How many boys you ever seen leave this place?"

Several boys agreed.

"Don't listen to him," Ring ordered. "Stay here and stay safe."

Cy felt like shooting Ring, anything to make him shut up. "Safe?" he retorted. "Safe from what? White man's whip? From him beatin' us to death like Prescott done to

West? From rapin' us?" The moment he spoke those words, Cy realized he was no longer ashamed. Shame had been replaced by rage.

There was a murmur from the boys, and suddenly Cy knew that he wasn't the only one who'd encountered Prescott in the icehouse.

"Like I said, I ain't gonna make nobody do this. But to me, it's the only way! If you got enough guts, take a chance! If not, stay here."

"Everybody who's stayin', over here by me," Ring shouted.

Cy held his breath. He hadn't taken the risk of killing the white men just to have his authority challenged. His finger felt for the trigger of the pistol. He hated Ring at that moment. The yellow coward had no right to frighten the others into staying.

Two boys moved in Ring's direction. Then a couple more.

Cy felt his power slipping away. "Jack," Cy cried, "join us. Your guys'll do what you say. Show 'em what's right!"

If Jack decided for Ring, things could end right then. Cy was not about to let that happen.

There was a moment of breathless silence. Then Jack walked across the yard and stood beside him. "I's with you," he said. "Cy right," he called out. "Anyone what want a shot at his freedom, come on! You ain't never gonna get another."

Relief swept over Cy. He put his hand on Jack's shoulder. "Decide now! We ain't got all night."

In a minute, half of the boys stood around Ring, who had suddenly become their leader. Cy realized what had to be done. "Back to the bunkhouse," he ordered, pointing the pistol at Ring's chest.

"What for?" he cried.

"Y'all got to be chained back. Can't take the risk you'll run squealin' to the white man."

"We won't!"

"Maybe not, but I ain't gonna give you the chance to change your minds. Now, go on. We leave you some food and water. 'Sides, somebody come around askin' questions in a day or so. Y'all can stand it until then."

Cy half expected Ring to charge him, and he was ready to shoot him down if he had to. What difference would one more killing make now, even though Ring was a black man like himself despite his white skin? But Ring told his new followers to obey. Once in the bunkhouse, they let Rosalee put them back in leg irons and lock them onto their beds.

Cy and Rosalee helped the remaining boys find clothes, and Rosalee said she was going to finish getting herself ready to go. The boys gathered in the yard, and Cy counted them: seventeen in all, including himself. Looking at them, he nearly smiled. They were a ragtag bunch, for sure, but at least the hated stripes were gone. In their arms and tied in bundles were as many supplies as they could carry.

Rosalee appeared from the barn, leading one of the horses. Bulging saddlebags hung from the saddle. At first, Cy didn't recognize her. She had cut her wavy brown hair very short and had somehow darkened the skin of her face. She was wearing a man's outfit: shirt, pants, jacket, and boots. Cain's pistol was tucked into her belt, and a slouch hat was clutched in her hand.

Rosalee had thought things out carefully. Cy respected her for that.

"You got 'em ready?" she asked.

"Yeah. We can go anytime. Which way we headed?"

"*We?* They ain't no *we*, Cy. You told these boys they got to go in small groups, two, three, maybe four. Go different ways, you told 'em. That what they got to do, if they wants any chance at all."

He could feel himself going tense. "I know that. But I figured you was gonna come with me." The words surprised him. Cy didn't remember ever having thought that, but now that the idea was spoken, he realized, embarrassed, that he wanted Rosalee to be with him. He *needed* her.

Something touched his hand and he jerked away. He turned to find it was Billy, searching his face with imploring eyes.

And he need me, Cy realized. What had Jess called out to him, about looking after Billy and Mouse?

Rosalee's voice brought him back to the world. "I ain't goin' with you," she told him coldly. "I done what you asked me. Now I got to look out for myself, and I can't have none o' y'all draggin' me down." She put one foot into the stirrup. "I reckon they get me sooner or later, but till then, I's gon' enjoy every minute, knowin' I got revenge on the man who killed my children."

With that, she swung into the saddle and tossed the keys to Cy. "Open the gate," she commanded him. He obeyed, too stunned to argue or refuse.

Rosalee urged the horse forward. Once in the road, she turned back, and her eyes locked with Cy's. "I hope it all turns out good for you," she told him. "The others too. And I thanks you for givin' me the courage to do what shoulda been done a long time ago." She kicked the horse's sides and disappeared into the darkness.

No one spoke for a few seconds, then everyone started

talking at once. Cy ordered silence, and the boys quieted down. Someone was whimpering.

Cy felt alone—and he felt scared. But now that the moment had arrived, he had to act.

Billy took his hand again, and Mouse left the other boys and came and stood beside him. They looked pitiful in their ragged clothes. Of course, Mouse's pants were too large, and he'd found a length of rope to use as a belt. Cy knew Mouse and Billy didn't stand a chance on their own.

"We got to get outta here," Cy told the boys. "Billy and Mouse is comin' with me. The rest of y'all, decide who you's goin' with. Older fellas, take a couple o' the younger guys. Some of you head north, up toward Tifton."

"What about the other horses?" Jack asked. "We can take them."

"Too risky," Cy said. "Somebody sure to recognize 'em. 'Sides, we got to stick to the woods, and horses can't go there."

"Where Tifton?" someone asked.

Cy wasn't sure, but he couldn't let on now. "Turn right on the road once you get outside camp. Some o' you go through the woods back o' here, and some go straight." He had no idea what lay in those directions, but that wasn't his problem.

"Which way *you* goin'?" a boy asked.

"Left, down toward someplace called Moultrie."

"To find my daddy," Billy said softly.

"We's comin' with you," another boy said.

Cy took a step toward the boys. His hand touched the pistol tucked into his belt. "No, you ain't!" he declared. "We's all goin' different ways, like we said. That the only way we got a chance. Long as it dark, you can pretty much stay on the road. If you go through the woods, just get as far as you can, then stop and wait till the sun come up. Then you can see where you's goin'."

"And where that?"

Cy didn't want any more questions. He had no answers, and he was desperate to leave.

"Look for folks to help you," he said. "Colored folks. They hates the white man just like you do. Tell 'em you runnin' away, and they hide you, find you places to live."

Maybe, said a voice in his head. *Remember Sam Arnold?*

It was time to quit talking. "If we doin' this, we got to do it now," he said. "It be dawn soon, and we got to be far from here as we can. Get movin'."

Silently, the boys moved forward and stepped into the road. Cy pulled the gate closed and snapped the padlock shut. Then he took the ring of keys Rosalee had given him and hurled it into the woods.

"Hurry now," Cy urged. One by one, each group

disappeared into the night, leaving Cy, Billy, and Mouse. Cy stood looking at the camp, wishing its fences would fall to earth, its bunkhouses crumble, all the chains and locks turn to powder and blow away in the wind.

Billy brought him back to the real world. "Thank you for takin' us with you," he said. "It ain't but a few miles down to Moultrie. We can get there for breakfast. Daddy gon' be right surprised to see us. He for sure gon' cook us up some hotcakes and fry up some bacon. And coffee—"

"Stop," Cy told him. He couldn't let himself think of such things—not yet. "Let's go," he said.

Off they went down the dark road to freedom.

TWENTY-ONE

CY LED THE WAY, STAYING TO THE SIDE OF THE
road so they could melt into the blackness of the woods at
the slightest sound of an approaching traveler. From the
start, Mouse had a hard time keeping up. It was torture for
Cy to wait for him to catch his breath, when everything in
Cy shouted that they must run. If Cy were on his own, he'd
be racing through the woods, panicked like a deer fleeing
a pack of hunting dogs.

Cy searched his memory for the directions to reach the
woman called Aunt Miriam. Somewhere, they had to leave
the road, turn off—he wasn't sure which way. He fought
down the thought that in the darkness, they would miss the
turnoff. In the gray half-light before sunrise, that fear was
replaced by another: getting caught. Soon they would have
to move into the woods.

*You just sent all the rest o' them boys to the Alabama
mines,* a voice in his mind accused him. *What chance they
got, not knowin' where they goin'? What make you think any*

black man or woman gon' offer them help? Them boys gon' be picked up, taken back to camp, whipped till the skin fall off they backs, and then sent off to die diggin' coal. They was better off the way they was.

I won't listen to you, Cy told the accuser.

But the taunting voice was not so easily silenced. *You gon' be caught too, lynched, and sent straight to hell. And for what?*

"Shut up!" Cy cried out loud.

"You okay?" Billy asked him. "Cy, you all right?"

"Yeah. Never mind. Follow me. We got to get off the road now."

They headed into the woods and stopped to rest. Cy had no idea how long they'd been walking. Dawn was coming quickly now, and rays from the rising sun turned the young spring leaves to gold.

"Eat somethin'," Cy told Billy and Mouse. "I can stand watch. Get some sleep if you want."

"I's too tired to eat," Mouse complained. But he did fall asleep. One moment he was awake, shaking his head to refuse the food Cy was coaxing him to try, the next second, he was out. Cy wondered if he himself would ever be able to sleep again. But as he listened to Billy's quiet breathing and watched Mouse curl up just the way he used to on the straw tick back in camp, Cy found his own eyes beginning to shut. Right away, images of Stryker's and Davis's bloody bodies loomed in his mind.

Cy's head jerked up, and he realized he had been asleep—for how long, he couldn't exactly tell, but the sun was fully up and the birds were in joyful song. He stood up and stretched, reaching for the sky. No matter what happened later, at this moment, he was a free man. *A free man.*

He let the others sleep while he crept up to the road and listened. No sound. Then he crawled back and lay down again.

The sun was overhead when he woke. Billy and Mouse still slept. Cy roused them. Now it was time to move, to find the turnoff that would lead them to Aunt Miriam—if she really existed. Failing that, they would make their way to Moultrie and find Billy's father—if *he* existed.

When Cy told them they were going to Aunt Miriam, Billy objected. He wanted to keep heading toward Moultrie. If they hurried, they could still get home by suppertime, he argued. Cy said no. They would go to Aunt Miriam first, and she could help them go the rest of the way.

They gathered their things and started through the woods, keeping the road to their left. Right away, Mouse complained of being thirsty. Then Billy did, too. They had brought all the food they could carry, but no one had thought about water. They looked for a low place where there might be standing water or, better, a creek.

A creek. Now Cy remembered. His daddy had told him the road crossed a creek, and beyond that . . . he wasn't sure. He would have to trust that when they got to the place, he'd know.

The going was slow because Mouse was so weak. Soon, Cy had to pick Mouse up and carry him on his back. That slowed them even more. The road was deserted, and Cy wondered why until he remembered that it was Sunday. God-fearing folks would be in church and sinners still lying in their beds, sleeping off last night's whoring and drinking.

Just when Cy was beginning to believe they'd missed the place his father had told him about, or that his memory was all wrong, the land started going downhill and the woods grew thicker. Cy knew it was a sure sign that water was ahead. They came to a creek, running brightly over a white sand bottom, and all three threw themselves face-down on the ground and scooped cool water into their mouths. Never had anything tasted so good, Cy thought.

When they had drunk their fill, Cy sat and tried to jog his memory. What had his father told him about the creek? He ventured up to the road and saw a bridge—yes, Pete

Williams had said there was a bridge. Looking left and right, Cy climbed up a weedy bank and scrambled onto the road. He crossed the bridge and—yes!—there was a turnoff to the right. That was the way to Aunt Miriam's!

In two minutes, he was leading Billy and Mouse along the narrow path that wound its way into thick oak woods. When they came to an enormous dead oak and an even smaller path to the right, Cy knew which way to go. His heart was beating fast again, but not from fear. Soon, he felt in his bones, they would be safe.

The path plunged into thicker woods, went down through a low place where the ground was soft and wet, up again to higher ground, and at last into a clearing. At the far end stood a shabby cabin. Behind it, a falling-down barn.

"Stay here," Cy told the others. "I'll go find Aunt Miriam."

"I's comin' with you," Billy said, grabbing his hand.

"Me too," Mouse added.

"Naw! Get behind them big trees and wait. If anything go wrong, run like hell."

Cy freed himself from Billy's grasp and took a few steps forward. When the door to the cabin opened, he dodged behind a tree and watched as an old black woman came onto the porch. She wore a shapeless long dress and was barefoot. Her white hair was pulled back and tied in a knot. Over the colorless dress she had on a bright red coat.

The woman reached the porch steps and stopped. She scanned the clearing and then, Cy was certain of it, raised her head and sniffed the air.

Cy felt himself trembling. Was the woman Aunt Miriam? There was only one way to find out. He came out from hiding and took two steps toward the cabin. Immediately, the woman had her eyes fixed on him. He kept walking toward her.

But he stopped short when the woman asked, "Cy Williams, that you?"

"Yes, ma'am."

She nodded, satisfied. "What done took you so long?"

He wasn't sure what the question meant or how to answer, so instead he said, "I got two others with me."

"And where they be?"

Cy felt sure it was safe. "Billy, Mouse," he called, "come out."

They appeared from behind their trees and stepped into the clearing.

"It's okay," Cy said. "We's here."

With slow steps, the boys advanced. Mouse was staggering with exhaustion, and his breath came in big, wheezing gasps. Billy rushed forward and grabbed on to Cy's arm. He began to cry.

"Aw, sugar, it's all right now," the woman said, making her way slowly down the steps. "Aunt Miriam gon' take care o' you."

Aunt Miriam. They were truly safe, then.

What happened next felt like a dream, the first good dream Cy could remember having in years. He had to keep reminding himself that it was real. He and the others had hot baths in the copper tub Aunt Miriam filled, emptied, and refilled so that each boy could wash in clean water. She fed them fish coated in cornmeal batter and fried crisp—redbreast and sunfish caught in the creek just that morning. She set out slices of yeast bread slathered with butter and peach jam, and a salad of fresh dandelion greens from the nearby fields mixed with sweet lettuces from her garden. And then there was hot coffee, served with sugar and fresh cream. Cy felt like weeping when he tasted that.

Mouse nibbled at the fried fish, but clearly he had no appetite. Cy noticed Aunt Miriam looking at the boy, and her eyes showed her worry.

Billy and Mouse were tucked into bed together in a lean-to room off the back of the cabin. Only then did Aunt

Miriam invite Cy to sit on the porch and talk. She brought out a corncob pipe from her apron pocket, filled it with tobacco, and settled down to smoke.

As soon as Cy sat in the comfortable rocking chair, he fell into a deep sleep. When he woke, at first he didn't remember where he was. Then he knew, but he couldn't tell how long he'd been out. Aunt Miriam was still there, the pipe clutched in her teeth, gazing at the newly greening trees on the far side of the clearing.

"How long I been asleep?" Cy asked.

"Pretty long time," Aunt Miriam replied. "I don't know 'bout clock time, but you done had a right good nap. Feelin' better now?"

Cy did feel better, but as he looked at this kindly, strange woman, he knew he had to tell her all he had done to make it to her place. But she spoke first.

"Yo' daddy was all tore up when he realize what that snake Arnold done to y'all."

"He knew? You knew?"

"Yes, child. Ain't much happen in these parts I don't hear 'bout sooner or later. I got my spies everywhere"—she laughed to herself—"and they report how Arnold turn you in fo' a couple dollars."

"Somebody told me Cain had him killed."

"'Deed he did! Can't say I shed no tears when I heard that." She spat over the porch railing. "When word come, yo' daddy carry on somethin' awful. All I could do to keep him from goin' back to Cain's camp and tryin' to bust through the gate and kill that devil. I got him to calm down after a while, and I made him see that they warn't no use in throwin' his life away. He kept sayin' that he didn't care nothin' about his life, 'cause it didn't have no meanin' without you."

Sadness washed over Cy, and he fought back tears.

"Finally, I got yo' daddy to agree that they warn't nothin' he could do. We jus' had to sit and wait to see what Father got up his sleeve."

"Father?"

"God the Father. You knows: 'Our Father, which art in heaven.'"

"Oh."

"After some few days, we got word that you was alive in the camp, that Cain didn't whip you to death or send you over to Alabam'. I told yo' daddy best thing for him was to go home and that you be followin' along behind him when you was ready."

"He went?"

Aunt Miriam put her hand over his. "Yes, child. Back

to Louisville. I know that a long way from here, but the farther, the better. Ain't nobody gon' think to look for you up there."

"But I don't know the way!"

"No more than the chillun o' Israel knew the way through the wilderness to the Promised Land. But Father show you the road."

Cy wasn't sure about that. It sounded strange to hear Aunt Miriam referring to God as Father.

"And Daddy be there now?"

She nodded. "He ask me to tell you that he be there waitin', if it take you ten years to get there. He say he ain't got nothin' to do now *but* wait."

Cy sat and thought things over. It warmed him to learn that his father had tried to save him and would have gone back to Cain's camp to try again, no matter how crazy that idea might have been. And now he was far away, waiting for his son to come back—to come home.

He could feel the old woman's eyes on him. He looked at her and saw deep compassion in the brown depths of her gaze.

"You ready to say how you and these boys come to be here?" she asked quietly.

He was, but having to remember felt terrible. Telling the story made it all come back again. Nothing would ever erase the images of Stryker's and Davis's faces, the open eyes, the blood . . .

Aunt Miriam showed no surprise, no horror. In fact, when he described the killings, she nodded satisfaction. "That Cain had it comin'," she said. "After all the evil he done. And the evil he let others do."

"You ain't mad at me for what I done?" Cy asked.

"Should I be?"

"The only other person I knows who ever talked about God an' the Bible an' all"—Cy groped for the words to explain himself—"he always said that killin' is wrong, and we got to wait an' let God fix things."

Aunt Miriam patted his hand. "Yo' friend had it right, mostly. 'Thou shalt not kill,' the book say. But it also say that Father don't like havin' his chillun whipped and starved and killed." She turned her eyes back to the trees across her yard. "And sometimes, when Father done waited long enough for wicked folks to turn from they evil ways and do right, he decide to fix things once and for all, and he call on us to do the fixin'."

It was too much for Cy to think about. Aunt Miriam seemed to sense his uncertainty. "Don't fret about it jus' now. We got other things to do. They's boys on the run, and I got to get the word out."

"How?"

"Come dusk, my grandson Simon be here. He check on me every evenin'. Been wantin' me to come live with him and his wife now that Aaron and Johnny Boy both gone."

"Who they?"

The woman looked out across the yard. "My husband and son. Aaron died 'bout a year back, just plain wore out."

"Johnny Boy?"

"White men killed him. Don't want to talk about that."

"I's sorry."

"Thank you, son. I miss 'em both real bad, but one day soon, I gon' be joinin' 'em on the streets o' gold, and then everything gon' be all right. Father gon' keep his promise, wipe away all our tears."

She talked the way Billy and the others had talked at West's funeral.

"Simon'll spread the word," Aunt Miriam went on. "He can get you boys started on y'all's way to Louisville."

"When can we go? Tomorrow?"

Just then, Billy came through the front door, wiping the sleep out of his eyes. "Home?" he asked. "Daddy be waitin' for me!"

"Where he be?" Aunt Miriam asked.

"Jus' down at Moultrie! Only couple miles from here. We can go this evenin', surprise Daddy before bedtime." Billy's eyes glowed with hope.

"Course you ready to get home," Aunt Miriam said. "But we gotta go slow. When Simon come, you tell him everything, and he can check things out in Moultrie. Find your daddy and figure a way for you and him to meet where it be safe. Come tomorrow, they gon' find out what happen at the camp, and then they be lookin' under every rock and behind every tree and bush to find you boys."

When Aunt Miriam sent Billy to check on Mouse, Cy asked the question he'd been wanting to ask all along. "Aunt Miriam, how you know it was me when you saw me in the yard?"

"Oh, yo' daddy tell me what you look like. He done a right good job, too. I knew the second I laid these old eyes on you."

"But it been a long time! How come you still waitin' on me?"

The woman smiled. "Any man brave enough—or crazy enough—to risk what you done that first time, bound to try it again. I didn't know how or when you'd do it, but I reckoned you would, when you wanted yo' freedom bad enough. And here you is."

"I got to find Daddy."

"I know, sugar. Louisville a long way, but that ain't nothin'."

Cy wasn't happy with what he knew he had to say next. "First, I got to help Billy."

The woman nodded agreement. "I figured you say that, too. What about that other one—Mouse? How he get to be so sick?"

Cy told her that Mouse had never had any strength, and that the whooping cough had just about finished him.

"Where he stay, 'fore Cain got hold o' him?" Aunt Miriam asked.

"I dunno. He say he from way down by Florida, near some big ol' swamp."

Aunt Miriam nodded. "Okefenokee," she said. "Long way from here, and that child couldn't make it a half mile, the state he in. Maybe we could get him down that way, but I dunno. It's a shame, seein' a child like that already used up. A real shame."

"I just want to get home. See my daddy."

"Course you do. And we gon' do everything we can to see to it you gets what you want."

Aunt Miriam's grandson Simon was a giant of a man with the biggest shoulders Cy had ever seen. He appeared just as darkness was settling over the clearing. Like his grandmother, he showed no surprise when he heard about what had happened at Cain's camp. In fact, he shook Cy's hand and thanked him. That made Cy feel better. So did the look of devotion on Billy's face as Cy retold the story.

Sitting close to a small fire that felt good even on a mild April evening, they talked until Mouse fell asleep in his chair and Simon carried him to bed.

The plan was for Simon to venture into Moultrie the next morning, taking Billy with him. Simon would look for Billy's father, and Billy could stay hidden under a tarpaulin in the back of the wagon. Billy liked that plan. When Billy couldn't keep his eyes open any longer, Simon led him to bed. He wouldn't let Simon carry him—said he was too old for that stuff.

Simon returned, poured himself some whiskey, and sat down again.

"Can I come to Moultrie with you?" Cy asked. The idea had been in his mind since Simon had first suggested it.

Simon looked serious, troubled. "I figured you might want to, but to my mind, it too dangerous. First thing tomorrow mornin', they gon' find out the state of affairs at that devil's camp, if they ain't already found out. Word gon' go out ever' which way, and you can bet they gon' send fast riders to Moultrie and up Tifton way too. Folks know me in Moultrie, so I got to be careful. I don't really want to take Billy with me, but I think we'd have to tie him to a tree otherwise." He sipped from his cup and said no more.

"What is it?" Aunt Miriam asked him. "Somethin's botherin' you."

"Granny, that boy say his name Billy Parrish, and his daddy name AJ."

"And?"

"I knows just about all the colored folks in Moultrie, but I don't know of no folks name o' Parrish livin' there now. But that name—AJ Parrish—soon as Billy mention it, I knew I recognize it for some reason, just couldn't call it to mind. But now I remember." Again, he was silent.

"You got to tell us," Aunt Miriam said. "Ain't no good holdin' back the truth."

"I know. But if I's right, it gon' be hard on Billy. What he told us 'bout how he end up in Cain's camp is most likely true. From what I recall now, they was a big mess in town some months back, and a black man made a big stink after his boy got arrested and sent off for stealin'."

"Right from the start, Billy told us his daddy was comin'," Cy said. "Said his daddy would get it all fixed with the court, or somethin', and then come get him. He went crazy when his daddy never showed up."

"He didn't make it 'cause he ran 'round town accusin' the sheriff and the judge o' framin' his boy. Got drunk and stood in the street in front o' the judge's house, callin' on God for justice. I didn't see it myself, 'cause I was workin' at the sawmill up in Ty Ty then. Heard about it later, though."

"And what happen?" Aunt Miriam asked.

"They run Mr. AJ Parrish outta town, that's what." Simon looked into his glass of whiskey. "We ain't gon' find him come tomorrow mornin'."

"What about the child's mama?" Aunt Miriam asked.

"He never said nothin' about havin' a mama," Cy replied. "I figured she was dead or gone away."

Aunt Miriam shook her head. "Po' child. If you can't find his daddy, he gon' be some disappointed."

As Cy listened, anger had been rising in him. Mouse was bad off. Billy would be destroyed if they couldn't find his father. Why did the white man have the power of life and death over colored folks? And why did colored folks have to risk everything if they ever dared to fight back?

"We can be in town first thing, and I can ask around, see what I can find out," Simon told them. "Maybe somebody know where AJ Parrish gone. Maybe he left word with somebody, case Billy ever come 'round lookin' for him."

"The way Daddy left word with y'all," Cy said. Hope rose in him a little. He had to keep believing it wasn't too late for Billy to find his father again, or for him to find his own.

TWENTY-TWO

SIMON LEFT EARLY WITH BILLY. AROUND DIN-
nertime, Aunt Miriam and Cy heard the wagon in the yard
and went out to the porch to meet it. They had gotten Mouse
up to eat breakfast, but he hadn't touched the hotcakes and
milk Aunt Miriam put in front of him. Complaining of
being too tired to eat, he'd returned to bed.

Simon had to help Billy down from the wagon seat.
The boy seemed to be in a daze. Cy remembered that look
from when Billy was new at Cain's camp. Lost and helpless, like a bird fallen from the nest.

"What is it?" Aunt Miriam asked. "It bad, ain't it?"

"Yes, ma'am," Simon answered. "When we arrived in
town, the place was already buzzin' like a nest o' angry hor-
nets. News about Cain's camp come last night, from what
all them told me. Rumors flyin' ever' which way, folks
talkin' 'bout bands o' black men armed with knives and
guns, roamin' around like Nat Turner and his men back
in the day, just waitin' to ambush white folks and cut 'em

down without mercy. I got dirty looks from some o' them white trash boys what hang out in the courthouse square."

"They been hatin' you long as I can remember," Aunt Miriam noted.

"Most black folks is stayin' off the streets, and I heard tell that the sheriff is callin' for volunteers to catch the killers."

Cy went cold when he heard that. *Killers.* That's what he and Rosalee were. Not the other boys, but now they'd all be rounded up and punished, if the white men could find them.

"What about Billy's daddy?" Aunt Miriam asked.

Simon shook his head. "More bad news. I remembered right. AJ Parrish *did* live in Moultrie, and Billy *was* accused o' stealin' some money. After the sheriff sent him off to Cain's, AJ went sort o' crazy. The city council ordered him to leave, and they took him to the city limits. Ain't nobody heard a word about him since that day. Was all I could do to keep Billy quiet till we got outta town. If they'd of heard him, I reckon we both be in the jail."

Aunt Miriam gathered Billy into her arms. "All right, now," she told him, her voice low and soothing. "It's all right, sugar. We gon' take good care o' you."

Cy wanted to shout that it *wasn't* all right. The whites would get horses and guns and dogs, and they wouldn't stop until every last runaway was found. Suddenly he was afraid, the way he hadn't been since he found himself standing over Stryker and Davis, the gun in his hand.

"We got to get these boys away from here," Simon declared. "Farther the better, and sooner the better."

"You's right," Aunt Miriam agreed. She stroked Billy's head. "But this child ain't fit to travel, and Mouse—"

"After dark," Simon replied. "I can take 'em. Back roads. Go 'round to the west, avoid Tifton, cross the Alapaha, head north."

"To Louisville?" Cy asked. Hope rose in him again.

Simon nodded. "Only other choice is to stay here and hide, but I ain't one to sit and wait for trouble to come to me. I say we take off soon as it dark."

Cy felt himself trembling, a wild mixture of fear and excitement running through him like icy water. "We got to leave," he exclaimed. "Billy, hear that? We got to go."

Billy didn't move.

"Billy, you hear me? You can come with us. We can make it to Louisville. Daddy take you and Mouse in."

Billy wiped his eyes with his jacket sleeve and looked at Cy. "You mean it, Cy?"

Cy realized that he *did* mean it. "Sure I do! Daddy be glad to have some more boys. You, me, Mouse—we can have a good time together. Hunt, fish—"

"Go to school," Aunt Miriam broke in. "Get you some education so you can grow up and be somethin' more'n a sharecropper."

"Yes, ma'am," Cy agreed. "What you say, Billy?"

"All right. Least for a while, until things quiet down and I can come back and find Daddy."

"That's my boy," Aunt Miriam said. "Just 'cause Simon couldn't find him today don't mean he lost from you. One day soon, you can come back and find him."

"Okay," Billy said. He sighed deeply. "I's ready."

Simon went down the porch steps. "We got to gather up supplies and make our plans. I'll fix up a load o' somethin' for the wagon so I can have a reason for goin' toward Tifton and beyond, case anyone stop me."

"How we gonna hide?" Cy asked.

Simon looked thoughtful. "I figure out somethin'."

"Come on," Cy told Billy. "Let's go tell Mouse."

They made their way to the small lean-to room at the back of the house. It was cool and dim. Afternoon sunshine filtered through the curtain drawn over the window. Mouse lay on the bed, one of Aunt Miriam's crazy quilts pulled up to his chin. He was so small and thin that Cy could hardly see him under the cover.

"Mouse?" Cy went to the bed and looked down at the boy. "Mouse, wake up. Billy an' me got some news. We gonna leave here soon as it get dark. Simon gonna take us. We goin' home, up to Louisville. My daddy can be yo' daddy from now on."

Mouse didn't answer. Then Cy noticed how still he was. There was no movement to show that he was breathing.

"Mouse!" Cy exclaimed.

Billy climbed onto the bed and touched Mouse's face. "Come on," he cried. "Wake up!"

Cy pulled back the quilt, but still Mouse did not move. His hands were cupped together at his waist. In them, he held the moth with the two dark eyespots on its wings.

Simon dug the grave in the woods in back of the cabin. Aunt Miriam washed Mouse and wrapped him in a clean sheet. As Simon gently placed the tiny body into the earth, Aunt Miriam read from a tattered Bible: "Behold, the tabernacle of God is with men, and he will dwell with them, and they shall be his people, and God himself shall be with them, and be their God. And God shall wipe away all tears from their eyes; and there shall be no more death, neither sorrow, nor crying, neither shall there be any more pain: for the former things are passed away."

Listening to Aunt Miriam, Cy realized she was the first black person he'd ever known who knew how to read. Again he was reminded of what Billy and the other boys had said at West's funeral. Like their words, these offered comfort, especially the part about God wiping away all the tears. Billy was standing on the other side of Mouse's narrow grave, not even bothering to stop the tears that coursed down his cheeks. Was there really a place where God, whoever he was, would put an end to all the pain of being alive?

When they were done, Aunt Miriam led Billy back to the cabin, but Cy wanted to help close the grave. He hated the sound of the dirt dropping onto the shrunken, sheeted figure at the bottom of the hole, but he was glad, in a way, that Mouse wasn't being buried by complete strangers.

Cy kept his eyes on the quickly shrinking pile of brown, sandy soil as he worked. The sound of weeping made him look up, and he was surprised to see Simon crying openly, like a child. Simon had known Mouse only a day, yet he looked as if his heart was broken. At that moment, love for Simon and Aunt Miriam flooded into Cy. He'd known them only a day too, but they had been kind to him and his companions, even at the risk of their own safety. Rosalee had been kind as well, bringing him water and bread when he was in the icehouse. His father had brought apples and molasses cakes, clean soft clothes, and a plan for his escape. And Jess—he had tried to help, even when all he had to offer was a word of hope, a cup of water, or a hand to hold Cy's forehead while he vomited from the whooping cough.

Such kindnesses had been rare in Cy's world for a long time, and each one shone in his memory.

Cy and Billy were helping Aunt Miriam gather food for their trip when Simon burst through the front door. He'd been loading the wagon in the yard.

"Quick!" he cried. "Get 'em into the hidin' place. They's folks comin'."

He pushed the eating table to one side and pulled back the rag rug. Underneath it was a trapdoor. Simon slid the blade of his knife into the space between the door and the floor and pried the door up enough to grab with his fingers. When the door was open, Cy could see a ladder leading down into a tiny, dark room.

Billy began to whimper.

"None o' that!" Aunt Miriam told him. "It the only way. They's some water in a jug and some food. You and Cy go on down, and we take care o' things up here. Don't you worry! Simon an' me won't let nothin' bad happen to you."

Billy didn't move.

"Let's go!" Cy grabbed his hand and pulled him to the opening in the floor. He went down the ladder first and caught Billy as he stumbled down after him.

"Not one word!" Aunt Miriam warned. "We get rid o' whoever it is, and y'all be back up here in no time."

Simon closed the trapdoor over them, and Cy could hear the rug being pulled back and the table put into place. Then the cabin door opened and the sound of footsteps meant that Simon and Aunt Miriam had gone onto the porch. Then silence.

The hiding place was pitch-dark, and it smelled damp but not bad. Billy and Cy sat down on the floor. Cy put his arm over Billy's shoulder and whispered to him to be quiet, to stay calm, that nothing would happen to them. He wanted to believe that himself.

As they waited, Cy realized that Billy was his responsibility now. Mouse was dead, and there was nothing he could do about it. The other runaways were being hunted down like animals, and there was nothing he could do about that, either. But so far, he and Billy had escaped. They were safe for now. Simon would help them all he could, but no matter what happened next, it was up to him to look after Billy.

He'd never wanted it this way. Only the day before yesterday, he'd dreamed of escaping by himself, free from having to think about anyone else. But he'd let Billy and Mouse come with him. To his surprise, he didn't regret it. Why?

Cy thought of Jess again and how the last thing Jess had ever told him was to look after Billy and Mouse. Cy hadn't wanted to do it, but somehow things had worked out differently. And now, he found himself glad that Billy was with him. Billy, who had also helped nurse him when he had nearly died with the whooping cough. He had shown kindness, too.

From above came the sound of loud voices in the yard. The voices rose and became shouts, and then they gradually died away into silence. Finally, the door opened and someone was moving the table and the rug. When the trapdoor opened, it was Aunt Miriam's face that appeared in the fading light of late afternoon.

"They gone," she told them. "It safe now."

The boys climbed up the ladder.

"Where Simon?" Billy asked.

"White men took him," Aunt Miriam answered. Her voice was shaky, and Cy sensed she was trying to be calm for their sake.

"Why?" he cried.

"No good reason. They just suspicious o' every black man what got a ounce o' courage, and Simon got more'n enough for ten men."

Billy dropped onto a chair. "They gon' get us," he said miserably.

"Don't you talk thataway," Aunt Miriam told him. "Simon be back. They said they gon' take him to Moultrie, put him in the jail for a couple days, just to make sure he ain't in on any plot. When this storm blow over, they'll let him go. He kept tellin' 'em he warn't part of what happen at Cain's place, and he didn't know nothin' 'bout no big plan for black folks to rise up and smite the whites. Maybe them men didn't believe him, but you boys know Simon tellin' the truth."

"What do we do?" Cy asked.

"Wait here. When Simon get out, he can take y'all up to Louisville."

"Naw!" Billy shouted. "If we wait, they gon' find us. Cy, please, we got to go!"

Cy didn't want to think of leaving this safe place. No one would suspect the hidden room under the table. They could stay down there for days if they needed to. But another part of him knew Billy was right. They might keep Simon in jail for weeks, not days. And when the white men let him out, they'd likely watch him. If he tried to take the wagon anywhere, they'd stop him, search everything. How could he and Billy hide in a wagon so that the white men wouldn't find them?

Cy knew Aunt Miriam and Billy were looking at him, waiting for his decision. "We got to leave," he said simply. "Soon as it dark."

"It risky," Aunt Miriam warned. "They be watchin' the roads."

"We sneak through the woods, then. Long as we know the right way to head, we be okay. Once we get past Tifton, it be safer. We can find black folks to help us, point the way up to Louisville. I know we can do it."

"Cy right," Billy agreed.

Aunt Miriam looked sorrowful. "You men all alike," she sighed. "Ain't gonna sit and hide when y'all can be out on the freedom road. In my time, I seen many a man do the same thing. Some of 'em made it all the way north, I reckon. Never heard back from 'em, though . . . Just helped 'em as best I could."

Evening was approaching fast. Aunt Miriam loaded them both with food, and she gave Cy a water bottle made of tanned leather. She told them of back roads, just narrow lanes, from her place up toward Tifton, and how to go around the town to the west. Eventually, they'd have to cross the Alapaha River, but that should be no problem, since the weather had been dry.

Memory taunted Cy. *Last time you come to a river, you let your friend drown.* Cy pushed the thought from his mind. It was time to go.

Aunt Miriam prayed for their safety. She held Billy

close and told him to be brave, that everything would be all right, and that he should come back to see her one day.

Then she put her hands on Cy's shoulders. "I ain't got to tell you that it a long road toward home. It gon' be hard travelin' at night, but at least the moon be full, and it can light yo' way. Look for places where black folks live and ask 'em to help you, if you feel like they's trustworthy. And God go with you, son. You took a stand 'gainst the powers and principalities what rule this dark world, and that count for a lot. One day, the freedom so many died for is gon' really come to us. I pray you lives to see that day."

Pride rose in Cy's heart. "Thank you for everything, Aunt Miriam." He threw himself into the woman's arms and let her hold him close.

TWENTY-THREE

THE JOURNEY WAS SLOW. AT FIRST, CY FEARED Billy wouldn't keep up, that he'd lose courage. But Billy did more than keep up. Sometimes he took the lead and then urged Cy to hurry.

By dawn, Cy figured they'd traveled several miles, although he couldn't be sure. As the sun rose, they left the narrow road and plunged into the thickest woods they could find. There they drank from the water bottle, ate some cold cornpone, and prepared to rest. Cy said he'd take the first watch, so Billy lay down, put his pack under his head, and dropped into sleep.

Now Cy had time to think. Tonight they would pass Tifton and make their way to the river. Beyond that, he believed they would be safe. Aunt Miriam had mentioned the names of other towns, but he couldn't remember them. They had to keep going north, and Simon had said to head east, too.

All at once, it felt like too much. Cy had never seen a mountain, but Louisville and his father seemed to lie at the top of a mountain so high he couldn't see it from the plain where he stood. The peak was there, but hidden in clouds, the road to the top narrow and steep. How could he ever get there? He had no choice but to try.

Cy meant to stay awake, but he couldn't keep his eyes from closing. When he roused, the sun was overhead. Billy woke up and they ate, found water in a low place, and felt safe enough to sleep again.

In the late afternoon, Cy decided it was time to move. They returned to the path, which had become a wagon road winding through woods and then skirting plowed land. Passing small farms, they had to be doubly careful. When more and more homesteads lined the roadside and the road joined another, broader one, Cy felt sure that Tifton lay just to the east.

They heard the sound of a wagon approaching and fled into the underbrush. From hiding, they watched as a wagon driven by an elderly black man passed by. Not far behind him, three white men on horses appeared. They had rifles on their saddles and they looked like men riding with a purpose. Cy sensed that these men were looking for him. They were his enemies.

He and Billy went back into thick pine woods and

found shelter. Not until well after dark did they start moving again.

Now Cy drove Billy forward. They had to get past Tifton and make it to the river. They returned to the main road but dared not travel on it. They kept it to their right, in sight but far enough away that they could find cover if someone came along. As the night wore on, they passed fewer and fewer farms, and finally saw no lights anywhere. Cy breathed easier. Exhausted from pushing through tangles of blackberry and wild roses, they went back onto the road. How far was the Alapaha, Cy wondered.

When the sky was beginning to lighten in the east, Cy could hear the sound of bullfrogs ahead. Then the soft sound of slowly moving water. The road dipped downward, and he could just make out the river.

"Let's get off the road," Cy told Billy. They moved to their left and then down an embankment toward the water. On the far side, a small, flat-bottomed ferry barge was tied. Somebody was making money from travelers who needed to cross.

"We got to swim," Cy told Billy. "You can swim, can't you?"

"Sure I can. Can you?"

"Yeah. Let's look for a place."

They kept moving to the left, searching for a spot that

looked both narrow and shallow. Cy knew that the narrow places in a river were often the deepest. The dark water worried him. Memories of trying to save Travis crowded back now, as clear and sharp as if that terrible day had been only yesterday. He didn't want to go into the water, soak his pack and the food in it, risk running into a snag or a cottonmouth.

Somewhere behind them a horse whinnied. Somewhere a man's voice said something and another man hushed him.

Billy and Cy dropped to the ground. The sound of voices had ceased, replaced by the sound of horses' hooves.

"We got to cross," Billy whispered.

"Let's go!" Cy urged.

They scurried down to the water's edge. The sound of hoofbeats grew louder. The riders were nearly at the river. Cy and Billy had to go now or risk being caught. But if they went together, the men chasing them could shoot them both as they swam. No, it would be better to let Billy go first while he, Cy, stayed behind to deal with their pursuers.

Cy turned to Billy. "You *sure* you can swim?"

"I told you! Why?"

"Listen. I want you to go—go now. Swim to the other side, hard as you can. Then hide and wait. I'll be along soon."

"Naw! You gotta be with me!"

"Too dangerous! Whoever is comin' is lookin' for us, and if they sees us in the river, they can shoot us both. We wouldn't have no way to fight back."

"How you know they after us?"

"I just do. Why else anybody be ridin' through the night? They lookin' for us, and they ain't gonna stop till they finds us. You got to swim for it. I can stay, see what's what. If I don't join you, you keep goin', you hear?"

"No, Cy! We's in this together!"

"Do what I say! If I don't make it, you keep goin' till you get up to Louisville. Find Daddy. Tell him what happened. Tell him—I love him. And you be his son."

Billy was crying. "Naw! I can't make it by myself."

"You can. You got to!" Cy's hand found the loaded pistol tucked into his belt. "I'll hold 'em off if I have to, give you a chance to get across safe."

Billy grabbed Cy's arm. "I ain't leavin' you!"

"Yeah, you are. This is the best way. Ain't nothin' gonna happen. Pretty soon, I'll join you. Please, Billy. Do this one thing for me."

"Cy—"

He pushed Billy into the water. "Quiet!" he whispered. "Don't let 'em hear you."

"I'll see you on the other side."

"Soon," Cy promised.

Billy waded in a few more steps, then started to swim, taking strong, sure strokes. Cy guessed he was trying to be quiet, but he was making plenty of noise, kicking hard for speed.

Behind him, Cy heard men tell their horses to stop. Then came the sound of low conversation. He crept through the underbrush back toward the road, then flattened himself in some tall weeds and listened.

There were two horses. Their riders had dismounted and stood surveying the river.

The sounds of Billy's swimming had stopped, and the men gave no sign they'd heard anything. Maybe Billy was treading water, trying to be silent until the riders went away.

"How soon you reckon the ferryman gonna show up?"

"It don't matter," said the second voice. "This river ain't deep. Horses can almost walk across, and we're in a hurry."

Horror washed over Cy, then deadly hatred at the sound of that voice. He would recognize it anywhere.

Prescott.

Cy pulled the pistol from his belt. This was his chance for revenge. He could ambush both men, drag their bodies off the road, and ride one of their horses across the river.

Then he and Billy could really make good time. They'd be in Louisville in a couple of days, instead of a week.

Kill two more white men. He thought about that for a moment. Well, why not? He'd started a job back at Cain's camp, and now he could finish it. Besides, Prescott had it coming.

Just then, there was a cry off to his left. "Help, Cy! I's caught!"

To Cy's right, the man who was not Prescott exclaimed, "What's that?"

"Pay dirt!" Prescott cried.

Cy heard frantic splashing from the river. If Billy had gotten tangled in something he couldn't see, he was struggling now to get free.

"Come on!" Prescott told his companion. "Let's find out what we got."

Cy saw the men start toward his hiding place. He jumped to his feet and darted behind a tree, pistol at the ready.

Behind him, the splashing continued.

The men came closer.

Cy stepped into the open. "Stop!" he shouted.

The men did.

"Put up your hands," Cy ordered.

They did that, too.

"You all right, Billy?" Cy called.

"Yeah," Billy called back. "I made it."

"Out of the water?"

"Yeah."

"Keep goin'. I be with you soon."

Prescott took a step toward him, and Cy aimed the pistol at him. "I told you not to move."

The other man was a stranger, and by the look of him, not much older than Jess. He was hatless, and his hair was so light that it appeared almost white. His face was smooth.

Prescott kept his hands up. The familiar, amused sneer appeared on his face. "Well, what have we here? A nigger with a gun." He looked at his companion. "You ever reckon you'd live long enough to see such a sight, Lem? Kinda like seein' a pig readin' a newspaper."

Lem's hand found the handle of the pistol holstered on his right side, but the man said nothing.

Prescott kept his eyes fixed on Cy. "Where'd you get yer new toy? Off Cain's body after you cut his throat? That the weapon you used to blow Stryker's brains out while he was sleepin'?" Prescott shook his head. "You're a real brave fellow, ain't you? More'n a match for defenseless men tryin' to get some sleep."

"If you don't turn around and leave now," Cy said, "you gonna end up just like your friends." He wanted to keep Prescott talking as long as he could, give Billy more time to get away.

"You might as well put that down," Prescott told Cy. "Ain't no way you can take both of us, even carryin' a white man's gun, which you stole from him after you murdered him, you yellow-bellied coward."

"Shut up!" Cy cried. "I's tellin' you to get on your horses and go back the way you come."

"You ain't got the guts to shoot a white man who's lookin' you in the eye," Prescott told him. He glanced at Lem, and Cy instantly understood the meaning of that look.

Both men went for their guns, and Cy fired at Prescott, who grunted and crashed over backwards. At the same moment, Lem's gun went off, and Cy cried out as the bullet tore into his shoulder. He staggered and fell, and then Lem was standing over him.

"Cy!" Billy cried from the other side of the river.

"Run!" he shouted back. "Don't stop until you safe!"

Just then, Lem drew back his foot and kicked Cy on the side of his head.

TWENTY-FOUR

IT WAS EVENING NOW, AND CY'S SUPPER PLATE,
the food untouched, sat on the floor of the cell. He was
hunched on the side of the narrow cot, his head down, a
hand touching the knot on his skull where Lem's boot had
smashed into it. What was the point of eating? They would
hang him in the morning.

He remembered coming to, finding his hands tied behind him—just the way John Strong had tied him the day
Travis had died in the Ogeechee River.

He had watched the man he knew only as Lem heave
Prescott's body onto the back of one of the horses and tie
it there. He remembered being hoisted into the saddle of
that same horse. He didn't like the touch of the dead man's
body against his.

Then the long ride to Moultrie, with folks stopping to
stare as they passed. Lem boasted how he'd bagged one of
the ringleaders of the uprising at Cain's camp and would
collect the bounty money.

As they rode, Lem had told Cy he would have shot him on the spot—that would have been easier. He'd been itching to put another bullet into Cy, seeing as how Cy had killed his friend Prescott; he could still have collected some of the cash reward for bringing in a dead nigger. But the authorities wanted the killers alive, if possible, to tell the truth of what had happened at Cain's camp.

Back in Moultrie, a mob of furious white men was waiting at the jail, calling for Cy to be lynched on the spot. But the sheriff made them back off. This was a civilized state, he told the crowd, and they were on the threshold of the twentieth century. There'd be no lawlessness in his town.

White men jammed the jail, demanding answers to their questions. Cy answered them simply and honestly. He knew there was no point in lying, not now. Yes, the whole thing was his idea. He'd put Rosalee up to it, and she'd done her part, then gone her way. Cy suspected she'd managed to escape. He hoped so, even though she'd left without him. Otherwise, someone would have let it slip that she'd been caught.

After three days, the sheriff had Cy brought into the courthouse. A judge listened to some men repeat what Cy had told them and pronounced sentence. The nigger Cy

Williams would hang by the neck until dead for the murders of white men Dawson Stryker, Love Davis, and Onnie Prescott, citizens of Colquitt County, Georgia. Sentence to be carried out in three more days.

From his cell, Cy could see two sheriff's deputies sitting at a desk, chewing tobacco and making frequent use of the spittoon. One of them whittled, leaving a neat pile of shavings on the top of the desk, the way Love Davis had sat whittling the day Cy and Rosalee had agreed to kill him.

Cy lay down, turned his face to the wall, and shut his eyes. If he pretended to sleep, maybe the men would talk freely. In the last couple of days, he'd learned a lot that way. He'd overheard that they'd caught six other boys from the camp, but that was all, so the others were still at large. For that, he was glad. He also found out that Prescott was hated by almost everyone who knew him, and no one was particularly sorry that he was dead. That the murders at Cain's camp would lead to an investigation of conditions there. That Simon and all the other black men they'd arrested had been released.

Most important of all, Cy had learned that no one had found Billy. Lem hadn't been able to go after him because he had a dead man and a live prisoner to deal with. By the time the searchers returned to the Alapaha, Billy was long gone.

Billy gone. That was the great thing. That made tomorrow worth it.

Once, Cy and a friend had come to a river. In a moment of fear, he, Cy, had turned yellow and fled from danger. Had leaped into the death waters of the Ogeechee. Travis, his friend, had followed—and had drowned. This time, Cy had stood his ground, giving Billy the chance to cross over into freedom.

The first time, Travis had paid with his life. This time, Cy would pay with his. After all the blood he'd spilled, he figured that it was a fair reckoning.

"Sheriff gonna let 'em have some fun with the nigger before they kill him?" one deputy asked.

The other chuckled. "I wouldn't mind seein' that myself. You know one reason they put off the hangin' this long is so folks from all over can make it to town for the big event. Them as travels from far away don't like it to be over so quick. Give 'em some of what they come for, know what I mean?"

Since he'd been caught, Cy had walled himself off from this world of white people who wanted to kill him. He had tried to keep himself from thinking, from feeling. Now that the end was near, he was strangely unafraid. Hanging didn't hurt. It was quick. One moment you were alive, noose around your neck, black hood over your face, and the next . . . it was over.

"Sheriff said he ain't gonna have none o' that tomorrow," the second deputy continued. "He don't care how disappointed folks might be. 'Hang the nigger and get it over with,' he says."

"Maybe he'll let 'em have the body," the first replied. "Some folks get a kick out of messin' with what's left over."

"You mean souvenirs? Shit. That's some kind o' sick stuff, Hank. I pray the sheriff don't let 'em get their hands on him. Just kill him and let the niggers in town take the body and bury it."

"I reckon you're right."

Cy opened his eyes and looked at the brick wall before him. How he wished he could use his strong arms to push through it. How he'd like to pull the building down, kill the two guards and himself with them.

He knew that if there was anything left to think about, now was the time. The night would pass quickly, and in the morning, he would face the world of white folks for the last time.

He thought of his mother and wondered if she was

alive somewhere, and happy. He thought of her pink bonnet. He felt sure his daddy had taken it with him when he left Strong's plantation.

Cy thought about his father, waiting for him in Louisville. He'd be surprised when Billy showed up instead. Billy would tell him what had happened, how Cy had been brave and done what had to be done. How he'd set some others free. His father would be sad, but Billy would be a good son to him.

He thought about dying. He hoped it would be fast, like he imagined it would be. And after that?

Aunt Miriam believed there was a heaven. God was there, waiting. When folks got to him, what did the Bible say? God would wipe away all their tears. There would be no more sadness, no more pain. Cy wanted to believe that.

And what would God say to him? "You killed three men. I can't let you stay here. You got to go to the other place." But hell couldn't be worse than Cain's camp, so Cy reckoned he could stand it if he had to. Or would God—Father, Aunt Miriam had called him—understand why Cy had killed, and forgive him?

Cy thought of West, who was always ready with a joke. And Pook, and the day he, Cy, had swung the child around and made him laugh. He thought of Jess, hoped he was still alive and would one day escape the coal mines of Alabama.

He thought of Mouse and the dark spots on the moth's wings, spots like eyes looking back at you from the strange, unknown world on the other side.

If what the deputy said was right, maybe the black folks could have his body. Maybe Simon and Aunt Miriam would take him to their place and bury him beside Mouse. And Aunt Miriam would put flowers over him. He'd like that.

And then he thought of Billy, whose life he had saved. *Let Billy find Daddy*, Cy thought. *Let him go to school, learn to read and write, make something good out of his life.*

He touched the brick wall. It was still hard and unmoving. Here he was in a jail cell, prisoner in a world he didn't make. They would kill him, but it didn't much matter now.

His thoughts drifted to the moment Billy would walk up and introduce himself to Pete Williams. Their new lives together as father and son would begin.

Cy, who never prayed, prayed for them now, that this would come true.

He hoped they wouldn't grieve over him for too long. After all, come tomorrow, he would be free.

AUTHOR'S NOTE

Some years ago, I was browsing in the Zach S. Henderson Library at Georgia Southern University and happened upon a book titled *The Rise and Fall of Jim Crow*, by Richard Wormser (New York: St. Martin's Press, 2003). Its cover caught my attention immediately: an archival photograph of black men in striped prison uniforms, chained at the waist and feet, working in a field. A closer look, however, revealed that the prisoners were not men but youths, some adolescent and others obviously still children.

From the book, I learned that by the end of the nineteenth century, between twenty and thirty thousand black Americans were caught in the system of convict labor. Perhaps as many as *one quarter* of them were children. Legal records show that some of these children received stiff sentences for petty crimes such as theft of small amounts of merchandise or money from retail businesses. Twelve-year-old Cy Williams got twenty years on a chain gang for taking a horse he was too small to ride.

We will never know what happened to the real Cy Williams and so many others like him. *Cy in Chains*, inspired by his case, was written to recall a shocking episode in our past and give voice to fellow Americans long silenced by time, forgetfulness, and our national shame. More important, however, this novel celebrates what poet Robert Hayden calls "the deep immortal human wish, the timeless will": our universal desire for freedom and our unchanging will to grasp it, no matter the cost.

Cy Williams, I am privileged to imagine and share your story.

ACKNOWLEDGMENTS

In 2004, editor Dinah Stevenson took a chance on an unknown and unpublished novelist and accepted my novel *The Bicycle Man* for publication at Clarion Books. I am deeply grateful that she did. As she guided me with patience, tact, and honesty through at least four major revisions of the book, she became my teacher, encourager, and friend. No one has taught me more about the craft of writing. As I sometimes tell people, my name might appear on the cover of my novels, but the finished books have Dinah's heart written all through them. Thank you for everything, Dinah!

So many people encourage me, love and accept me despite myself, and express their kindness in countless ways every day. Colleagues, friends, family—to all of you, including those whom I can't name here because the list would be too long, my gratitude and my love:

My brother Chris, his wife, Kellie, and their children, with a special nod to Sam; Katie and Tim Mather, all the Mather clan, and everyone dedicated to the work of Bear Creek Ranch; my brothers and fellow kings Justin, Jason, and David; my Georgia Southern University colleagues, especially all the members of the Department of Literature and Philosophy; my administrative assistant Rebecca, without whom I would be lost.

My children and their families, of whom I am enormously proud: Chris, Amanda, and Noah; Joy, Daniel, Aiden, Emma, and Madaline; Michael; and Will. I love you beyond my powers to tell you so.

God my Father.

And Eileen, my life's companion, Father's extravagant gift to me, my biggest fan, and the greatest hero in my life. My love always and forever, my dear. Couldn't have made it without you!